ICE COLD SAINT

New York Times & USA Today Bestselling Author

CYNTHIA EDEN

PROLOGUE

"She has to be stopped."

Saint Black stared at the picture before him. A beautiful, smiling woman gazed back up at him. The smile on her full lips was taunting, sensual, and it never touched her eyes. Unusual eyes, a mix of topaz and brown—almost gold. Her gaze in the photo seemed oddly luminous as she peered back at him.

"I get that she doesn't look like a killer," the would-be client who paced in his office said, her breath catching. "That's part of the problem. Or—or maybe it's part of her appeal. I don't know. Men fall at her feet. Always have. Men like my brother, Donovan. They fall for her, and then..."

Saint forced his gaze to lift. To lock on the lady who'd surged into his office five minutes ago, right before he'd been preparing to cut out for the night.

"Then she kills them," she finished as she lifted her hand and swiped a tissue under her left eye.

Tracy Eldridge. That was her name. She'd been late for her appointment with him, and he'd been fairly certain she'd just be a no-show.

His fingers slid toward the picture she'd dropped on his desk moments before. "You haven't told me who she is."

"Alice Shephard." The name came out like a curse. "I tried to warn Donovan that she was trouble. I knew it from the first moment I met her. But he wouldn't listen. Now he's gone, the others are gone, and she's still out there. It's only a matter of time until she strikes again."

Curiosity trickled through him. Curiosity—always a dangerous thing. Because once he became curious about something...Saint's gaze slid back to the photo. He frowned when he realized that his finger was sliding lightly over her smile.

What in the fuck?

He immediately stopped the odd movement.

"I want to hire you," Tracy announced. "Money is no object for me. You have to catch her."

Now they were getting down to business. "Did she jump bail? If there are warrants out for her—"

Tracy rushed toward his desk. She slapped her hands down on the surface. "No! No, there are no warrants, that's the problem! They never arrest her! The cops fall under her spell just like everyone else, and they let her go." Pain and rage shook the words even as tears glittered in her pale blue eyes. Her blond hair had been pulled back into a severe twist. "They let her go," she repeated in a seething voice, "and no one will help me stop her."

Tread carefully. "I'm a bounty hunter. If this Alice Shephard is not wanted for a crime, there really isn't much I can do."

Her lashes flickered. Her mascara had run, darkening the skin beneath her eyes. "I'm not trying to hire you in your bounty hunting capacity."

Yes, he'd suspected as much. So he waited for her to continue.

"I've heard about your...your connections."

Saint didn't let his expression change. He never did. When it came to being stone-faced, he was a master. "What connections might those be?"

"You solve cold cases."

Occasionally. "When I'm bored." An easy, dismissive response.

Her chin lifted. "Are you bored right now?" Then, before he could answer, she shoved her hand into her purse and yanked out a checkbook. Diamond rings glittered on her fingers, weighing them down. She snatched a pen from his desk. Scribbled an amount on the check and shoved it toward him. "Or...how about now?"

One hundred thousand dollars. "If you're referring to my involvement with the Ice Breakers..." Saint shrugged. "My involvement with that online group is purely minimal. And they don't get paid for their jobs."

"I know. I've tried reaching out to the others. They were no use to me. They—they told me they would try to help when they had *time*." She tore up the first check. Wrote another. "We are running out of time. I know she'll kill again. She *always* kills again. Men fall for her. She lures them in, and then she kills them. Three dead lovers. Soon, she'll pick a fourth." Tracy pushed another check toward him.

Two hundred thousand.

Saint straightened in his chair. "What is it—exactly—that you want me to do?" He knew people—quite a few of them actually, thanks to his bounty hunting work—who would literally kill for that much money.

He, however, wasn't in the killing business.

But he did dabble in some crime solving. A man needed a hobby, didn't he?

"I want you to find proof. That's what you do, right? You find proof. You find the victims. She made them all vanish. That's why the cops just—they won't help me without bodies. Alice made my brother vanish. She made the other two men vanish."

Once more, his gaze flickered back to the photo. Alice Shephard appeared to be a small woman, built along delicate lines. It was never easy for a woman to make a much larger individual *vanish*. At least, not without help.

"You always catch your bounties, and with the Ice Breakers, you don't give up. I want that. I *need* that. Alice Shephard is a killer." Her breath heaved in and out.

He made no move to take the check. His gaze lingered on Alice's image.

Beauty can hide a monster.

"I know she did it!" A sharp crack in Tracy's voice. "And if you won't help me to prove it then—then I will just stop her myself!" Rage and stark desperation twisted in her words.

He took the photograph. Put it in his desk drawer. Slid the check into the drawer, too. "I'll see what I can do."

Tracy's jaw dropped. "You—you—" Her eyes lit with what appeared to be feverish hope. "You'll take my case?"

His mind had already started to assess the possibilities. "You're describing a black widow."

"I—what?"

"A black widow. She chooses her mates, then she kills them." He'd never had a black widow case. Should be interesting.

Again, curiosity stirred. Stronger this time. Curiosity had always been his weakness. Maybe because he spent so much time just feeling bored—or feeling fucking nothing—that when curiosity came along, he tended to get hooked.

"Thank you." Tracy's thin shoulders slumped. *"Thank you."*

"I haven't done anything yet." And he would make no promises. "I'm just going to dig around a little bit. See what I discover." About the beautiful and potentially deadly Alice.

"I want her locked away."

Too bad. We don't always get what we want.

"I want her to lose everything that she cares about in this world," Tracy continued passionately. "I want her to *hurt* just like I hurt. She thinks she's gotten away with murder, but we'll show her that she hasn't."

If Alice was guilty, then, yes, he would see her locked away. Jail was a real bitch. He should know. He'd spent too much time there himself.

"You'll be careful?" Tracy asked quickly. "You won't let her trick you?"

Saint couldn't help it. He laughed. "Don't worry. I'm not about to fall into her web." It took one hell of a lot more than a pretty face to fool him.

CHAPTER ONE

"What's the password?"

Are you shitting me? Saint glared at the guy who'd just opened the small, metal grill in the wooden door before him. The door itself looked like something straight out of the 1920s, but then, that was probably the point. He was standing in front of a speakeasy in Savannah, Georgia, and the jerk squinting at him from behind the small viewing area in the door wasn't going to let him in, not unless Saint had the magic word.

"Password," the man repeated impatiently.

Fucking annoying. Saint grabbed a fifty from his wallet and shoved it toward the man's eyes. The eyes were all he could see beyond that grill. "I'm pretty sure it's Grant." The president on the bill.

The cash disappeared through a small slat. "Nope. Tonight, the password is *misdirection*. Remember that in case anyone else asks." Then the big door swung open as he allowed Saint to step inside.

"Welcome to Abracadabra," he told Saint. "Get ready for some magic."

Saint barely contained an eye roll as he strode past the bouncer—a tall guy wearing all black—and down the dark corridor that waited for him. Gas lanterns flickered on the walls, and he realized that heavy stone rested beneath his feet. He had to give the place points for atmosphere, if one had been going for a grim and cold atmosphere. Then he rounded the corner, saw the dark, red drapes, and Saint pushed them aside...

Well, well, well.

It was truly like walking back in time. Because Saint could have sworn that he was staring straight at an old-school speakeasy. Exposed brick showed on all the walls, a long, twisting bar ran down the right side of the room, and high-back chairs and round tables were scattered along the perimeter.

A stage—with black curtains and a black floor—waited to the left. On that stage, a woman stood in a circle of light, holding tight to a microphone, and crooning for all she was worth. And the place was *packed*. Men and women filled the joint, but they were dressed like they were at a fancy ball. The men were in tuxes, while the women were in designer gowns. And the drinks were definitely flowing.

Okay, so Alice Shephard knows how to make a killing.

Because this was her place. He'd spent the last six days researching her. Learning every possible detail that he could about the mysterious Alice. The details had certainly made her look dangerous.

It seemed to be common knowledge that Alice was a killer. That she'd gotten away not with just one murder, but potentially three. And as he passed the packed crowd and made his way to the bar, he even caught a few excited whispers about her...

"Do you think she'll be here tonight?"

"God, could you imagine? Sharing a drink with a real killer!"

"I want my picture taken with her."

His brows pulled low at the comments. In his experience, people weren't excited about the prospect of hanging out with a killer. Or, at least, they shouldn't be excited.

Alice seemed to be eliciting an unusual response from these individuals. People he realized were packing the speakeasy just because it *was* her place.

When he got to the bar, he took the only open stool he saw. He reached into his wallet and pulled out another fifty. A woman with dark hair had her back to him. She was mixing a drink, humming slightly, and he cleared his throat to get her attention.

"Don't worry, handsome," she said without looking back, "I'll be with you next. But I'm already guessing you're an old-school whiskey guy. An old-fashioned? That what you're after? Because you hardly seem the pretty-drink type to me."

He'd been looking at the crowd, but at that low, husky voice—a voice that seemed to sink into his skin—he jerked his head back toward the bartender. He realized she was wearing a shimmering, silver dress. Very much flapper-like. It dipped low at her back, plunging in a daring V that stopped right over her perfectly rounded hips. When he leaned forward a bit, he could see beyond the bar's edge, and he got a glimpse of her toned legs and the high heels that—

"Like what you see?"

She was still not looking at him, but she seemed absolutely certain he was looking at her. His gaze immediately whipped up, thinking there must be a mirror on the wall there so that she could peer at him, but—

No. No mirror. Just bottles and bottles of alcohol.

"I'll take that as a yes." A throaty, seductive laugh. "But, sorry, my dark and dangerous new friend, I am not on the menu." Then she turned toward him.

And it was as he'd suspected.

Fucking Alice Shephard.

The heels had given her extra height. At least two inches extra. Maybe three. And her hair was different. In the picture he'd viewed of her, Alice's hair had trailed down her back and been shot with blond highlights. Now, her hair skimmed just below her shoulders. It was much darker, but when she stepped forward and a shaft of illumination hit her, he realized there were still golden highlights in her hair.

Golden highlights. Blood-red lipstick on her full, sensual lips. Luminous eyes that had been carefully shadowed to make them appear even deeper. Even bolder. Cheekbones sharp enough to cut.

Her head tilted to the right, and her hair slid over her shoulder. "You're not wearing the appropriate clothing for tonight's affair."

He was wearing jeans. A black shirt. His old jacket.

"You bribed your way inside." A nod. "Typical. Well, I'll let you stay, but just because I am an incredibly nice person. Next time, download our app so that you know what the theme is for the evening. The theme and the password."

So there was a theme? That was why everyone was so fancy? Whatever. He didn't give a shit about being fancy. He cared about her. "*Are* you nice?"

Someone at the end of the bar called out to her.

She ignored the person. Saint could have sworn a spark of interest lit her eyes as Alice sharpened her gaze on him. Then she was leaning toward him, sliding her upper body over the edge of the bar, and Saint found himself leaning toward her, as well. He caught her scent—light, floral, kinda reminded him of freshly cut roses he'd scented once or twice—and he drank it in.

"No," Alice replied, her voice going low and even huskier. "I'm not nice."

He smiled at her. "Good. Because I'm not, either." Fair warning.

Her gaze, even more luminous in real life than it had been in the photo, dropped to his mouth. "You have one of those gorgeous, disarming smiles," she noted, not even seeming to miss a beat. "Very dangerous. I'm sure you flash that smile and women drop their panties at your feet."

He peered down at the ground. "Don't see any around me at the moment."

When he looked back up, she was pushing an old-fashioned toward him. He noted the curving shell of the orange peel in the amber liquid.

"You don't see them because I'm not the type to drop my panties just for a grin. It takes more. A lot more than that for me."

Saint wrapped his fingers around the drink. As he did, he brushed *her* fingers because she was pulling back. A hot, hard surge of lust drove through him at the contact. *Yeah, I was afraid of that.* He ignored the lust and the aching dick he had and tried the drink.

It was perfect. Actually, the best he'd ever—

"Best you ever had?" she murmured. "I get that a lot." She sent him a smile. One that, like in the photo, never reached her eyes. "Enjoy the drink." Alice turned away.

"What does it take?" He savored the drink. You didn't down an old-fashioned of this caliber. When something was special, you took your time with it.

Alice paused. Glanced over her shoulder at him. "Trust me when I say that you can't handle me."

"You'd be surprised at what I can handle."

She motioned toward the crowd behind him. "Go try that smile out there. I'm sure your luck will be outstanding. Lots of women go for that dark-and-dangerous vibe."

"But not you." Another taste of his drink. His eyes remained on her.

She turned to fully face him. "I'm not interested in wannabe danger."

Oh, this was intriguing. No, *she* was. "You only go for the real deal?"

Once more, she leaned over the bar. Her scent teased him. But she didn't speak. Instead, she searched his gaze. He wondered just what it was that Alice was looking for as she stared at him so hard with those topaz eyes of hers.

"You want real danger?" he rasped as the tension seemed to stretch between them. "How do you know I can't give you that?"

Her lips parted. She was going to—

"That's her." A woman's voice, coming from right behind Saint. One of the excited voices he'd caught before as he made his way through the crowd. He was pretty sure that was the woman who'd wanted—

"May I please get a picture with you?" The woman leapt toward the bar. "Please? It would be so great. I mean, I have these friends who would not believe that I was actually brave enough to stand right beside—"

Alice's gaze turned to the woman. Hardened. No smile curved Alice's lips.

The woman stopped talking. Her voice just broke off in that unnatural, nervous way that always showed clear embarrassment.

"Beside what—exactly?" Alice asked with a faintly quizzical air.

Saint glanced at the woman who'd nudged her way so close to Alice. The woman's hair was jet-black, and her skin had flushed dark red. He could smell the alcohol drifting off her, and he realized a lot of her boldness came from the booze.

One of her friends tried to grab her arm and haul her back. "Genna!" A low, warning hiss.

"Ah...she meant right beside the owner of the speakeasy!" Another friend hurried to exclaim. "That's all Genna meant.

Just because the place is so popular." She grabbed the flushing woman's other shoulder. "Genna, come *on*."

Genna stumbled back. She clutched her phone in one hand, and she still seemed to be trying to take a photo—

The phone was plucked out of her hand. "Alice doesn't take pictures with guests." The man who'd taken the phone shook his head, and the light glinted off his blond hair. "How about I call you ladies a cab?"

Which Saint realized was polite speak for...*Your asses are getting tossed out.*

"Thanks, Logan," Alice murmured. "I think a cab is exactly what they need."

Logan led the women away. Saint quickly assessed him. Big, muscled, and with an attitude that pretty much screamed bouncer or bodyguard. The guy had slid silently toward the bar to reach Alice. *My money is on bodyguard.* But in order to have a bodyguard, Alice would need enemies.

He turned back to ask her about those enemies—

But Alice was gone. He blinked. Looked again. Even leaned over the bar to make sure she hadn't just bent down to get something but...no, gone.

Saint slowly lowered back onto his stool. He lifted his glass once more, and as he did, he noticed the little napkin that Alice had slid under the drink. Black, with white letters emblazoned across the top.

Abracadabra.

Fuck. He was even more curious about her now.

✳✳✳

Two a.m. meant closing time. A few stragglers always remained, but Logan knew how to handle them. He was good at getting people to do what he wanted. Mostly because her manager could be intimidating as hell.

"You just like to play with fire, don't you?" Logan asked as he walked her to the back door. The private exit.

"I have no idea what you mean." Yes, she knew exactly what he meant.

"You know crazed Alice fans will want to get close to you. You're supposed to stay out of sight when the place gets too packed."

She reached up and patted his cheek. "But if I'm out of sight, then how are they going to rush back and tell their friends that they saw me?" She let her eyes widen. "Infamous little old me." Infamous in certain circles. The crime-obsessed circles. "You know I always come out for a bit." Working the bar let her take stock of everyone in her place, and, sometimes, people didn't even realize who she was. At least, not until after they'd spilled their secrets to her.

Bartenders learn all the best secrets. Something she'd discovered years ago.

"The crime tour is starting to come this way," he grumbled. "I saw a group out front, staring up at the building on my way in tonight as some guide rumbled on and on."

She had to laugh. "You act like that's a bad thing." Alice pushed open the door. "Tourists just mean more money. Something you used to love." Behind the building, her precious cherry-red convertible waited about twenty feet away.

"I still love money," Logan assured her. "Money is my favorite thing in the entire world."

Yes, she knew it was. Logan had grown up with nothing, just as she had, so when it came to acquiring wealth—and all the glorious trappings that came with that wealth—he was quite passionate. "Then why are you complaining?"

"Don't you get tired of them all whispering about you?" The words seemed to explode from him. "I sure do!"

She shook her head. "I don't care what they say. As long as they are coming in my place, giving me their money, they can whisper all they want."

"Alice..." His phone beeped and vibrated. He yanked it out. Swore when he saw the screen. "Got to head back in. Marcel needs me at the front door." But he lingered.

She sighed. "You've walked me to my car. Done your due diligence. I'm safe and sound. Go." She motioned with her hands. "I'm *fine.*"

And he finally went. Grudgingly. Alice held her keys in one hand, and she waited until he'd disappeared inside, waited until the door had closed behind him and... "Is there a reason you're hiding in the shadows?" she asked, pitching her voice to carry, but making sure she still sounded calm and relaxed. "Or do you just enjoy stalking women you've just met?" Her head turned to the right. Toward the darkness on the edge of her building.

Toward the man that she knew waited in the darkness.

There was a faint rustle of sound, and then she heard the soft pad of footsteps. Alice found herself holding her breath as he slowly emerged.

Big, bad, and wannabe dangerous. The man from the bar. Her old-fashioned customer. He walked from the shadows as if they were a part of him, and Alice had to admit that he could certainly create a dramatic scene.

She held her ground as he approached. Mostly because these days, Alice made it a point not to retreat from anyone or anything. After all, when you were the monster in the dark, what did you have to fear?

Only other monsters.

He smiled at her. She'd had lights installed over the back door, and those lights let her see his grin. Still as amazing as before. How wonderful for him. She truly did think that grin had opened all sorts of doors for him in life.

Meanwhile, doors had been slammed on her again and again. *But not any longer.* "Just so you know, in case this is one of those situations in which you think you will rob me or do something else...nefarious..." What a fun word that was. "You should know that you are on video right now. And if I want help to come running, all I have to do is press a little button on my keychain." A security alert that would go straight to Logan.

But, obviously, she didn't want Logan running to the scene right then. Otherwise, why would she have waited for this little talk? She'd known all along that her stranger was in the shadows. She'd heard the faint rustle of his step and saw the outline of his body the moment she'd exited the building.

His body was rather unforgettable.

He stepped even closer to her. So close that she could practically feel the heat emanating from him. He was big—even bigger than Logan by at least an inch or two—and his shoulders were wide and strong. Even in her heels, she had to tip her head back to stare up at him.

"Nefarious." A shake of his head. "Why do you think I'm the bad guy?"

"Because you're lurking in shadows. Because you stared at me with recognition in your eyes when we first met." She easily clicked off the items on her list. "Because you didn't come into Abracadabra by chance, and you're not a crime groupie."

"A crime groupie?"

"Um." Annoyance flashed through her. "Don't pretend. It's a waste of my time. You know who I am."

"Alice Shephard."

"You know *what* I am," she added deliberately.

"The woman suspected of killing three men. A serial killer."

That response gave her pause. "I'm not a serial killer."

"Well, the definition of a serial killer is someone who has murdered multiple people in a rather predictable manner—"

Laughter spilled from her. Real laughter, despite the heaviness that so often pulled at her.

He jerked at the sound, as if he'd been caught off-guard.

She let the laughter linger because it felt good, and she enjoyed feeling good. Then she said, "There is nothing predictable about me."

A nod. "I'm coming to see that."

"I don't think there is much that is predictable about you, either." A point in his favor. "Because most men who want to fuck me don't straight-up accuse me of being a serial killer. Sort of ruins the mood, if you know what I mean. Sure, they may think it, but to actually just say those words outright…" A shake of her head and she absolutely could not resist saying, "Mood *killer*."

His lips twitched. Not a full smile, but definite amusement. For just a fleeting moment. "What makes you think I want to fuck you?"

She almost laughed again. Alice realized she hadn't enjoyed this much fun in…hmm, she couldn't remember when. Ages. "Seriously? I know lust when I see it in a man's eyes. When you looked at me inside Abracadabra, let's just say your gaze was blazing."

His jaw hardened.

Well, well. Someone didn't like being called out on his desire. Too bad.

"I guess you're used to men wanting you," he said, his voice a deep and dark, utterly delicious rumble that slid over her. "So you just assume we're all the same."

She would never make that fatal assumption.

"But I'm not here to fuck you, Alice."

"No? Then what are you here to do?"

His hand lifted. She tensed, automatically, then wanted to curse herself. His fingers reached out and stroked her cheek. The caress was as gentle as a breath of wind on her skin. She could feel the calluses on the edges of his fingertips, but his touch was ever so careful. She even wanted to turn into his touch, as crazy as that—

"I'm here to take you down." His voice was serious and a bit sad. And utterly, utterly certain.

So she did turn into his touch. She nuzzled a little against his hand and heard the swift inhalation of his breath. But Alice didn't smile at his reaction. Now wasn't the time for a smile. However, it was time for a little bit of truth with her mysterious stranger. Testing, she let her lips skim over his hand.

She saw him tense. Felt it.

His hand jerked back from her.

Alice lifted her chin. "You said that wrong."

His hands were at his sides. The one she'd touched with her mouth? That hand had curled into a fist. So very telling. For a moment, she admired the dark swirls on his fist. His tats were interesting. Something she'd noticed while he'd drank his old-fashioned inside. The tats covered the back of his hands. Slid up his wrists. Did they go all the way up his arms? Hard to say since he was wearing that ancient-looking jacket.

Focus. Right. Because she needed to set this poor man straight. Alice let a little sigh slip from her. "What you meant was that you're here to fall in love with me."

"That's damn well *not* what I meant."

Alice stepped toward him. She put her hand on his chest.

"Lady, you are playing with fire," he warned.

"I'm not playing." His heart raced beneath her touch. "I don't play. That's probably the first thing you should learn about me."

"I already learned plenty."

Alice filed that revealing bit away for later. "You bust into my life and say that you're here to take me down."

"There *is* the little matter of three murders tied to you."

She pressed up on her toes. She liked his mouth. Firm but sculpted lips. She liked his jaw, too. Hard and strong. There was a little cleft in his chin that she found delightful. It didn't soften his fierce, handsome face, though. If anything, the faint cleft somehow made him seem sexier. His dark, thick hair had been shoved back from his forehead, and faint stubble covered his jaw. "You're not a cop."

"No?"

"No. You don't look like a cop, and you certainly don't act like one."

"You don't know me. Don't make assumptions."

"Ah. I could say the same thing to you." She was staring at his mouth. Definitely considering kissing him simply for the hell of it. "Damn." Regretful. She began to ease off her toes and back down. "I know what you are."

"And what am I?"

Obviously... "The bad guy." Another sigh. More forlorn this time. "That's the only kind of guy I'm attracted to." She was most certainly attracted to him. "Sort of a talent I have. Some women go for men who bring them flowers and treat them to candlelight dinners. Me? I tend to get drawn to the men who are trouble."

"Are you sure that *you* aren't trouble?"

Oh, she was. "The worst kind of trouble," Alice affirmed without hesitation. "Remember that about me and stay away, would you?"

"Why? If I don't stay away, will I end up like your last three lovers?"

She didn't flinch. Didn't gasp. Didn't put her hand to her heart dramatically as if those cutting words had just, well, cut *her*. Even though they had.

Deal with it. "End up like them?" She pondered that. Pretended to ponder it. "You mean enormously satisfied and ruined sexually for everyone else?"

A beat of silence. He cleared his throat. "No." A rasp. "I meant dead."

Oh, she just had to do this. The man was entirely too tempting. Once more, Alice shot up onto her toes. This time, she also curled her hands around his shoulders so that she could tug him down to meet her. He was a big one, after all. She had to pull him close. When she had him in position, her mouth moved toward his left ear. "What makes you think those men were my *last* three lovers?"

"*Alice...*"

Ah, had he felt the brief lick of her tongue over the shell of his ear?

"You're so wrong," she told him huskily. *About many things.* Not that he'd discover her secrets.

No one ever did.

He'd tensed against her. She could feel the tightness in his shoulders and because she was wicked and being wicked could be fun, Alice lightly licked the edge of his ear once more.

He hissed out a breath. His hands flew out and curled around her waist. Fast. Tight. Strong. He—

"There a problem out here?" Logan's hard voice.

She almost jolted in surprise. Almost. Such a near thing.

When had Logan come outside? She didn't remember hearing the back door open, yet she could now clearly discern the rush of his steps toward them.

"Alice?" Logan called.

She eased back, but the man before her didn't release his grip on her waist. "No problem," she said without looking away from his deep, dark eyes.

Logan rushed closer. "Get your hands off her, asshole!"

But the grip on her didn't ease.

So her stranger wasn't intimidated by Logan. Something else to remember. She tilted her head toward Mr. Dangerously Sexy. "Take your hands off me."

Immediately, his hands dropped. "For the record," he murmured. "You put yours on me first."

Had she? She distinctly remembered him touching *her* cheek. But, then, yes, she might have been a bit touchy after that.

"You can touch me anytime, Alice. As long as, you know, you aren't touching me with the intent to kill."

Her lips pressed together.

"Is that shit supposed to be funny?" Logan locked a hand on the stranger's shoulder and heaved him back. "Bastard, get the hell out of—"

"Name," Alice said, voice flat. Because she wanted a name. Needed it.

His eyes were still on her, and he didn't seem to notice Logan at all. "Call me Saint."

He had to be joking. "Sinner," she called instead. Because she was well acquainted with sin, and, staring at him, she knew this man was, too.

Like called to like. Darkness to darkness. Alice knew she carried a strong darkness inside of herself. There was no use denying that stark truth. Or denying the fact that she was drawn to this man.

Like to like.

Together, they might be incredible. Her attraction to him was off-the-charts electric. They could burn down a bed.

Or burn up the world. Because...he was dangerous. Not a wannabe as she'd first charged. But the very real deal. She knew it, deep inside.

Yes, they might be incredible together. Or they could just be another nightmare.

She already had enough nightmares and wasn't particularly in the mood to have more. "I would like to say that meeting you has been a pleasure." A careful exhale. "It hasn't. I hope our paths do not cross again." Brisk now, she turned on her heel and headed for the waiting car.

"They will." A drawl from...*Saint.*

She glanced over her shoulder.

"Our paths are definitely going to cross again. Count on it." A pause. "And as far as I'm concerned, it was a definite pleasure. I'll be seeing you soon." With that, he sauntered away.

Whistling. The man actually whistled as he strode into the darkness, as if he didn't have a care in the world.

How wonderful for him.

She stood beside her car, gripping her keys too tightly, until she could no longer hear the pad of his footsteps or the sound of that too cheery whistling.

Logan edged closer to her. "Want me to give orders that he isn't ever to be allowed in your place again?" Low, barely a breath.

Alice considered that option, and, for the moment, discarded it. "Dig into his life. I want to know everything possible about Saint."

"Good, bad, and all the stuff in between?" Mocking.

"Something tells me there will be plenty of bad." Stuff that she could potentially use against Saint, should he become a problem.

He already is a problem.

Still, she'd always believed in the old adage to...*know thy enemy.* Know him but try not to fuck him. No matter how incredibly tempting he may just be.

***

She stood on the edge of the ravine, with her heart racing so hard that it shook her chest. Her breath heaved in and out, and her whole body shuddered. She forced herself to look over that edge, to inch just a bit closer.

Her tennis shoes hit a few loose rocks and sent them crashing down below. She peeked over the edge, looking for him. He had to be down there, and he—

A hand flew up and locked around her ankle. He grabbed her and she fell forward, tumbling down, down—

Alice fell out of the damn bed. She hit the floor hard and cursed. Sweat covered her body. The stupid dream. It would never stop haunting her.

The covers had fallen with her and twisted around her body. Alice shoved them aside and climbed to her feet. Faint rays of light trickled through her curtains, and she knew there was no point in trying to sleep more.

She'd get dressed. Go for a run.

There are some things you can't run from. But you could sure as hell try.

In moments, Alice had on her jogging shorts, her sports bra, and her sneakers. She slipped from her house, made it down to the street, then immediately took a right.

Five minutes later, Alice realized she was being followed.

No, not followed. *Stalked.*

The day had not gotten off to the best start...

CHAPTER TWO

Alice stopped running. She sucked in a deep breath. Then another. And when she was ready, only then did she turn to face the threat.

Saint. Wearing jogging shorts. A compression shirt that looked truly amazing on him and displayed more of his wonderful, swirling tats. And, of course, he was sporting that killer grin of his.

"What a coincidence," Saint said. "You come this was for your morning run, too?"

She was not in the mood for bullshit. Alice headed straight for him. "Do you always stalk the women you find attractive?"

His eyes widened. "You think I find you attractive?"

"Saint, stop being adorable."

"Excuse me?"

"You're tenting the jogging shorts." She waved down his body. "Of course, you find me attractive. So attractive that you are being stalkery, but I have to stay, you should have just saved yourself some trouble this morning. I told you already that I didn't want our paths to cross—"

"But you were lying."

Yes, she had been. Part of her had very much wanted to see him again. "Fine. I'd like for them to cross, but you and I..." Her gaze dipped over him. Over all those delicious inches and those tenting shorts. *Settle down, woman.* She couldn't help it. There was something about him that called to her. A purely primitive reaction that she'd never had before. She saw him, and she ached. She could all too easily imagine having hot, dirty sex with Saint. Maybe on top of the bar in her speakeasy. Maybe against the wall of an alley. Maybe...*right here.*

No. Bad idea. He wasn't someone she could trust.

And he certainly couldn't trust her.

"You and I..." Alice repeated once more as she tried to get on solid footing with him, "we are not meant to be. Sorry to crush your hopes and dreams, but I suppose someone had to do the dark deed."

"You do lots of dark deeds, my Alice?"

She'd caught the possessive *my*. Had it been deliberate? When she looked in his eyes, she couldn't tell if it had been a slip of the tongue or an intentional push. Either way... "Yes. Yes, I do. But not this morning. This morning, I'm just going for a lovely run."

"Do you run this way every day?"

Her brows climbed. "Why? You think I should vary my routine because I might have *stalkers* following me?" She barely paused. "If it's a true stalker, he'll just follow no matter what path I take. I like going this way. Takes me to the park. Why give up something I enjoy for someone else?"

"Because it's safer?"

Cute. There he went, being adorable. "Do I look like the safe type?"

His gaze slid over her. Slowly. Heat filled his stare.

"Hmm." Saint made a show of stretching. Seemingly casual, he asked, "Do you get a lot of stalkers?"

He certainly had a lot of questions. "I'm staring at one right now."

That hard jaw of his clenched. "I mean it, Alice. Do you have a lot of people like that woman last night? People who want to get photos with you? People who want to be close to you?"

She stepped toward him. "What is your deal?" Enough games.

"My deal?" He rolled back his shoulders. Powerful, broad shoulders.

"Yes." Slightly hissing. "You said you were here to take me down. Down for what, exactly?"

"Ah, there are three missing men linked to you."

Damn you, Saint. Anger snapped through her. "Who made you my judge, jury, and executioner?"

His eyelashes flickered. He had the deepest, darkest brown eyes. No flecks of gold. No softness. Just the tempting dark. "Did you kill them?"

Alice laughed, but not with genuine amusement. Mocking, cold laughter. "Really? You think that's how this works? You follow me while I jog, and I suddenly spill every secret that I have to you? I did *not* take you for an amateur."

"What did you take me for?"

The area was so quiet. Too empty. It wasn't even six a.m. yet. The faintest light had begun to spill onto the historic street. She was completely alone with Saint. A man she didn't know. A man who had to outweigh her by almost a hundred pounds. A man who was big and scary and who seemed intent on following her.

She should have been afraid.

So why wasn't she? "Not a cop." She knew this with certainty. But she hadn't gotten her report back from Logan, not yet, so everything else was just a shot in the dark. "Maybe a PI? I've had more than my share of those dodging my steps. All thinking they'd magically be the one to solve the big mystery that is little old me." She touched her chest.

His gaze followed the movement. Lingered. Heated even more. Ah, yes, the spell-binding power of a sports bra. You'd think he hadn't seen one before.

"Did I kill those men? Make their bodies disappear? Am I as bad as the stories say?" Her hand dropped. "Or is there a different side to the tale?"

Saint didn't deny being a PI. Didn't confirm it, either. Instead, he said, "At first, I thought someone of your size would have trouble with the bodies."

Her temples began to pound. It was truly too early for this.

"Then I realized that making people vanish was a specialty of yours. Sort of a family trait." He crossed his arms over his powerful chest. "Almost as if...by magic. *Abracadabra.*"

Alice laughed. Once more, the sound mocked him. "Bravo. You've cracked the case. You've somehow managed to figure out—probably by doing a basic Internet search—that my father was a magician. Not a very famous one. Dear old dad never made the big stages, but he did enjoy his work. And, yes, my speakeasy is named in honor of him. Your sleuthing skills are top-notch." She looked at her wrist. At the watch that kept track of her steps and her heartrate and...

My heartrate is way too high. That escalation had nothing to do with her run and everything to do with the man in front of her. But she kept her expression controlled and her voice cool as she told him, "Chat time is over. I have to finish my run, and then get busy with my day." She dropped her hand. Smiled brightly. "You know the old saying. I have places to go—"

"And people to kill?"

Do not tell him to fuck off. Do not. "Fuck off." It just felt so good to say. She gave him a salute. Then went on her way.

He didn't follow her, but she could feel his eyes on her. Watching her so very carefully.

That man is going to be such a problem for me.

***

"Murder."

Alice looked up from the extremely boring paperwork in front of her. Accounting sucked, but someone had to go over the books every now and then. Logan stood in her doorway, managing to appear both satisfied and grim at the same time. An interesting combination.

She fiddled with the pen in her hand. "Care to elaborate?"

"Oh, you know...*murder*...That would be why your new friend Saint went to jail."

Jail. Her spine straightened. She stopped fiddling with the pen. "You have my full attention."

Logan sauntered inside. "Thought I might. Did I mention it was *multiple murders?*"

The plot thickens. Her heart raced a little faster. "You're mentioning it now. And you're about to tell me more. By more, I mean everything."

He pulled out the chair in front of her desk. Flipped it around, straddled it, then sat. "Your *Saint* was eighteen at the time."

"He's not mine." Why had she even said that? Why did it feel wrong?

Logan hummed. "Quite brutal crimes. Someone with a whole lot of rage committed the attacks. Saint was implicated because there was a witness who swore he was at the scene of one of the attacks. That he'd fought with the victim."

Alice barely breathed.

"But Saint apparently has friends in high places."

A dangerous point in his favor.

"He was eventually cleared of the charges. Funny thing about that, Saint was cleared by the very bounty hunter who tracked his ass down and tossed him in a cell."

Her brow furrowed. That was odd.

"Saint joined the bounty hunter in his business. Been doing the job for years. Has a reputation for taking on the worst of the worst." He steepled his fingers beneath his chin. "You know what they say. Sometimes, it takes a monster to catch a monster."

"I don't think anyone says that."

"You sure?"

"No." *I am so screwed.* "Why is a bounty hunter after me? I haven't been charged with any crimes, and I'm certainly not fleeing from the law." Because there had never been any evidence left to conclusively link her to the crimes. Alice had made sure of it.

"Oh, didn't I mention it? No? Turns out your Saint has a side gig."

"Stop calling him mine."

There was no amusement on Logan's face. "But he is yours, Alice. He's your problem, and you are going to have to eliminate him."

Her eyes narrowed.

"Ever hear of a group called the Ice Breakers?" Logan asked.

"No. What are they? Some hockey team?"

"They would be his side gig. A group that likes to solve cold cases. You know, find the missing and stop the evil murderers who got away with their crimes." The faint lines near his mouth deepened. "I'm sure you see where this is going."

Anyone could see where it was headed.

"Word is that Saint likes a challenge," Logan added.

That name again. *Saint.* "He's no Saint. Tell me his real name."

"Sebastian. Sebastian Black." Anger hummed in his voice. "I assume that with all of this newfound knowledge, he will no longer be allowed entrance to Abracadabra?"

Alice shook her head. "You assume wrong. In fact, I want you to roll out the red carpet for him when Sebastian makes an appearance tonight."

Now his lips parted. "You're kidding me."

"Do I ever kid?"

Logan glanced upward as he seemed to consider the situation. "I...no." His bright gaze shot back to her. "This is a mistake. I said *eliminate* him. Not throw a party for the asshole."

She didn't plan for a party. "I want to know more about the murders that got him locked up. I want to know how long he was in jail. I want to know why he was so special that he got out." She shoved her chair back and stood. "Whatever file you've got going on him, I want to read it." Every single detail mattered because the more she knew about Saint, the better she would be able to manipulate him.

Some wars were fought outright. You saw the attack coming.

Not really her style.

She preferred to get very, very close to her enemies. That way, they never saw the threat, not until she was ready to draw blood.

Muttering about mistakes she'd live to regret, Logan made his way out of her office. The door closed quietly behind him. Alice remained standing behind her desk.

Not a PI.

A bounty hunter. Someone who chose to chase monsters. Someone who'd once been accused of murder himself. Saint— Sebastian—was no easy prey. In fact, he might just be the strongest foe she'd ever faced.

In some ways, that made him...absolutely perfect.

***

Saint knew the password. He'd even dressed the part. The tux had been a rental, but it fit like it had been designed for him. Once upon a time, he would have laughed if someone had told him that he'd be dressing up in an outfit like this one.

Back when he'd been poor. Scraping by on the streets. Pickpocketing his way through the tourists and making sure that he'd be able to get enough cash so that he and his mom could eat.

He'd been trouble, back in the day. He still was trouble.

And so is she.

Alice Shephard was very dangerous, very seductive trouble. The more he learned about her, the more his curiosity grew.

His hand lifted, and he rapped against the wooden door that would take him inside Abracadabra. Saint was ready to spit out the password—

The door swung open almost instantly.

"Alice is waiting for you," the bouncer said with a wave of his hand. "Go right in."

Instead of going in, Saint frowned. "I don't have to say the magic word tonight?"

"*Alice* is the magic word. She wants to see you." The big, burly fellow—again, wearing black—jerked his thumb over his shoulder. "What Alice wants, she gets."

"Is that the general rule for her?" He didn't enter. Just kept waiting. Saint wondered just what this guy knew about his lovely boss.

"Yeah, that's the rule."

Nice to know. "How long have you worked for Alice?"

The bouncer offered him a grim smile. "Ever since I got my ass out of prison, and she gave me this job."

"Out of curiosity..." His flaw again, rearing its head. "Just what were you in prison for?"

"Assault."

Saint's shoulders tensed. He wasn't particularly surprised to discover that Alice liked to hire dangerous employees. But what did surprise him was the odd surge of protectiveness he felt...

Toward fucking Alice. Like that made a bit of sense. "Make sure you keep your hands *off* her."

"What?"

"I think you heard me just fine." He held the bouncer's stare—correction, glare.

"I wouldn't hurt her. Ever." A sharp retort. "No one else would hire me when I got out. Alice gave me a chance. I'd do fucking anything for her."

Saint suspected Alice hadn't hired this man out of the goodness of her heart. At this point, he wasn't sure there was goodness in her. In fact, he wasn't quite sure what to make of Alice. "Would you kill for her?" A question he just threw out to see a reaction and—

"Alice doesn't like to be kept waiting." A sharp warning that had been delivered by her other flunky. The blond who'd been at her side so quickly the previous night.

Saint shifted his attention to the man who'd appeared behind the bouncer. Logan Becker. Saint had done research on him and discovered that Logan had been in Alice's life for quite a while, going back to when her father had still been alive. Logan had been her father's assistant, until her father's untimely death right after one of his biggest shows. Just when his act had attracted attention, he'd given his final performance.

"And before you ask, sure, I'd kill for her." Logan smiled coldly at him. "Not that she'd ever ask. Alice is the kind of woman who likes to take care of her own problems."

How close was Logan to Alice? He was older than her, maybe by five or six years. Were they lovers? If not now, had they been in the past? This man kept her secrets, Saint was sure of it. Perhaps Logan could be a weak link that Saint could use.

But Logan turned away before Saint could say anything else, and he began marching back down the corridor. Saint cast one more look at the bouncer, then followed him. Like Saint, Logan was also wearing a tux. The evening promised to be a formal, decadent affair. At least, that had been the description on the app. Alice's business was quite high tech. People who wanted to get in her speakeasy downloaded the app and then Alice picked a lucky number of individuals to gain entrance. She sent them the password and dress instructions for the night.

When he followed Logan into the main area, he wasn't surprised to see that the place was packed. But the scene was a bit different from the night before. Ice sculptures had been added. A giant ice dragon that had alcohol pouring from its mouth and into waiting glasses. A snarling tiger that crept down frozen stairs as he stalked his prey.

There was also an overflowing chocolate fountain for the eager guests, and a classical band played on the stage.

The middle of the speakeasy had been transformed into a dance floor. Elegant couples moved in graceful time to one another. He looked toward the bar, but a man was preparing drinks. Not Alice.

"Hurt her, and I will fucking kill you."

The warning was given quietly.

Saint turned back to Logan.

Logan grinned cheerfully at him, as if he hadn't just issued a death threat. His words had been so low that Saint knew no one else had overheard them.

"And she won't have to ask, of course," Logan continued in the same, low tone. "I'll do it for fun."

"Do you often kill for fun?"

Logan's grin merely stretched.

"Do you often kill *for* her?" Saint pressed. "Because someone has hurt her, and you're looking to get payback? Is that what happened with the other men in her life? They hurt her, so you jumped in to handle them?"

Logan took a step closer to Saint. "Why act like there are no sins on your soul?" A wry shake of his head. "We both know that is not the case. And it doesn't matter how hard you try, you can't make up for what was done before."

Saint felt a faint tickle along the back of his neck. Logan looked entirely too pleased with himself. *He knows who I am.* Well, big damn deal.

Someone tapped Saint on the shoulder. He spun around.

And almost didn't breathe.

Alice smiled at him. Her hair has sleek and straight, parted in the middle and sliding down to make her cheekbones look even sharper than before. Her eyes did that peculiar luminous thing where they looked even more gold than normal topaz, probably because the dress she wore was a tantalizing mix of gold and black. Her lips were red, a dark, lush red, and she stared at him as if...as if she was actually glad to see him.

Impossible, of course. A lie. But...

I'm glad to see her. Because she was his prey. His target. Because this was another chance to interrogate her. Because...

"Would you like to dance with me?" Alice asked him.

He could feel eyes on them. Saint was pretty sure everyone in that speakeasy watched him—or, rather, her. "Can't think of anything I'd like to do more." He reached for her hand. Curled his fingers around hers and was oddly aware of the fragility in her fingers. Such a delicate hand.

She was delicate. He knew her mother had been a ballerina, back before she'd fallen in love with Alice's father and become his assistant. For years, she'd worked with him, using her small form to easily escape and create illusions. Alice was built along similar lines. As he drew her onto the dance floor, and his left hand went to her waist he had the odd feeling that...

I need to touch her with her care. Can't hold her too tight. Can't bruise her.

So he kept his hold gentle. One hand on her waist. One hand gripping hers.

"We're not at prom," Alice said, and he could hear the hint of laughter in her voice. "No chaperones are going to tell you that you're too close or that you're holding me inappropriately."

"Wouldn't know about that. Never went to prom." Not exactly his scene.

"Really? Hmm. Neither did I." She tugged her hand free of his, but only so she could then place both of her hands around his neck. She wore heels again. Incredibly high heels but she moved with ease on the dance floor. "Wrap your arms around me," she said.

He did because it was what he wanted. He pulled her flush against him. Loved the way she felt against him. As if she fit. A lie. No one ever fit him. No one could handle the darkness he carried.

Alice has plenty of darkness.

"I won't bite," Alice promised him in that husky, seductive voice that made him think of a wrecked bed and silken limbs wrapped around him.

"I will."

She gave a little jolt. Then laughed. "Promises, promises."

His hold tightened on her a little bit more. "Yes." She smelled just as good tonight. No, even better. He could all too easily imagine stripping off her clothes. Kissing her skin. Tasting her, everywhere.

"Is seducing me part of your master plan?"

Her words pulled him from the fantasy that had taken root in his head.

"Is it like, Ice Breaker 101 to seduce your prey and get close to her?"

He maneuvered her away from the other dancers. Didn't ease his hold at all. "There is no Ice Breaker 101."

"Then maybe it's just your standard procedure. Do you always try to seduce your marks?"

Now he laughed. "Most of the marks I chase don't look quite like you. They tend to be bastards with brutal fists who have rap sheets that stretch a mile long. They're violent and dangerous, and someone needs to toss them in a cage so that they can't ever get out."

She looked up at him. "And that someone is you?"

"Some days, it is."

Alice held his stare. He realized that they weren't moving any longer. No more gentle swaying. They'd stopped, on the far side of the dance floor, and were just gazing at one another.

Her tongue swiped over her lower lip. "Is that what you want to do with me? Toss me in a cage so that I can't ever get out?"

He could think of a thousand things he wanted to do to her in that instance, but locking her away...*no*. Not at the top of his list.

Unless she did it. Fuck, but he didn't want her to be guilty. The thought shocked him, and Saint let her go.

"I will take that as a yes," Alice murmured. "Pity. I wanted to do other things with you. Locking you up wasn't on my agenda. But you know what? Maybe it will be fun."

What?

She eased from his grasp, but then surprised Saint by taking his hand. "Come with me."

He had the unsettling idea that he just might follow her anywhere. The thought pissed him off. Was that how it had been for those other fools? They'd gotten drawn in by her? Hadn't cared that she was taking them straight to hell?

He was better than this. Stronger. He didn't get taken in by a pretty face, and lust sure as hell didn't rule him. Yes, he wanted Alice. His desire for her worried him because it was dark and heated and too *primitive*. Almost savage. He had never reacted this way before. Maybe because...He'd always held back with other lovers. Been afraid of frightening them if they saw him for who—what—he really was.

But instinct told him that he didn't need to hold back with Alice.

Without another word, she led him away from the crowd. Down another corridor, this one through a hallway that curved, and into a backroom. There was a keypad near the door. A modern bit of technology that stood out in the hallway that seemed to have been frozen in time. She tapped in a code, and the door opened. "I only bring a select few back here." She sent him a glance that held too much mystery. "Consider yourself a VIP." She pushed the door open wider. Stepped inside.

He wasn't sure what he expected but...

Magic.

That was what he found. A room filled with magic. Or rather, filled with old magic tricks and props. A black table held a top hat. Gleaming, silver rings surrounded the hat. To the right, he recognized a water torture cell, minus the water. A brown trunk had been pushed into the corner of the room, and a large, red box—one with what appeared to be swords cutting through its center—rested close to the trunk.

She shut the door behind him. Made her way to the desk that sat near the window. She reached into the top drawer.

He looked around. "Quite the collection. Did it belong to your father?"

"Creditors took nearly everything my father owned the day after I put him in the ground. With the exception of that rather large, magical red box, these are my own collection pieces. That water torture chamber actually once belonged to Harry Houdini."

Saint edged closer to the cell. He could easily imagine a magician hanging upside down in that chamber, bound, and surrounded by water. Twisting and turning to get free as the crowd watched. "Impressive."

"Glad you think so."

He glanced back at her. "Can you do any tricks?"

Her lush mouth tightened. "Don't really like the term 'trick' personally." She had something cradled in her hands. He caught a glimpse of silver. "You can call them 'illusions' or 'effects,' those words fit better." She came around to the front of her desk. Propped her hip against it. Studied him.

His gaze fell to her hands. "Are those handcuffs?"

"Why, yes, they appear to be."

His stare returned to her face. He quirked a brow. "Feeling kinky, are you?"

"I'm actually feeling like I'd enjoy answers from you."

"And you think I'll give them to you if you cuff me?" He closed in on her. More like stalked toward her. He seemed to be pulled straight to Alice. Saint didn't stop. Not until he was right in front of her.

"Why tease?" She tilted back her head. "We both know it's not the first time you've been cuffed, Sebastian."

"Don't really like that name. Much prefer Saint." No one ever called him Sebastian. That was the name for another time, another man. Sebastian had died ages ago.

I killed him.

He tried to shake off the past. "How about this? I won't call them magic *tricks* if you don't call me Sebastian."

"But we already agreed that the title of 'Saint' doesn't fit you."

He took the cuffs from her. Stared down at them. They were heavy. Solid. And, yes, too damn much like the cuffs that had once surrounded his own wrists. "I told everyone I was innocent. No one believed me." The past rose again, even stronger this time. "Sure as shit not the other inmates. They made life a living hell for an eighteen-year-old kid, and they started calling me Saint just to mock me."

Her lashes fluttered.

Why the fuck had he just told her all of that? Frowning, he glanced down at the cuffs. Not like it was the first time he'd seen cuffs since his arrest. Hell, he used cuffs all the time on the perps he hunted. But for some reason, this moment felt *different*. Because she was different?

"I bet they didn't get to mock you for long." Alice's voice had turned musing. "I would imagine that even at eighteen, you were quite strong. A junior badass in training."

He had been. Yes. "Each day was a fight." More talking. More secrets that he hadn't even told his own brother. "I'd get put in isolation and left there. When I'd get out, it would be the same routine. They thought I was prey, so I showed them that I wasn't." Until he'd gotten out for good. Until he'd been able to prove that he wasn't guilty.

Until Memphis proved it for me.

"And now you hunt the monsters," Alice concluded. "Like you were once hunted."

He stretched out the cuffs. Tested them. They felt like the real deal, and he didn't see any hidden mechanism to open them. "I hunt them because I'm a predator, and they're prey."

"Is that what I am to you? Prey?"

He reached for her wrist. Such a fragile, delicate wrist. He put one cuff around her. Closed it with a click. "I don't know what you are."

"But you have a suspicion." She showed no alarm at being cuffed. Like it was a normal occurrence for her. "That's why you're here. Why you think you will take me down. Because I'm one of the monsters you like to hunt. You think you'll get close to me, and you'll trick me into spilling all my deliciously deep and dark secrets to you. Then you'll lock me away."

He reached for her other wrist. Didn't cuff her. Instead, his fingers slid along her inner wrist. He could feel the beat of her pulse. Fast. She sounded so cool and controlled, but her racing pulse gave her away.

"You were innocent," she said.

He'd leaned over her. Been pulled even closer to her by that crazy, invisible magnet she seemed to exert.

"If you were innocent..." Breathy. Soft. "How are you so sure that I'm not, too?"

He wanted her mouth. He wanted her. *Stay focused. Keep her talking.* "Is that what you're telling me? That you didn't kill those three men?"

Three men.

Three men who'd been drawn to her, just as Saint was now drawn to her?

Thinking about them had his body tensing.

Donovan Eldridge. The first man to vanish. Alice had been nineteen. He'd been twenty-one. They'd gone hiking together at Providence Canyon State Park. Only Alice had returned home. She'd told authorities that she'd gotten separated from Donovan. Saint had read the reports. She'd been tearful. Bruised. Cut. Dehydrated. Even had a broken rib. She'd stumbled onto a park ranger and said that Donovan had disappeared in the middle of the night.

Donovan—a skilled hiker, according to all accounts—had never been found again.

An accident. Tragic. Everyone agreed. And, at the time, Alice had been cast as the victim.

Until the second man went missing. Two years later.

Twenty-one-year-old Alice had been engaged. She'd been planning to marry—

"Usually when a man is this close to me, I have his complete attention."

Saint blinked.

"But you are far, far away from me, and I find that rather annoying. And that's why you're cuffed."

His gaze shot down. Sure enough, Alice had managed to unlock the single cuff he'd put around her wrist, and now both of *his* hands were cuffed. He hadn't even felt the slight movements. Damn. He couldn't help but be vaguely impressed. Okay, fine, more than vaguely.

"I guess I caught you," she noted with an arched brow. "Now what do I get to do with you?" Her hand rose and her index finger tapped against her bottom lip as she seemed to consider the matter. "Oh, I have an idea. Like I said, I do like to have a man's complete attention." Then she curled her hands along his jaw, pulled him toward her, and put her mouth against his.

CHAPTER THREE

The kiss wasn't supposed to matter. Passion was just a tool, one she used if necessary. A kiss was a kiss. But...

This was different. Part of her had feared it would be.

The instant her lips touched his, she could feel the change in the atmosphere. The room felt hotter. Smaller. He felt bigger. Tension snaked through her body. His lips parted, so did hers, and when his tongue swept out—

Desire.

Lust.

Hunger.

She stopped playing a game. This wasn't about seducing him. Manipulating him. For just a moment, it was merely about letting go. Feeling the rushing tide of need blast through her in a way that it hadn't in so long. Suddenly, Alice couldn't get close enough to him. Her hands dropped so that she could touch his chest. Feel his muscles. Absorb more of his heat and power.

He picked her up.

Wait, wasn't he cuffed?

Saint sat her on the edge of the desk. Her legs were spread, and he stepped between. Dazed, she pulled back. *Out of control. Slow down.* Her gaze dropped to the hands—*his* hands—that had curled around her waist to lift her.

The cuff dangled from only one wrist.

Alice started to smile.

"I want more." Saint's voice. Guttural. Demanding.

So do I. Her smile died.

He took her mouth again. Harder. Deeper. He stood between her legs, and the skirt of her dress had hiked up. His arousal shoved toward her. Her nipples were tight and aching, and her hands pressed eagerly against him. This wasn't about a game. No one-upmanship. This was just raw need.

A beautiful, stark craving.

His hand dropped to her thigh. She felt the cold touch of the handcuff sliding over her skin as he pushed up her dress even higher. She could have stopped him. She didn't. She was enjoying this far too much to stop.

"Alice..." A murmur against her lips. "Is that a knife strapped to your thigh?"

"Of course. I always like to have it close." She nipped his lower lip. "I'm sure you have one strapped to your ankle." As if that would be his only weapon. Not if she'd assessed him correctly.

He slipped her knife from the sheath. She heard the faint clink as he put it on the desk, then those wicked fingers of his went back to her thigh. The calluses on his fingertips were wonderfully rough against her as—

Pounding on her door broke the lust-filled spell.

Dammit.

"Alice!" Logan's growling voice. One that hit her like a splash of icy water. "I need you, now."

He'd known that she planned a private meeting with Saint, so for him to interrupt, she understood it had to be bad. Swallowing, she eased back a little from Saint. She made sure her expression was schooled and hoped that no emotion showed in her eyes. "That was delightful. Perhaps we can resume again at a later date? Provided, of course," Alice could absolutely not resist adding, "that you haven't managed to lock me away in a jail cell."

His eyes gleamed. A mix of dark lust and...amusement? "We will be resuming. Count on it."

"*Alice.*" Logan sounded even more frantic. Unusual, for him. She knew, though, that he wouldn't burst into her office. Even if she hadn't locked the door, Logan would never invade her privacy that way. They had rules, after all.

Sighing, Alice pressed against Saint's shoulders. He eased away. As he did so, his right hand slid toward the cuff that still circled his left wrist. His fingers moved quickly, and the cuff opened.

"You got the paperclip from my desk." She'd caught a glimpse of it. "I'm impressed."

"Not yet, you're not. But you will be."

She would not smile at him. She'd already given him enough of her smiles.

"Did I pass the first test?" Saint wanted to know.

She reached for her knife. Took her time sliding it back into the sheath that she strapped to her upper thigh. Alice could feel his eyes on her as she slowly—very, very slowly—lowered the skirt of her dress back into place. "I have no idea what you mean."

"Don't you?"

"Alice. Check the security footage. Exterior. *Your lot."*

Her chest tightened. Enough playing. She rushed back around the desk and tapped on her keyboard. A moment later, she was viewing the security footage. What she saw had her huffing out a breath of frustration.

"What's going on?" Saint asked.

Her head lifted. "Your client is pissing me off."

A faint line appeared between his dark eyebrows. "Excuse me?"

But she wasn't in the mood to excuse him or anyone else. She'd gone from glorious passion to cold rage in an instant. Sometimes, enough was just enough. "Don't insult my intelligence. I hate when people do that." Alice marched toward her door. Hauled it open.

Logan filled the entranceway. "Took you long enough," he groused. "What the hell did you do, stop for tea?"

Cute. "I'll deal with her." She started to push past him.

He just moved to better block her path. "Nope. Let the cops do it. You've handled her with kid gloves too long. She's out of control. If you don't watch it, she'll become as dangerous as he was."

"What's going on?" Saint repeated his earlier question with a distinct edge in his voice.

Alice realized that she could still taste him. And that Saint very well might have been aware of what his *client* had been doing. Perhaps the confusion was an act. She glanced back over her shoulder, trying to judge for certain. "Were you aware that

Tracy Eldridge had followed you to Savannah? Or did the two of you come here together?"

"What?" He bounded toward her. "No, no we didn't come together, and no, I didn't realize she was here." Saint shook his head. "What in the hell is she doing in town?"

"At the moment, she's spray painting my car."

His jaw dropped in surprise. "Tell me that you're shitting me."

"She's not shitting you," Logan snapped back. "Your client is a psycho. Doesn't exactly speak well for you, does it?"

Alice didn't give Saint a chance to respond to that retort. She ducked around Logan and stormed for the back exit. With every step, her heels clicked, faster and angrier. She'd tried to be nice. Or at least, tried to appear nice. She was dealing with the grieving sister and all that drama. But enough was enough.

Alice was highly conscious of the two men following her. They could come and enjoy the show. She knew that Logan would have her back. He always did. Saint's reaction to the scene he was about to see—that was what interested her.

Which side would he chose? Tracy's? Or hers?

Alice shoved open the back door. Marched for her car. "Red is my favorite color," she called out, and her sharp voice had the woman with the spray can jerking and spinning around in shock. "But I don't particularly enjoy having red paint all across my windshield." And that was where it was. The paint had been carefully applied across the front, and thanks to the lights out back, she could easily discern the word...

Killer.

"How incredibly original," Alice said as she closed in on Tracy and—

Tracy sprayed the red paint at her. It was a fast burst, right to the chest and arms, and Alice staggered to a surprised stop.

"What in the fuck?" A furious snarl—not from Logan, but from Saint. He bounded in front of Alice. Shielded her with his body. "What in the hell are you doing, Tracy?"

Alice spread her arms as she looked at the paint on her. "I believe it's obvious. She's giving both my car—and me—a new paint job."

Saint's head whipped toward her. "That's not funny."

"No." Flat. "It's not." Alice stepped to the side. She didn't need him to shield her. She'd been fighting her own battles for a very, very long time.

Logan rushed forward. He snatched the spray can from Tracy's fingers. She let out a sharp cry. He ignored the cry. "I'm calling the cops! Your ass is getting arrested!"

"No!" A cross between a yell and a sob. Tracy pointed at Alice. The tip of her index finger looked dark, probably because she'd painted herself when she'd held down the top of the spray bottle. "She's the one who belongs in jail, not me! *Not me!* She's the killer!" A scream. "A *kill—*"

"Stop." Saint's voice. Low. Commanding.

And she stopped. Tracy blinked. Looked at him. Seemed confused.

"You shouldn't be here," he told her.

Tracy tossed a glare at Alice. There was no missing the hate on her face. It was, after all, a familiar sight. "How long is it going to take? You were supposed to lock her away."

Right. Like she hadn't already known that was the master plan. After all, as soon as she'd realized that Saint worked to solve cold cases, Alice had known exactly who had reached out to him. The grieving sister. "I'm getting a restraining order," Alice announced.

She felt all eyes on her.

"If you come near me again, I will have you arrested. I've put up with your accusations, your stalkings, and your defacement of my property long enough." Because this was not the first time Tracy had gotten spray-can crazy. In fact, Alice had planned for this situation. She raised her hand and pointed back toward her building. "Smile, Tracy, you're on camera."

Tracy didn't smile. She screamed and launched herself at Alice.

Alice didn't move at all. She thought a nice hit, maybe a slap on the cheek, would play well in the video that she planned to show to the cops and then leak to the media. After all, a woman had to do what a woman had to do.

But Tracy didn't get to make contact. Saint grabbed her. Locked his arms around her stomach and hauled her back against him. "You are not touching her," he growled to Tracy. "*Calm down.*"

Alice almost told him that situation would not occur. In all the time that Alice had known Tracy, the other woman had rarely appeared calm. Or, if she did, it was just a facade. Donovan had been great at facades, too. Had to be a family trait.

"I could call the cops on you right now," Alice said. A true statement. "You just destroyed my property. You assaulted me—"

"I did *not*—" Tracy fired back.

"My dress would say otherwise." Talk about a waste. But, it had given her the evidence she needed. Some people were so predictable. "Your money won't make this evidence disappear. I'm tired of your harassment. My goodwill only goes so far." People like Tracy thought that they could control everyone because they had money to burn.

You can't control me.

"There is nothing *good* about you!" Tracy spat. "You're a killer! I know what you did! You hurt Donovan, and then you left him to die! He loved you, and you killed him."

"You're wrong." That was all she'd ever said. *Because Donovan had not loved me.* Alice didn't think that Donovan had been capable of loving anyone.

Or maybe Alice was the one not capable of love. Some days, it was hard to know for certain. Alice rolled back her shoulders and focused her attention on Saint. He still had a tight grip on Tracy. "Why don't you take your client back to her hotel? Perhaps you can convince her that staying away from me is truly the lifestyle choice she needs to make."

His jaw hardened. "Alice..."

She didn't want to talk more. She needed to clean off the paint that felt too sticky on her arms. "Good night." Alice spun toward the speakeasy.

Logan closed in right behind her. "You're being too soft," he gritted as he trailed after her.

All part of my master plan. But she couldn't reassure him, not then. Not when others were watching. So she just kept putting one foot in front of the other. She reached for the building's back door.

"*Alice.*"

Saint's voice. Ignoring his call, Alice opened the door and went back inside. "Keep the spray can," she quietly instructed Logan. "It will have her prints on it." Something they might need later.

He caught her arm with his left hand. Tugged her around. "I get that you like your games..."

Actually, she did enjoy them. But in this particular instance... "This isn't a game."

"She's getting bolder. This isn't her parking across the street and glaring at you all night." Anger shook each word. "What if she'd had a gun instead of the spray can? What if, when she'd turned, she'd shot you? What the hell then?"

It was a scenario she had considered—right as the spray paint hit her body. "She is not going to be a problem any longer."

"Because you're getting a restraining order? Yeah, I understand that you wanted proof she was causing trouble, but you need more than a piece of paper. People like her don't care about the law. Fuck, she probably thinks she's above the law because of her money. Probably thinks that she can—" He stopped, no doubt because Logan realized what he had *almost* said.

Alice exhaled slowly, then finished for him, "Probably thinks she can get away with murder?" She swallowed. "What an incredible idea. Wonder if that ever happens in real life." Her heels tapped on the floor as she headed back to her office.

***

This was a clusterfuck. "You should not be here," Saint snapped.

"Let me go!" Tracy heaved against his hold.

He lifted her up and carried her from the scene.

"What are you doing?" she cried. "Stop it! Put me down! Now!"

He cleared the building. Let her go.

She immediately whirled to confront him. Fury had her face—

Her eyes widened. She was staring at his mouth. They were under one of the bright streetlights on the main road, and she seemed utterly horrified. "There's lipstick on you."

What? His hand lifted. He dragged the back of his hand over his mouth.

"You came out with her." Tracy seemed to be putting the pieces together. "OhmyGod, were you in there, *kissing* her?"

Like he was going to answer that question. Like he would admit he'd been in fucking heaven until hell came crashing down on him. "Why are you in Savannah?" Saint kept his voice low. "I told you that I'd investigate Alice."

"Oh, right, that's what you were doing. *Investigating* her."

She may as well have said...*Fucking her*. But, no, he hadn't been. Yet. "Did Alice and your brother have problems before he vanished?" A deliberate push to see how she would react.

"What? He—he *loved* her. That was the problem! He was blind, and he couldn't see her for what she really was. Just like you can't."

He could see just fine. Twenty, twenty. "Your brother got into a lot of fights when he was younger."

"What in the hell does that have to do with *anything?*"

It had to do with everything.

"Are you investigating *him?*" Stunned. "He's the victim! She's the killer! You are supposed to bring her down, not listen to some old dirty laundry about Donovan and his temper."

And there it was—paydirt. "Your brother was noted for having quite the temper." He thought of the scene he'd just left. "Guess it's a family thing?"

She didn't back down. Instead, anger poured from her as Tracy snarled, "Yes, it's a family thing. Our father raised us to take no shit. To stand up for ourselves. He ran the city, and he told us that you never, *ever* tolerate disrespect."

He'd known a few assholes like that in his time. "And did he also teach you that you were better than everyone else?"

"Damn right, we were."

Yep, Saint had definitely met assholes like that one. "Let me guess. Your brother grew up to be just like him? That is, until your parents died."

She sucked in a shuddering breath. "Tragic accident. One tragedy after another...It won't ever stop. It won't stop because Alice is getting away with his murder and you were supposed to help but you aren't. You're just sniffing after her and you want—"

Enough. "Number four."

"What?"

Was he gonna have to draw the woman a picture? "You said she'd be moving on to the next victim. That it was only a matter of time until she picked some other dumb bastard and got him in her web." He looked around, didn't see anyone close. He'd spell shit out for Tracy so she would back the hell off and stay *away* from Alice. "I need to get close to Alice. If I'm going to find out the truth, screw it, why not put myself in the line of fire?"

"You...you aren't serious."

Maybe he was. Maybe he wasn't. Right now, all he wanted to do was get this woman far, far from Alice. When she'd sprayed that paint at Alice—

Fuck me, what if that had been a gun? He'd been so busy checking into Alice's life that he hadn't investigated his own client well enough. That situation would be changing, ASAP. Because Alice was his—his *case*—and no one was going to threaten her. "You're going to stay away from her."

"You're putting yourself up as her next target?" Now Tracy was all breathless. "That's brilliant!"

No, it wasn't. And had he just caught the scent of a cigarette? Saint stiffened.

But as if a switch had been flipped, Tracy now seemed almost giddy. She edged closer to him. "She'll tell you everything, and you'll stay on your guard because you know what she is. She won't be able to catch you unaware, not like she did Donovan. You can stop her. *We* can finally stop her!" She threw her arms around him. Hugged him tightly. "Thank you!"

Hell, no. He grabbed her hands, pried them off him, and pushed her back. "You can't be anywhere near Alice. Get out of town. Stay away from her. I'll take care of her from here on out."

A frantic nod. "Absolutely. I understand. I've got it now."

No, you don't.

But she whirled away. Rushed down the street and toward a long, black limo that waited. *She came to the scene in a limo? Are you freaking kidding me?*

She hopped in the back. The limo's headlights turned on and shot right toward Saint. And when those headlights turned on, he was able to see the figure who'd been lurking about ten feet away, in the shelter of an arched doorway.

A figure he recognized.

The bouncer. The ex-con. Fuck.

The guy stared straight at Saint. He slowly lifted the cigarette in his hand. Took a puff. Red flared from the end of his cigarette.

I am so screwed. Saint reached into his pocket. Hauled out some cash. "How much is it going to take?" Saint asked as he closed in on the man.

The bouncer dropped the cigarette. Crushed it beneath his feet. "More than you've got."

"Don't be too sure of that."

***

She kept spare clothes at the club. Alice did her best to wash the paint off her arms, then she dressed quickly in a pair of black pants and a black top—the same clothing she ordered for her staff. There was a reason for the black, and it wasn't just some esthetic. It was an old magic secret. Black curtains lined all the walls of her place, and if necessary, her staff members could easily blend with those curtains in the dark. They could slip close. Pick up conversations. Secrets. All you had to do was slide on a black cap and you would practically vanish in the right lighting...

"Let me take you home," Logan said as she met him at the bar. His voice was pitched low, just for her. "Not like you can drive your car."

No, at the moment, she couldn't. "I'll get a ride. You keep an eye on things here."

His lips tightened, but he didn't argue. Logan knew she needed him on site. Alice inclined her head, then slid toward the curtains on the right so she could—

"Uh, Alice?" Hesitant.

It was her main bouncer, Marcel. She managed to offer him a quick smile. "I'm sorry, but I'm in a bit of a rush—"

"He's using you."

"Excuse me?" The voices around her were loud, so it was a bit hard to hear him. She moved closer.

"That guy who's been coming around. Last night. Then tonight. You gave him permission to come right in, but you shouldn't have." Marcel's big hands twisted in front of him. "He's using you. Heard him say it myself."

Marcel had her complete attention.

"He was talking to that woman in the limo."

A limo? Really? Tracy had taken a limo to the scene of her crime? So typical. Didn't she understand that you should try *not* to be seen when breaking the law? Some things should be obvious. *Amateur.* "What did he say to her?"

"That he was...was gonna get close. Learn all your secrets." His Adam's apple bobbed. "Said he was putting himself up as your next target."

Her target? Fabulous. *So he's decided I'm guilty.* "I would certainly hate to disappoint Saint."

"You can't trust him."

Someone was going to get a bonus. "Don't worry, Marcel. I don't." Marcel Taylor. He'd served two years for assault because he'd nearly beaten a man to death. That man had sexually assaulted Marcel's sister. Left her shell-shocked and suicidal. Marcel had found her after she'd slashed her wrist. He'd been able to save her, barely, and then he'd gone after her attacker.

When he'd gotten out of prison, he'd turned up on her club's doorstep, looking for a job. Maybe because of her reputation, he'd thought she wouldn't be too choosy about who she hired. He was wrong, of course. She was extremely choosy. In all facets of her life. Marcel just happened to fit all her necessary qualifications, so she'd hired him on the spot.

And he certainly kept proving himself to be just the kind of person she needed. Admiringly, she noted, "I swear, you've got management written all over you."

"You...don't seem worried."

What good would worry do? Worrying had never once solved a problem. But action on the other hand? Action eliminated problems. "I appreciate you coming to me. If you happen to hear anything else useful, please do let me know."

His intense stare held hers. "I don't care what they say about you. You were good to me when no one else was, and I won't ever forget that."

Ah, but Marcel was wrong. She wasn't particularly good. She just knew how to look after her own self interests. She didn't let people get close without knowing exactly who they were, deep down. Past the veneer that could fool so many. Once upon a time, Alice hadn't known to look so deeply. She'd believed the lies and easy promises.

No more. Not ever again.

"I won't let him back inside," Marcel promised.

Now why would he do that? "But if he's not inside, how can I use him?"

Marcel's brow furrowed. "Say again?"

She leaned even closer to him so she could make a confession. "I'm not really a turn-the-other-cheek type of person."

A nod. "Neither am I."

Something they had in common. "When someone uses me, I use them right back."

A slow nod. "I see."

She thought he did. "Have a good night, Marcel." Alice suspected that her own night would be very interesting, to say the least.

Alice slipped from the crowd, made her way outside, and wasn't particularly surprised to find her big, bad Saint pacing on the sidewalk near the main road. As soon as he saw her, he closed in.

"Listen," Saint began, his voice tense and hard, "I need to explain—"

"You're taking me home."

He stiffened. "What?"

"You're out front because you were going to offer me a ride home. How very gallant of you." Her nose wrinkled as she lifted her arms. "I couldn't get all the paint off in the bathroom sink, and I'm sticky. I need to shower desperately, so a ride would be great. Thank you."

Saint slid toward her. "You...you don't want an explanation?"

She wanted plenty from him. For now, she strove to look tired. Perhaps even a wee bit vulnerable. Unfortunately, Alice knew that she didn't do vulnerable so well. "It's been one hell of a night. What I'd really like is a ride home before someone appears and asks to pose in a photo with me."

Saint jerked his head in agreement. "I'll give you a ride."

Well, of course, you will. That had been part of her plan. Her fingers lifted and touched his cheek. Felt the press of the stubble against her skin. "My hero."

"Haven't exactly ever been called that before."

"No? Then maybe you've been hanging around the wrong people."

His eyes glinted. "Or maybe I'm not the hero."

CHAPTER FOUR

Alice was down the hallway, in the shower. Absolutely fucking naked. Well, of course, she was naked. People were naked in showers. Normal occurrence, but for some reason, Saint kept getting stuck on a repeated mental image of Alice, sliding out of her clothes. Stepping into a massive shower, letting the spray fall against her body. Slide over her pert breasts and down, down to her—

"Did you know that when red spray paint washes down the drain, it looks a lot like blood?" Alice asked from behind him.

Well, shit. So much for the sexy fantasy in his head. Alice was obviously in the mood to play. Though the game she seemed to want wasn't quite what he'd had in mind.

"Not that I'd know, mind you," she continued in her sensual, husky voice, "not speaking from personal experience or anything. I just imagine that's what it *would* look like."

He spun toward her.

She smiled at him. Blinked innocently. Perhaps the innocent blink would have worked, if she hadn't been wearing just a silky black robe that skimmed the tops of her thighs. The fabric was thin, and he could easily see the outline of her nipples thrusting against the silk. Her wet hair had been combed back from her face. She'd removed all her makeup, and she was fucking stunning.

His jaw locked. "Not happening."

"Excuse me?" So very prim and polite.

"You must own a different robe. Something thick and fluffy and made of terry cloth."

Her brows rose, then fell. "Why are you concerned about my choice of robe?"

"Because you're trying to make me drool, and we need to have a deep conversation. Being able to see your nipples isn't exactly conducive to deep chit-chat time."

Alice's head tipped forward as she looked down at herself. "You can see my nipples? Sorry. The shower was a bit cold." Her head lifted. "But you don't have to stare. My eyes are up here, you know." She waved a hand toward her eyes.

He smiled at her.

And saw the flicker of unease in her gaze.

"Yeah, first off, I'm not like the other dumbasses you might be used to manipulating in your life, my Alice. You can't waltz that sexy ass of yours out in a silky robe and then just have me drop at your feet." Though, he would admit, she had cute feet. Her toenails had been painted a deep, bold red to match her nails.

"What makes you think I manipulate people?"

"Because it's probably like breathing for you. Second nature."

Her lips tightened. "You're hurting my feelings."

Was he? He could *almost* believe that had been a breath of pain in her voice, and, shit, he didn't want to hurt her, he didn't want—

Saint caught himself as he took a step toward her. "You are lethal." He couldn't help the admiring tone.

Alice shrugged. "I've been told that before." While he had frozen, she advanced. Alice's bare feet slid across the lush carpeting, not making a sound, and she stalked forward until she stood right in front of him.

They were in her den. The den of an obviously expensive historical home that was located not too far from Forsyth Park. Two stories, with massive, white columns out front and sweeping porches that circled both levels of the house. He'd smelled jasmine and roses when he walked up the steps outside, and as soon as he'd entered her home, he'd noticed the rich luster of the hardwood floor in the foyer. Elegantly decorated, the home seemed to scream money. Money—and security. Because he'd glimpsed the security cameras that had been installed at all corners of her home.

"It took a little longer than I anticipated to remove the leftover paint." She offered him a wide-eyed gaze. "If you're truly uncomfortable by my attire and you don't think that you can manage to control yourself, then I can go and change."

Nice. He liked the way she'd tossed things back at him. "Don't change on my account. I just thought you were...cold and might want to warm up with a bigger, fluffier robe."

"Oh, is that what you thought? How considerate you are."

Fuck it. He wasn't in the mood to dance around with games. *My client attacked her.* "No, I thought you looked sexy as hell. I wanted to pull you into my arms and take right back up where we left off in your office. You know, before Tracy Eldridge decided to spray paint your car and you."

She bit her lower lip. "You're not pulling me into your arms."

He could hear the thunder of his own heartbeat. "Is that what you want?"

"Yes. I think sex with you would be quite fantastic. You have this barely leashed sensuality that hits me on a primitive level."

What the—

She turned away. Headed for the fireplace that wasn't lit. "But I don't like to sleep with men I don't trust." Her hand rose. Her fingers tapped against the dark wood of the mantel. "I also don't like to sleep with men who want to cage me. Call it a quirk."

"Cage you?"

"Lock me away in a little tiny jail cell for the rest of my life. Strip my freedom away and leave me broken."

He found himself edging toward her. "The last thing I want to do is break you." Talk about a crime.

No one will break her. The thought was deep. Unsettling. So was the heavy fury that filled him at the idea of a broken Alice. *What is happening to me?*

"Good to know. But we still have that pesky trust issue to work out." Alice glanced over her shoulder at him. "Frankly, I'm disappointed in you."

He lifted a brow. "Want to say why?"

"Did you do any research on your client? Did it completely slip your notice that the woman is extremely unstable?"

So they were putting their cards on the table? Fine with him. "I focused mainly on you."

"Sure, you did. Because I'm the dark temptress who has eliminated three lovers." A sigh. She turned to face him, moving so that her shoulders pressed to the mantel. "I must point out that, of the two of us, you are the one who was charged with murder. Multiple murders, at that."

"Noted." He eliminated the last bit of distance between them. "But those charges were dropped. I was cleared."

"Because you were innocent?"

Innocence was relative. "I hadn't killed those men."

"But you did assault multiple individuals while you were being held in custody, correct? Broke one man's ribs. Another's jaw. Had to be secured in solitary confinement—"

"You've done research on me."

"Seemed only fair," Alice returned softly. "Since you were investigating me. Know your enemy and all."

What about fuck your enemy? Dammit. He did not like his reaction to her. He'd never responded this way to anyone, and his primal desire raised every red flag in his mind. He didn't touch her, but Alice's heady scent reached out to tease him. "I fought the people who came after me. They thought they could take me down because I was some eighteen-year-old punk kid. They were wrong."

"Certainly, they were." Her hand rose to trail over his chest.

He flinched at her touch.

"What's that about? Surely, I'm not hurting you. Not after you stood so strong against everything else. They came at you with fists, and I'm barely touching you."

It wasn't pain he was feeling. "You like to be dangerous."

"What makes you believe that?"

His gaze held hers.

"You were innocent, Saint. Is it so impossible to imagine that maybe I am, too? That maybe the stories are wrong? That maybe I don't belong in a jail cell?" A soft sigh. "That maybe your client—as crazy with grief as she is—that she's wrong? That I've just had incredibly bad luck and maybe I'm the victim in all of this?"

He didn't speak.

Sadness came and went on her beautiful face. The flash of sorrow was so brief that he could have imagined it. "You've made up your mind about me. Must be weird, being attracted to someone you believe is so evil."

"Are you evil, Alice?"

"I'm what I've needed to be."

And Saint thought that might just be the most honest thing she'd said to him. "I haven't made up my mind about you. I'm here to find out the truth. Tracy presented the case to me. Offered me two hundred thousand dollars to get the proof to lock you away."

She swayed. Caught herself. "Two hundred grand? Wow. She is certainly stepping up her game. That's an awful lot of money. For two hundred grand, some people might just invent evidence. Do whatever was necessary to get the payday."

"Her check is still in my desk drawer. I'm not here for the money."

Laughter. Bitter. Mocking. He'd heard real laughter come from her before, and he liked it when her amusement was genuine. He liked the way her laughter sounded, and the way it seemed to warm a coldness he held inside.

"Right." Alice gave a little eye roll. "You came busting into town because you were—what? Curious? Like the people who come into my speakeasy, you wanted to put your eyes on me? You're just here for the thrill?"

"Curiosity is my weakness, and I'm here to get the truth. Not Tracy's truth. Not whatever truth is convenient for people to believe. I want to know what really happened to those men, and I'm not leaving Savannah until I find out."

Her lashes lowered to conceal her eyes. "There's a reason they're called cold cases, you know. The trail has gone cold. No one knows what happened to the victims."

"And there's a reason my team uses the name Ice Breakers."

He saw the faint tremble of her lower lip. "You think you're that good?"

He waited for her lashes to lift before he answered. He wanted her eyes on him. When those thick, dark lashes finally rose and her gaze met his... "Baby, I know I'm that good." His hand curled under her delicate jaw. His thumb brushed over her cheek. "If you don't have anything to hide, why don't you work with me? Don't you want to know what happened to the men you loved?"

"Saint." A breathless sigh. "What makes you think I loved them?" Her head turned. Her lips brushed lightly against his thumb.

He released her and stepped back because the touch of her mouth on him—

No. Don't play her game.

"I'm giving you a chance." He ignored his aching dick and the lust that burned so hot when he was near her. "But there can be none of the bullshit that you enjoy so much. You and me— we can work together. If you're innocent, if you want me to think that you were the victim, then you'll work *with* me. No tricks."

"I told you already, we don't call them that in the magic world. Effects, that's what they are."

He hadn't been talking about magic.

"You think I'll open up my life to you? Knowing that you're just trying to tear my world apart?" A negative shake of her head that had a wet lock of Alice's hair sliding over her shoulder. "Number four. That's supposed to be you, isn't it? You're bravely putting yourself in the line of fire to save all those poor bastards out there who would just be helpless against my amazing charm."

"First, I haven't found you to be overly charming."

She blinked. Then...laughed.

And he jerked a bit because that was her real laughter again. The warm, rich laughter that wrapped around him. Sank into him. Made him yearn for her. As she laughed—for just a moment—her icy demeanor melted away, and he had the feeling that he was staring at the true Alice. Or, maybe at the woman she'd been, long ago. Her laughter was rich and warm and sensual, and it made him want to pull her close.

To hold her tight.

And never, ever let go.

"Now which of us is lying?" A smile still tugged at her full lips. "I am absolutely charming."

"No." He was adamant on this. "You have plenty of charms, don't get me wrong. There's no doubt that you're gorgeous."

"Thank you so much for noticing." She winked at him.

"But you haven't exactly gone out of your way to charm me." His head tilted. "Huh. That's interesting. Why *haven't* you tried to charm me? Because I think if you wanted to do it, you could wrap just about any guy around your little finger."

Alice moved her shoulders in a careless shrug. The top of her robe dipped. Slid a little off her right shoulder. "Maybe I didn't think you'd respond well to charm, so I decided to try a different tactic with you."

"That tactic would be...?"

"What you see is what you get. If you don't like it, screw off. I don't have to prove anything to you."

"You kind of do, considering that I'm investigating you. I can be a major pain in the ass that you do not want." But his gaze darted to her right shoulder. He'd just caught sight of something on her skin...

She started to pull the robe back into place.

He caught her hand. Froze the movement. "What in the hell?"

She tugged her hand from his.

He touched the silky edge of her robe. Slid it a bit more to the side so that he could see clearly. A long, thin white line. Raised skin. "Knife scar."

"Excuse me?"

Anger pulsed through him. No, more like rage. A dark and twisting brew that had his back teeth clenching and him gritting out, "Who the fuck used a knife on you?"

"Settle down."

What? No, no she had not just—

"It's an old scar. One I've had a very long time."

His index finger was on the wound. Testing the length. Stroking it. Wait. Why the hell was he caressing her scar? He immediately stopped. "If you were attacked—"

"It was an accident. Happened years ago. A real sword was mistakenly used instead of a fake one. No big deal."

His heart thundered in his ears. "You worked in your father's magic act when you were a teenager."

"Ah, yes, you did all that wonderful research on me. And you're right, after my mother died, I joined my father's act."

Saint had done plenty of research on her, and there had never been a mention of Alice being hurt in a magic show.

"It was the sword box routine. I'm small enough that I could fit easily in the box and shift around when the swords were placed inside." A pause. "For safety, my father preferred to use fake swords for a portion of the trick. The sword that he first showed the audience was real enough—he would even use it to slice open some random object like a piece of fruit. But certain swords that he put into the box were...let's just say made of a more flexible material so that they could bend and contort inside. They gave me a little more room."

He'd started caressing her old scar, almost helplessly.

"But something was off that particular night. When the second sword came through, I wasn't paying enough attention. It didn't flex. It sliced me."

"Dammit."

"After that, I knew to be extra careful with the others. I slipped around them. Made myself as small as possible. Somehow, my father's real swords—which should have been all backstage for a trick that would come later—were used in that act." Another shrug. As if it didn't matter. "There was space inside the box. With real or fake swords, I could still fit. I just—as I said before, I wasn't paying enough attention, or I never would have been sliced."

His rage didn't cool with her words. "Let me make sure I've got this straight. You were a teenager—"

"Eighteen. The same age you were when you were sent to jail."

He kept going. "And you were bleeding in a fucking tiny box while your father smiled for the audience? You didn't cry out? You didn't ask for help?"

"What would have been the point in doing that? I would have ruined his illusion, and the crowd would have been disappointed." She wet her lips. "I made sure my hair covered the injury when I came out, and I got patched up backstage. End of story."

Her skin was softer than the silky robe. And she felt so warm.

"Why are you so bothered?" She sounded genuinely confused. "It happened a long time ago. Ancient history."

"I don't like to think of you hurt." That was why he was so bothered.

"Oh." Her lips parted in surprise. "Well, if that's the case," Alice rallied, "then you should probably stop trying to prove that I'm guilty of multiple murders. Because heading down that path? It will lead to hurt for me."

"Only if you're guilty. If you're innocent, I can finally get you some peace."

"Is peace what you think I want? Sounds rather boring to me," Alice said as her nose scrunched.

He didn't think anything that involved Alice could ever be boring.

"Besides, I don't want to shatter your illusion of me. If you discovered that I wasn't the heartless villain, then you *would* go falling in love with me. And we both know what happens to men who love me."

Was he supposed to be scared? Not happening. Saint didn't get scared. Hadn't, not in a very, very long time. "I'm not like the others."

"Right. Because you don't think I'm charming." She pouted.

"Don't." He kept right on touching her. "I don't like it when you pretend. Be cold. Be outrageous. Be sexy. Be you." And a pouting Alice? Not a real thing.

"I think you just insulted me and...complimented me in the same instance." Alice studied him. "How interesting. I'm afraid, though, that I must tell you...I don't find you particularly charming, either."

"No, but you do find me sexy." No sense dancing around it. "We have one of those electric attractions."

"Oh, is that what we have?" Alice demurred with a flutter of her lashes. "Hadn't noticed."

Right. "It makes me want to rip off your robe and take you against the wall. Or the mantel, seeing as how it's closer. I suspect the same attraction makes you want to rake your nails down my back."

"And have you roaring my name?" she finished softly. Sensually.

God, she was something. *Something dangerous and delicious.* "I can want you and still take you down if you're guilty."

"How lovely for you. Must be wonderful to be able to compartmentalize one's life that way. But, alas, *my* Saint, you're wrong. You can't."

His brows lifted.

"Do you even know that you're still touching me?"

Shit.

"Want me too much and you'll do anything to protect me." She seemed to be giving him a warning. "You won't be the guy who tosses me into a cell and walks away. You won't be that heartless."

Now he laughed, and the sound was grim. "My own brother tossed me into a cell once upon a time. Trust me, I can do what needs to be done. Family trait."

Red burned in her cheeks. "What a bastard! I hope you kicked his ass as soon as you got free."

He blinked. Her anger sounded genuine. Anger, because of what had happened to him? "Memphis came back for me," he told her, speaking slowly as he considered her. He pulled his hand back. Balled his fingers into a fist so he wouldn't give in to the temptation to touch her again. "He believed my story, but the guy follows the law."

"How boring. And you know how I feel about boring things."

He laughed, not so grim.

Surprise flashed on her face.

Hell. He'd just given a real laugh, too. "Memphis is many things, but I'm not sure boring is one of them." Saint sobered. "He proved my innocence. Got me out of there. Gave me a job working with him."

"Oh, so he's an Ice Breaker."

"He's a bounty hunter. Or was. But, yeah, he works as an Ice Breaker, too."

"And is he helping you on this case? My case? Just how many Ice Breakers are working to take me down? I'm dying to know."

"Damn." Admiring. "You are good." His head leaned toward her. "Afraid that's need-to-know info."

She rose onto her bare toes. Because he had leaned so close, her movement brought her mouth dangerously near to his. "But I very much want to know."

And he very much wanted her mouth. "If *you* work with me—"

Something crashed through her window. The glass shattered and almost immediately a loud, piercing alarm blasted through the house. Saint whirled, even as his arms swept out and he made sure that Alice was secured behind him. Safe.

He heard the squeal of tires outside. "Stay here." He lunged forward, stepping over the broken glass and...was that a freaking brick?

"No, I think I'll run to greet the bastard out there. That plan sounds awesome."

Saint whipped his head toward her. Growled.

"Joke." She wrapped her arms around herself. "I won't move, but from the sound of those screeching tires, he's long gone." A pause. Her lips pulled down. Not like the faint pout from before. Real sadness. "They're always gone before help arrives."

He didn't like that statement—or what it implied—not one damn bit, and Saint rushed outside. Sure enough, he could only see the distant taillights from a vehicle. Looked like maybe an SUV. Sonofabitch. He put his hands on his hips and glared. But...Alice had security cameras everywhere. She would have caught the vehicle's image. He whirled for the house. Noted the broken window right in front.

Two attacks, one night.

Just how often did this shit happen in her life? From the way she talked...*They're always gone before help arrives*...Hell, it sounded like this crap went on far too often.

He bounded back into the house and found Alice still standing near the mantel. Her arms were still wrapped around her body. "Not wearing any shoes," she said. "I was afraid I'd get cut on the glass."

Because the glass that *had* been her window now littered the floor. And right in the middle of all that broken glass? A brick.

"Not very original," she muttered. "But I suppose it got the job done."

He crouched near the brick. Something red had been spray painted on it.

"Let me guess..." Alice's voice held no emotion. "Killer? Two notes in one night. Your client certainly is persistent."

No, that wasn't the message.

"Saint?" Her voice roughened.

"Die."

"Wh-what?"

He shot to his feet. Turned toward her in time to see Alice take a stumbling step forward. Before she could stagger into the glass, he was in front of her. He scooped her into his arms and held her easily. "The message is... 'Die.'"

He could feel her fear. The tremble shook her body.

His hold tightened on her. "Not happening," he swore.

"Saint?" She looped an arm around his neck.

He carried her out of the living room. "Don't worry. No one is going to hurt you."

"Promise?" Breathless. Hesitant. And...

"Yes, I promise." Because he'd found her. She was his case. He'd be the one who decided if she was innocent or guilty and no one—*no one*—would hurt her.

She's mine.

No one hurts what is mine.

"Thank you," she said, voice so soft that he had to strain to hear her. Her lips brushed lightly over his ear with her husky whisper.

And Saint knew he was in serious freaking trouble.

CHAPTER FIVE

"Come on, come on, answer the damn phone," Saint muttered. But the annoying tone just kept ringing in his ear. Tracy Eldridge was not picking up his call and—

Voicemail. Again. Seething, he choked back his impatience and said, "I told you to stay away from her, Tracy. We had a deal. I don't care how much money you think you can throw at me, this ends. Understand? Let me do my job. Leave Alice alone. This is the only warning I'm going to give you." He hung up.

"Well, that certainly seemed like a productive call."

Alice.

His shoulders stiffened.

"Let me guess, voicemail again?" She made a tut-tut sound of sympathy. "Your client is dodging your calls. Never a good sign. If I didn't know better, I'd think she wasn't satisfied with the service you are giving her."

He turned toward Alice. Before the cops had arrived, she'd dressed. Black pants. Black shirt. Black heels. When the officers in uniform had come knocking at her door, she'd looked perfectly in control. As if she was only reporting a mild annoyance. Yet, earlier, when he'd held her in his arms, when he'd felt the tremble that shook her, Saint had seen her control break.

"Thanks for boarding up the window for me." She inclined her head toward him. "I'll have a team out in the morning. I know some people I can use—a group that worked to help me get the speakeasy turned around in near record time. Can you believe the building was just a hollowed-out shell when I bought it? That meant I got it at a cut-rate deal. Shane helped me to negotiate it."

Shane Madison. The last man to vanish who'd been tied to Alice. Missing lover number three.

She pressed her lips together. "I appreciate your help." Her tone was very formal. "And it's getting extremely late."

Or early, depending on how you looked at the matter.

"You should go back to your hotel. Or whatever it is you're staying in while in town. I'm about to crash, so I want to hit the bed. I'm sure you do, too."

A dismissal. Fair enough. But he wasn't leaving just yet. Saint walked toward her. Saw the shadows in her stare. Hated them. "You don't like to be afraid."

"Actually, I don't mind a little fear every now and then. Isn't that why horror movies are so popular? A little fear is supposed to be good for us?"

"Not the same thing. I'm not talking about some controlled, fake fear. I'm talking about the fact that you are sick and tired of whoever the hell has been stalking you." He was close enough to touch her. He didn't. Not this time. Touching her was dangerous. "You need me."

"I've found that I don't need many people in this world."

"You need *me*." He was adamant. "Or do you want to go through the rest of your life having bricks thrown in your window and finding spray paint on your car?"

"So, it would seem the two incidents you listed are tied to your client. If you could control her better, then none of this would happen to me. Or perhaps I should look at controlling her, instead." A nod. "I must confess, my patience with her is at an absolute end."

He knew the feeling.

"I felt sorry for Tracy, at first. Her grief was so real. The only person who was crying about Donovan's disappearance."

Now that had been one hell of a telling statement. "You didn't cry?"

Her lashes flickered. She knew she'd just been caught. He waited for her to try and twist and manipulate and—

"Donovan Eldridge was a bastard."

Was. Past tense. Another tell. As far as Alice was concerned, Donovan was dead. "Interesting." He cleared his throat. "Because the reports I have on him all said quite the opposite,"

Saint noted carefully. And not quite truthfully. He wanted her to talk more.

"I can guess what your reports said. Amazing football player in high school. Academic all-star. A Good Samaritan who donated both his time and his family's money to an assortment of worthy causes. Amazing Donovan. When his parents died in that tragic car accident, he picked up the pieces of his broken life. He raised his sister. Inherited all that wealth but still remained such an amazing, down-to-earth individual." Her delicate nostrils flared. "Who was driving the damn car?"

"Excuse me?" He was completely focused on her. *Tell me everything, Alice.*

"His father was driving. Not Donovan. Of course, not Donovan. He was in the back, right? Isn't that what the police report said?"

Yes, it had been what the cops noted.

"And he tried to call out a warning to them," Alice continued almost feverishly. "Tried to say that he saw something in the road, but it was raining and dark, and they didn't heed his warning." A pause. "Isn't that what was claimed in all the papers? Not like there are ever lies printed. Or not like reporters just get the story *wrong* sometimes."

His body had turned to stone. "You're saying Donovan drove the car."

"Is that what I'm saying?" Her eyes widened. "I have to be careful, you see. Don't want to slander anyone. Even though the world loves to slander me." A beat of rage pulsed in her voice. "But maybe that golden boy wasn't so perfect. Maybe he didn't like it when people told him no, and maybe his parents had just told him that they were cutting him off because they knew what he was really like. Maybe..." A shrug of one shoulder. "Or maybe not."

"You called him a bastard." Saint wanted to hear more. "Did he hurt you?" Now he was the one with rage pulsing through him.

"Yes." A whisper. Pain swirled in her eyes.

He lifted his hands toward her.

She blinked. Seemed to catch herself. Alice cleared her throat. "He hurt me terribly when he vanished. I was so grief-stricken that I must have been in shock during those early days after his disappearance. The shock stopped me from being able to shed even a single tear for my dear, dear Donovan."

Damn. "Nice save there, Alice. For a minute, I thought you might actually tell me the truth."

"I did." Flat. "Maybe one day, you'll understand that." She brushed back her hair. "Now, I'm dead tired. Even too tired for the amazing sex that I am sure we could have together. So we'll just rain check that, shall we?"

His brows climbed. "Yes. We'll rain check that."

"Excellent." She turned and headed for the front door. He followed slowly behind her, and when she opened the door, Alice waved him out. "Drive safely. Watch out for flying bricks, and be aware that spray paint can come at you when you least expect it."

She was certainly handling this...*In a way just designed to intrigue me more.* "Maybe you were right."

Her gaze was on the dark road. None of her neighbors had come out when the cops arrived, but then again, she had a yard that stretched at least two acres, and the house down the street had been dark when he arrived. Maybe she didn't have any close neighbors who could be nosey.

"I'm usually right about lots of things." Her head tilted as she searched first toward the left, then to the right. "You'll have to be more specific," Alice added.

"If you're worried about staying alone, I can stay with you."

Her head whipped toward him. "I thought...we'd taken a rain check."

"I can sleep on the couch. This isn't about sex." Yeah, and he couldn't believe he'd just said those words to her.

She inched closer. "Then what is it about?"

"I don't want you scared." Simple.

But she acted as if he'd just slapped her. Alice jerked back. Her move was so sudden that her feet slipped on the porch—her right heel twisted, that crazy, high heel on her shoe—and Alice would have slammed down onto her delectable ass, but he grabbed her. Saint locked his hands around her arms and steadied her.

Her breath heaved in and out.

"You okay?" he asked softly.

"You're not good."

He'd barely heard those rasped words.

"You hunt your prey. You bring them in to jail kicking and screaming. And you go after the worst of the worst."

He didn't let her go. He did shrug. After all, she was right. He did those things. He also enjoyed the hell out of his work. When you had a talent, it was always good to use it. Use it or lose it, wasn't that the way the old saying went? Or, in his case, what he'd always feared...

I like the hunt too much. If I'm not careful, I might—

"Why the hell would you care about how I feel, Saint?"

His hand rose. He slid a thick lock of her hair—dry now—behind her ear. "Because like I said before, maybe you were right."

"About what?" Breathless. "The amazing sex?"

He had no doubt it would be fantastic. "We'll find out soon enough."

"Promises, promises..."

He took her mouth while her lips were still parted. Kissed her right there, with her porch light shining on them and her boarded up window steps away. His tongue slid past her plump lips, and he kissed her deep. Slowly. Fully. Took his time about it because he wanted the job done right. He wanted her to know this wasn't playing. This was owning. Taking.

Because he intended to take her.

Was she dangerous? Oh, hell, yes, he knew she was.

Did he care? Fuck, no.

Because she'd intrigued him. Pushed up his curiosity. Reached the dark, deep parts of him that he tried so hard to keep hidden from the rest of the world. The parts that sometimes made him worry about his sanity. That made him think he wasn't wired just like everyone else. No matter how hard he pretended, he just didn't feel things like everyone else did...

Until her.

Until now.

Because, no, he didn't want Alice afraid. He just wanted her.

She trembled against him. Her body leaned into his. Her hands rose to touch his chest. Not to push him away. To slide over him. To stroke. And he kept kissing her. Tasting her. Feeling his desire surge even stronger because Saint knew one thing for certain—they were going to be different. For better or worse, being with Alice was going to change him.

It might just wreck them both.

Her tongue slid over his. A ragged groan tore from him, and he wanted to lift her into his arms. She was so much smaller than he was. It would be easy to lift her up. To let her wrap her legs around him. To carry her back inside.

To fuck her until the sun rose.

Not yet. Not. Yet.

He forced his head to lift. Her breathing came in ragged little pants, and he knew she'd been just as impacted by the kiss. He stared down at her.

Innocent?

Guilty?

Didn't really matter. He wanted her just the same.

"S-Saint?" Uncertainty.

The more he was with her, the more he could see through her mask.

"Maybe I will fall for you," he mused.

Her lips started to curl.

"But if you're guilty, sweetheart, I will still lock that sweet ass away."

Her smile froze. Then...laughter. The rich, real laughter that reached inside the cold, dark parts of him and made him feel so reckless and wild.

Her laughter continued, ringing out into the night, and it made him want her even more.

She stroked his cheek. Pressed a quick kiss to his lips before smiling again. "No, you won't, but it's cute that you think so."

"Don't play with me, Alice."

"Why not? We'll both have fun if we play together."

"I'm not like the other men you knew."

She slipped away from him. Headed for her open door. "God, I certainly hope not." A final glance his way. "Good night, Saint."

"Sweet dreams, Alice."

She'd started to close the door, but at his words, she stopped. "They're never sweet."

The door shut.

He stared at it a moment. "Yeah, neither are mine." Saint walked away, still tasting her. Still wanting more.

Knowing that sooner or later, he *would* have more.

***

"What in the hell did you do?" Alice peeked through her curtain and watched Saint drive away. Her fingers rose to her swollen lips.

She'd forgotten herself during that last kiss. Let go. Wanted to believe...

That he might fall for me.

But he wouldn't. And she couldn't afford to make mistakes.

"I don't need help," she gritted into her phone. "Just stop, okay? I have things under control." She hung up the phone, heaved out a breath, and cast a glare toward her boarded up window.

Enough. She was so sick of this madness. If the world wanted to think she was a villain, then maybe she needed to give them something to fear. Something they would never forget.

***

She saw the blood drops as soon as she opened the front door. Alice stared down at them, the champagne bottle gripped tightly in her hand. The euphoria she'd felt only moments before gave way to instant worry.

"Shane?" Her voice cracked. "Did you cut yourself?"

Her heels tapped across his marble floor. The tile was normally immaculate, as was everything in Shane's home. But this time, someone had made a mess.

A spatter of deepening blood drops.

More and more blood.

And she wasn't just worried any longer.

Alice was nearly at the kitchen. She still gripped the champagne bottle in her hand. "Shane?" She turned the corner.

And nearly slammed into the figure standing there. The figure with the knife. She screamed and swung her champagne bottle.

Beep. Beep. Beep.

Alice opened her eyes. Glared up at the ceiling. "I fucking hate memories." Especially when they snuck into your dreams. Because in a dream, you were helpless.

Alice couldn't stand to be helpless.

***

Tracy Eldridge hadn't returned Saint's calls. He wasn't going to just wait around for her to pull another stunt, so he found out which hotel she was staying at—freaking child's play—and he headed there to meet her. Swanky, of course. A place that reeked of money. As if she would stay anywhere else.

It was simple enough to get her room number from the helpful lady at check-in. He flashed a smile, told her a story about surprising his girlfriend, and a few moments later, he was heading up in the elevator.

But when the doors opened and he reached the fourth floor, he saw that the door to room 408 was open. Frowning, he quickened his pace. What was Tracy up to—

A maid hummed from inside the room as she stripped the bedding.

He rapped on the open door, and she gasped, spinning around to face him. "Sorry." He offered her a faint smile. "Didn't mean to scare you. I was looking for the woman who stayed in this room last night."

"Oh, she left early today. Had errands." Her hand fluttered around the bedding. "Called housekeeping and asked if someone could come first thing today to clean the room. She wanted it fresh for when she returned."

Saint frowned. Tracy had wanted someone in her room at 6 a.m.? Because that was the time. Actually, a little after six. "That kind of call isn't normal. It messes up the schedule—"

"Mrs. E is a big tipper," the maid confided. "She stays here pretty often. Always requests the same room." An incline of her head toward the window. "She likes the park view. And sometimes, she calls about an early morning cleaning. We all know how she is."

Yes, I'm learning how she is, too. Obsessed. Determined. Dangerous? All her visits to town were a bad sign. And when she was in Savannah, he'd bet she spent her time watching Alice. Harassing her?

Hell. He had screwed up on this one. He should have dug deeper on Tracy. He would be taking care of that error immediately. Saint thanked the maid, then slipped out. He wondered where Tracy was.

Probably close to Alice.

And that meant he needed to get his ass close to Alice, too. Because he wasn't going to let his client—or anyone else—take shots at her.

In silence, he rode the elevator back down to the lobby. As soon as he walked through the revolving door at the posh hotel's entrance, he hauled out his phone. There was one man he trusted above all others, and the guy would probably give him hell about this case, but, well, the situation couldn't be avoided.

In moments, he had his half-brother, Memphis Camden, on the line.

"Saint. How the hell are you?"

"Been better. Been one hell of a lot worse, too." He headed toward Forsyth Park as streaks of light began to trickle across the sky. If Tracy liked the view so much, had she taken an early stroll in the park? He saw the moss hanging from the heavy limbs of oak trees and could hear the faint call of birds. Maybe Tracy had just gone for a walk...

Or maybe she'd gone after Alice.

"What's happening?" Memphis suddenly seemed a lot more serious.

"The case I'm working is...taking a few unexpected turns."

A grunt. "That's what cases do. They twist and turn." Memphis paused. "This a bounty or—"

"It's a cold case." Saint waited to catch hell.

And it came flying at him. "What the fuck? You didn't tell me you'd taken a cold case. Are you working with a partner?"

Potentially. If you counted his chief suspect as a partner.

"You got backup?" Memphis wanted to know. "How dangerous is this case? How—"

"You and I both know the bounties I hunt are usually a lot more dangerous than the cold cases we try to break." Truth. But, this time... "You ever hear of a woman named Alice Shephard?" Saint hadn't known about her, not until Tracy had slid Alice's photo across the desk toward him and set this case into motion.

"The Black Widow?" A whistle. "Yeah, I've heard about her. Never had the pleasure of meeting her in person, probably a lucky thing for me because guys who get too close to her tend to..." His words trailed off. "No."

"No...what?"

"Tell me you aren't close to her," Memphis pleaded.

He scanned the area. Old-fashioned streetlamps still burned even as the sun began its struggle to rise. "Technically, right now, I'm several miles away from her."

"Funny, jackass. Real funny. Tell me that you are not involved with Alice Shephard."

He thought of the way her body felt against his. The way her mouth felt when it opened for him. "Define involved."

"Oh, Christ."

"That's not a very thorough definition," Saint pointed out. "Want to try again?"

"Tell me you're not fucking the Black Widow."

"I'm not fucking the Black Widow." *Yet.* "I'm just trying to find out if she's guilty or not. Though it certainly seems that you have already formed an opinion about a woman you haven't met. A woman who was never charged by cops." *Holy fuck. I'm defending her.*

"I have a file on Alice."

Surprise rocked through Saint. "Since when?"

"Since the second guy disappeared. The stories came up in my news feed. Caught my interest. So I started keeping tabs." A long sigh. "She's trouble. I don't like what I've learned."

"I want your file."

"Aren't you doing your own research? You're damn thorough, you—"

"Not thorough enough. I want to see what you've got." It was always good to look at something from a different perspective. "And I need your help."

"Oh, sorry, we must have a bad connection. I missed what you said," Memphis drawled, and the prick sounded almost gleeful. "Can you repeat that part again?" Nope, there was no *almost* about it. Memphis was definitely gleeful.

"I need your help," Saint gritted out.

"Hold up. Let me put you on speaker. Maybe that will work better. Hey—hey, Eliza," he called.

Saint closed his eyes. Wonderful. Now Memphis was bringing Eliza into the mix. Though he wasn't particularly surprised. These days, Memphis tended to stick very, very close to Eliza.

"Eliza, I think I'm mishearing my brother," Memphis continued.

"Such an asshole," Saint muttered.

"He said you're an asshole," Eliza said in her careful, cultured tone.

Saint found himself smiling. Ah, so he was already on speaker. He liked Eliza, even if the woman had tazed him the first time they'd met. In her defense, she had been desperately trying to get to Memphis and she hadn't known that Saint was on her side. She'd thought he was the bad guy.

Not an entirely wrong assumption.

"That's hardly the way one asks for help." Memphis sniffed. "And I'm sure he was asking—"

"Cut the BS. I need your help." Saint could see the fountain now. The big centerpiece of Forsyth Park. The towering tiers. The wading bird statues. The powerful sprays of water.

"You heard that, right?" Memphis seemed to ask Eliza for confirmation. "He clearly said—"

Enough bullshit. "I want you to use your super skills and dig up info for me on a woman named Tracy Eldridge."

Silence.

Hmmm. Maybe Memphis really did have a bad connection?

"That's the sister. Victim one. Donovan Eldridge."

Nope. No bad connection. Memphis had just been clicking through his mental files. People tended to underestimate

Memphis. Probably because he seemed all easy going and charming. He wasn't. The man was a viper, always waiting to attack. "Yeah, that's the sister." The area around him was deserted. "She was the one who first came to me," he added. "Told me about the case. She offered me two hundred grand to investigate Alice."

"Damn."

"What I didn't realize was that she'd been harassing Alice. Caught her spray-painting Alice's car last night, then a brick was thrown through Alice's window. It smashed not two feet away from us when we were standing near her mantel and—"

"Back up. Where were you standing?" Memphis demanded to know.

"He said he was standing near the mantel," Eliza responded. "You must have heard him. The connection is crystal clear."

"Fine. I did hear him." A grumble from Memphis. "But I want to know *why* he was standing inside the Black Widow's house, all cuddled up to her and—"

"Saint!"

His head whipped around. He stared at the thick oak trees with their dripping Spanish moss. Alice stood beneath one of those trees. She wore jogging shorts and a sports bra. Tennis shoes. And abject horror was on her face. "Get out of the way!" Alice screamed even as she broke into a run and came barreling straight for him.

"What's happening, Saint?" Memphis barked. "What are you doing?"

"Alice..." His gaze darted around. What had her so scared? What was she doing? And he—

Saw the figure in black. A figure who was raising a gun. A fucking ski mask covered the shooter's face, and he was aiming his weapon at Saint.

Saint realized he stood right in the open. The fountain was the closest cover. Shit. He was—

Alice hit him. They both tumbled back because the woman hit him with the force of a football player coming in for the tackle. His leg slammed into the stone edge of the fountain, and they tumbled into the water even as a bullet thudded into the statue that sat so proudly just a few feet away.

CHAPTER SIX

The water was freaking *cold*. Alice shivered but did not push up. The tall side of the fountain's wall gave her a little bit of cover, and she was afraid that if she popped her head up, the jerk with the gun might decide to fire at her. Better to just stay low...and soaking wet.

Saint bobbed beneath her. His black hair had been soaked, as had his clothes. Drops of water slid down his face as he gaped at her. "Did you just save my life?" he growled.

Yes, she had. *And* risked her own in the process. Jeez. What in the hell had she been thinking? "I—"

Footsteps. Racing away. A very distinct thud that was a fabulously good sound to hear in that instant. Or, at least, she thought it was a good sound, but Saint's face took on a particularly savage edge as he pushed her to the side and leapt over the fountain's small wall.

"What are you doing?" Alice cried after him as she splashed in the water. "He has a gun!"

"So do I!"

He did? A wet one now and...she peered after him, barely poking her eyes over the edge of that wall. If Saint wanted to run off and chase after danger, that was none of her affair. She had already gone above and beyond by trying to help the man. Obviously, she should have saved herself the effort because he clearly had a death wish if he was so intent on charging *after* the person who'd just attempted to kill him.

And it had been very deliberate. The gun had been aimed straight at Saint. She'd burst from the trees, breathless and surging with her runner's high, and she'd come upon the sight that had nearly sent Alice to her knees. The fear and worry she'd felt in that moment still stunned her. She didn't get involved. Didn't play hero—heroine—whatever. She didn't do that bit.

Yet, she had. For him.

And for all her trouble, she'd been left soaking wet in a fountain and not even given so much as a thank you. Sighing, Alice hauled herself out even as she made a mental note to not perform any Good Samaritan acts ever again because they just were not worth—

A phone was ringing.

She stood just beyond the fountain, water dripping down her body, and her curious gaze landed on the phone that had been discarded just a few feet away.

Saint's phone?

It kept ringing.

She picked it up. Saw on the screen that the call was from... *Memphis.*

The name clicked for her. Memphis Camden had been the bounty hunter who collared Saint—and dumped him in jail. His brother. The same brother who had later cleared Saint.

The phone rang again.

"Hello?" She put the phone to her wet ear and scanned the park. "I'm sorry," she said, without waiting for a reply, "but Saint can't come to the phone right now."

"What?" A sharp, rumbly retort. "Who the hell is this?"

"I'm Alice." She saw no sign of Saint. Or his attacker. Was that good or bad? Deciding to look after her own self-interest— it was what she should have done to begin with—Alice hurried toward the shelter of a massive oak tree. No one else was out yet. Too early. If the attacker came rushing back this way, at least she had a good hiding spot now.

"Alice? Alice Shepherd?"

"Oh, you've heard of me. That's nice. I knew that when Saint started falling for me, he wouldn't be able to wait on telling the world about how he felt." Sometimes, it was just too easy to play with people.

"Excuse me?" Memphis seemed to be choking.

She smiled.

"Where is my brother?" Memphis snapped. Oh, but someone sounded dominant and demanding. Must be family traits.

Alice risked a glance around. "I don't see him at the moment, so I suspect he's still chasing the person who just tried to shoot him."

"*What?*" Guttural. Enraged.

"Don't you worry, I saved him." Well, perhaps Memphis should worry. "But then Saint ran off without me, so I guess he's on his own now."

A growl.

"I'd suggest calling back in about ten minutes or so. You might be able to reach him then."

"Have you called the cops?"

"Why would I do that?"

"Because...*someone shot at my brother.*"

"True. But that someone is long gone now. He was wearing a ski mask. And only Saint and I saw the person. We won't have much to go on, not unless your brother magically comes dragging the attacker back. Don't have much hope of that, to be honest with you," Alice continued breezily. "He had a bit of a head start because I had to shove Saint into the fountain."

Footsteps thudded. Alice tensed. Those footsteps were coming her way, and they had better belong to Saint. And if it *was* Saint, she didn't have much more time for phone talk. Time to get to info that mattered to her. "So, was it hard sending your brother to jail? Did you hesitate at all? Because I've got to tell you, I think it was a real dick move."

"Wh—"

She didn't catch whatever else the growling, rumbly Memphis said because Saint had just burst onto the scene once more. Still soaking wet and clutching his gun, he bounded toward the fountain and peered inside.

Had he seriously thought she'd just stay in there? "Hey, gorgeous, I'm over here."

Saint whirled toward her. He'd shoved his thick, wet hair back, but one lock had fallen forward to tease his brow in an oddly endearing Superman sort of way. She smiled at him.

He glared back at her. "What the fuck are you doing?"

"Well, first, I was saving your life." She shivered. It was *cold* out there when one was soaking wet. "And second, I've been having a lovely chat with your brother." She held out the phone. "Want to assure him that you're all right?"

He tucked the gun into the waistband of his wet jeans and took the phone from her. Their fingers brushed, and Alice pretended that she didn't feel that maddening spark of electricity shoot through her fingertips.

His lips tightened—delectable lips that she shouldn't be noticing at that particular moment—and he put the phone to his ear.

Since he was stopping for a chat, Alice figured it was safe enough for her to be making her exit. She took a few steps forward.

Saint's left hand flew out and manacled around her wrist. "You aren't going anywhere." Then he swore. "No, dammit, Memphis, I was talking to Alice. She was trying to slip away."

"Sure I was," she returned. "When there is a madman with a gun running around, it's never a good idea to just stay in the place where the individual was shooting. I'm pretty sure that's Survival 101."

His hold tightened. "I can't talk now," Saint said into his phone. "I need to get her to safety."

Alice lifted her brows. "You should probably get yourself to safety. You were the one being targeted, after all. I was just out doing a lovely morning jog." Which brought to mind a new question. "Were you following me?" Such a stalker. "Why were you out here—"

"I was following Tracy."

Following Tracy and, for his trouble, had nearly been shot? "That will teach you to follow her." She tugged against his hold.

He didn't let go. He *did* start sounding just as growling and rumbling and dominant as Memphis as Saint blasted into the phone, "Calm your ass down! I'm all right! Alice got me out of the way." His gaze locked on her. Seemed to heat. "She saved me."

Her chin lifted. "It was the least I could do. If I'd just stood there and watched you get shot, I'm sure the sight would have ruined my entire day."

His lips twitched, but... "No, she was kidding. That's how she is."

"I was not kidding. A bloody you would have ruined my day." *It would have ruined more than just my day.* She brushed aside the uncomfortable thought. "Maybe I'll just go out and rescue a cat from a burning building next. Maybe this is the start of a whole new me."

"Memphis, I have to *go*. The shooter got away, I need to talk to the cops, and I want Alice safe. She's talking about saving cats, so I have to stop her."

She held up her free hand. Counted on her fingers deliberately. Yes, she'd come in *third* on his list. After the shooter and after the cops. Way to make her a priority. Obviously, they still had quite a way to go in their relationship. But, he was alive. So was she. Alice would take that as a sign of progress.

"Dig into Tracy's life. I'll call you again as soon as I can." He hung up, even though Alice heard Memphis still talking. But before Saint could start in on her...

"Oh, look," Alice said with a demure smile. "A patrol officer." Her free hand was still up—because of her counting—so she waved at him. "Officer, I think my friend here wants to report a shooting..."

The officer rushed forward.

If only you could have been making these particular rounds about ten minutes ago. But, better late than never, she supposed.

The cop started firing questions.

And there went the rest of her morning.

***

"Thanks for taking me home." Alice stood in front of her door. Her hair had dried. No more water droplets slid down her body, but every few moments, she'd shiver.

He'd already given her his jacket. When he'd gotten her into his rental car, he'd bundled her into the jacket that he'd left inside previously. It swallowed her, covered some of her delectable skin, and, oddly, just made her look sexier.

"I suppose you'll be wanting this back." She began to slide off the jacket.

"Keep it." Okay, he needed to be a whole lot less growly. He cleared his throat. Tried again. "I can get it later."

"Oh, are we making a date to see each other later?"

He put one hand on the doorframe near her head and deliberately leaned in toward her. "You're inviting me inside."

"That sounds like an order. How odd."

Through clenched teeth, Saint said, "Alice, will you *please* invite me inside? Because I've had one real bitch of a morning that involved some bastard shooting at me and an unfortunate dip in a cold-ass fountain. I need to dry off a bit." Lie, he was plenty dry. "And we need to talk." That part was the truth.

Her lips curled in a slightly taunting, but ever-so-sexy smile. "I like it when you beg."

Fuck, he had not—

"Sure, you can come in."

Baby, one day soon, I'll have you begging.

"That way, you can thank me properly."

She turned away. Unlocked the door. She'd had the key hidden in the tiniest pocket imaginable inside the waist of her shorts. And because he was on edge, because she'd just pushed him, he decided to push back a little.

Two can play this game. "You want me to come inside and fuck you properly? Is that what you said?"

She went very still.

Okay, fine. Shit. Too far. He'd back off. Apologize. He'd—

Alice glanced over her shoulder at him. Her gaze was deep and mysterious. Her tongue slid over her lower lip. "Yes." Soft. Husky. "I think I'd like that."

Every muscle in his body jolted. "Don't tease." Bitten off.

"I wasn't." A pause. "Were you?"

He...

She was heading inside. He followed because there was no force in this world that could have stopped him in that instance. When it came to Alice, no, he wasn't teasing. But he knew just how dangerous the situation was between them.

"Be sure to shut and lock the door, would you?" Alice called back to him. "The world we live in is so very unsafe."

He'd already kicked the door shut. Locked it. Now he pressed his shoulders against it so he would not spring at her. "We need to talk."

"I thought you wanted to fuck. You're a confusing man." With her back to him, she grabbed the edge of her sports bra and just did some sort of shimmy with her body as she tugged the tight material over her shoulders and head. Then dropped it. The bra hit the floor. Her back stayed toward him the whole time, so he couldn't get the view he truly wanted.

Saint choked down his lust. "Why did you save me?" He needed to know before anything else happened.

"Maybe I thought you were worth saving."

Those words pierced straight through him.

She kicked out of her tennis shoes. Ditched the socks. Shoved her shorts off her hips so they could rustle onto the floor. Alice stepped daintily out of them. "I smell like fountain water, and I'm pretty sure they dump a ton of chlorine into that thing, so I'm going to shower. Join me if you like."

He could not take his gaze off her ass. "This is a dangerous game."

"But that's the only kind of game we both like, isn't it?"

She never looked back.

He watched her ass sway away from him and just as she turned for the door on her right, he surged after her. He ripped off his shirt as he chased Alice. Kicked away his shoes. Then he rushed into the room after her—*Alice's bedroom*. He was in her bedroom. He could smell her in there. That sweet, light, flowery scent. White furniture. That fashionable, chalk white paint. A decadent bed with sturdy posts and high mattresses. A few books on her nightstand. No photos. Jewelry to her right and the thunder of a shower already coming from the left. She'd left the bathroom door open.

Saint could think of a thousand reasons why this was a mistake, and one very real reason why he wasn't going to walk away.

I have never wanted anyone more. There was something about Alice that called to him. Something that had pulled at him from the very first moment. Something that had awoken within him when he'd first seen her picture. And when he'd met her in real life...

Like to like. Was that what it was? Was he pulled to Alice because he could feel the same darkness in her that he carried? Because with her, he could stop pretending to be so fucking good?

Who am I kidding? I've never been the good one. Memphis was the good one. The one who did things right.

Saint...He was the one who liked to hunt in the dark.

His steps were silent as he headed toward the bathroom door. Steam already drifted lightly in the air. Alice stood beneath the spray of the water. He could see her, standing behind the glass door of the shower. She turned toward him slowly. Gave him a fantastic view of the most perfect breasts he'd ever seen. Alice smiled at him...

And the shower door clouded over because of the growing steam, obscuring his sight of her.

Fuck that.

He finished stripping in record time. His fingers curled around the long bar handle for the shower door, and he yanked it open.

"I get it," Alice murmured as the steam wrapped around him, too. "This changes nothing. When you get proof that I'm an evil murderess, you will still lock me away. It's the heat of the moment."

His gaze swept over her. Tight, pert nipples. Curving hips. Sensual legs.

"We're riding an adrenaline high. We're not in perfect control. It's not every day that you survive an attack on your life," Alice continued in that same, soft voice. "It doesn't mean anything. It's just sex."

He stepped closer to her. Pulled the shower door shut behind him. Saint drank her in, memorized the sight of Alice, even as he shook his head.

"Do I have something wrong?" Her voice took on a careful edge. "I thought I'd covered the basics well for you."

"You have everything wrong." He advanced.

She retreated, just a little. Just enough that she was pinned between his body and the shower wall. Water sprayed onto them both.

Her chin lifted. "Then why don't you explain things to me?"

He'd rather be kissing her. But, sure... "I ride adrenaline highs all the time. They don't make me want to fuck the nearest woman."

A laugh sputtered out of her. That elusive, real laugh that he'd discovered he was hungry to hear. "Good to know," Alice said.

"I don't think you want to fuck the nearest man, either." Jealousy twisted in him. Surprisingly sharp and deep. *Don't think of her with someone else.* His hand rose and brushed back the wet hair on her cheek.

"How do you know that?" Her eyes held his. "Because there are only three missing exes?" Annoyance flashed. "Maybe I don't kill all my lovers, did you think of—"

"Stop."

Her lips pressed together. He wanted her mouth. He was about to take it. Take her. "You think I didn't dig? *You* have been my priority." His mouth lowered. Pressed first to her neck. A light little kiss. "You haven't been with a lover in a very long time."

Her hands rose. Curled around his shoulders. "Maybe I just...kept the lover secret."

He kissed her neck again. Licked the skin. Bit lightly.

She shuddered. Pressed closer.

"No, baby," he said. "No lies. Not right now." His head lifted. His dick was so hard the thing *hurt.* Stiff, long, full, and her thighs had parted already. It would be so easy to lift her up. To get her to wrap her legs around his hips as he drove into her over and over.

Until they both found oblivion.

But, not yet.

"Not adrenaline." He did not look away from her. "And not just sex."

"Oh, do you love me already?" He saw the careful mask slide back over her face. "I did warn you about that—"

"No lies. That's the rule. *No lies now.*" His mouth took hers. Her lips had been parted, and he thrust his tongue inside. The kiss wasn't careful or gentle. Maybe it should have been. But there was a savage edge to the need he felt for Alice. Or maybe he was just savage at his core, and he'd finally found someone who understood him.

Because Alice didn't try to pull back beneath the onslaught. If anything, she just met him with a ferocity that matched his. Her hands curled tighter to his shoulders, and she pushed up on her toes. Her slick, hot body brushed against his—brushed against his dick—and he just wanted her all the more. The water pounded, but he ignored it. What mattered was Alice. Kissing her. Touching her. Branding her.

Taking her.

Lust burned between them. In every desperate kiss and touch. Her nails sank into his skin. His hand slid between their bodies. His fingers teased her nipples, and she gasped into his mouth. Nice. But...

He'd take more.

He grabbed her waist and easily lifted her up.

"Saint?"

She was so small compared to him. He could move her where he wanted and right then...

He lifted her and took her nipple into his mouth.

A stronger gasp. A moan. Her nails bit deeper into him. He laved that nipple with his tongue. Sucked. Let her feel the edge of his teeth in a sensual caress. Then he turned his attention to the other breast. Her nipples were fucking amazing. So sensitive. She twisted and arched against him, and her moans drove him on and on.

Her legs curled around him. His cock pushed right at the entrance to—

Fuck. Condom. They needed protection.

Hating it. Fucking *hating it*, he pulled back his head. The water sprayed onto his back. "Tell me you have condoms."

"Fresh box, in my nightstand drawer," she rasped.

Hell, yes. He didn't let go of his hold on her waist. "Turn off the water."

She blinked. "But...but you didn't get to—"

Screw getting clean. He'd rather be dirty. "Turn it off, Alice."

She did. As the rush of water turned into a drip, drip, drip, he carried her out of the shower. Her hand reached for a towel, but he didn't slow.

"Aren't we going to dry off?" Alice asked, breathless.

"Why bother? I like you wet."

"Ah, a dirty talker."

Actually, he wasn't much for talking during sex. He was more for action. He carried her to that lush bed. Spread her out. She smiled up at him and he—

His hands went to her thighs.

Her smile dimmed a bit. "Saint?"

"Let's make sure you're wet enough." Because he wanted to go hard and deep, and she had to be ready. Plus, he just freaking wanted to taste her everywhere.

He leaned down, spread her a little more, and put his mouth on her. At the first lick of his tongue, her hips surged up toward him. His hand clamped around the edge of her hip to hold her steady. "Easy."

"I..."

"You can trust me," he breathed against her core.

"No." Sad. Helpless? "I can't." But her hips arched a little more toward him.

His tongue licked over her. Stroked. Tasted every single inch. Thrust into her. Then went back to her clit so that he could lick and lick and—

"Saint!" A sharp cry. Not of release. She wasn't there yet, but he knew she was close. His left hand came down so his fingers could thrust into her even as he kept licking and licking and—

She bucked beneath him.

There it is. He could almost taste her pleasure as she came beneath him. Not some light pop, but a body-shaking orgasm that had her crying out for him.

He kept licking her and tasting her through the release, and when the aftershocks died away, when he knew he could not hold back another moment, Saint pulled from her. He yanked open the nightstand drawer—rather, yanked the whole drawer out of the stand.

Another laugh sputtered from her. "My, you are a strong one."

The drawer dangled from his hand. The condoms had fallen onto the carpet. He dropped the drawer. Grabbed the condom box and had a packet open and out seconds later.

"Strong *and* big."

He looked over and saw that Alice's gaze had landed on his dick. Yeah, he was big. "We're gonna fit just fine."

A wide smile teased her lips. "I knew that from the first moment I saw you."

And I knew you were mine. The thought settled heavily around him. A truth that had been there the whole time, but he hadn't wanted to acknowledge it because he never saw things—surely not people—and thought they belonged to him. Abandoned by his father, left with a mother who struggled every damn day, he'd never had anything that belonged to him growing up. Not unless he stole stuff from others but...

She does.

She will.

Alice sat up. She took the condom from him. Stroked his dick. Teased him before slowly rolling the condom on him. Her tongue slicked over her bottom lip. "How long do you think you are going to last?"

She'd seen the moisture already on the head of his cock. But he did enjoy a challenge. "Long enough for you to come again."

"Promises, promises." A husky taunt.

"A guarantee." A guttural vow.

He tumbled her back onto the bed. Positioned his dick at the entrance to her body. She wrapped her legs around him again and arched toward him. He'd made sure she was more than wet and ready, and he sank deep and hard. Just like he'd wanted. And she felt freaking fantastic around him. So tight and hot that, for a moment, he thought he might lose all control. That he'd just drive into her relentlessly in a surge of blinding need—

No, she comes again first. Because he wanted the sex to be good, better than good, for her. It would the best of her life.

Step one in getting her addicted to him.

He withdrew, only to plunge back in even harder. His fingers slid between them so that he could stroke her as he thrust. Over and over. Her frantic breaths filled the air. The drumbeat of Saint's heart echoed in his ears. Then he felt it. The clenching of her inner muscles around him. Her head tipped back against her pillow as pleasure washed across her face.

"Saint."

He kissed his control goodbye. His hand pulled from her clit, and he grabbed her legs so that he could lift them over his shoulders. Frantic passion took over in the fierce drive for his release, and when his climax hit, it detonated through his entire body. The pleasure was so intense it felt as if it consumed him, and all Saint could do was hold tight to the woman beneath him and enjoy the hell out of the ride.

***

It was quite possible that she had made a strategic error.

Alice stared up at the ceiling and tried to catch her breath. Pleasure hummed through her. Not a soft afterglow of sated bliss, but more of a body-shaking quake that would shiver along her nerve endings every now and then.

She'd expected good sex. All the promise had been there, in the heated, instant attraction that she'd felt for Saint. Giving in this once had seemed...okay. Safe enough.

A miscalculation on her part.

One that, Alice hoped, would not come to bite her in the ass.

Saint pressed a kiss to her forehead. An oddly tender gesture that she hadn't expected from him. They were more about hot lust, not tenderness. The kiss made her feel funny. Uncertain. But she didn't get to analyze that uncertainty because he pulled out of her, and her greedy body resisted the withdrawal, clamping around him.

"Ready again?" Saint murmured, as he flashed her that deadly smile of his.

Oh, yes. But she didn't say that. Because once had been too tempting. Twice—twice would be dangerous.

He padded into the bathroom. She knew he'd gone in there to ditch the condom. She didn't want to just be lounging in bed when he returned, so Alice hopped up and rushed to her closet. She grabbed her silk robe and wrapped it around herself as—

"You didn't have to cover up on my account."

Yes, she had. Alice belted the robe and stared down at her hands as she did the small movement in order to buy a little time to school her expression. The truth of the matter was that Alice felt off-kilter. Unsettled. She *hated* to feel that way. "I dressed so I could walk you out." Her head lifted. "I'm sure you have quite the busy day planned. I do, too. Places to go, people to kill and all that."

He was still naked. Dammit. He was *gorgeous* naked. Sometimes, men could look all awkward when they were naked. Too hairy. Too pale. Slack muscles.

Uh, no. That wasn't Saint. Saint looked incredible naked. As in, the man should never, ever wear clothing again because she was pretty sure that covering him up was a crime.

Alice knew a thing or two about crimes.

His muscles were magnificent. Enough to make a woman drool. And those tats...they swirled up his arms. Over his powerful chest. Twisting and turning and looking tough as hell. "Love the tats," she heard herself say.

"Some people don't like them. Say they make me look too rough."

"I'm not some people." Why was she talking about his tats? She'd planned to get him *out* of there, and instead, she was thinking that she should lick the tats to show her appreciation. So wrong. "But then, I often like what others don't."

"Are you saying you like me, Alice?"

Her heart beat a little faster. "Well, we both know you *adore* me." She waved vaguely in the air. "But time is ticking, and as I indicated, I have quite a number of things on my to-do list so..."

His hands went to his hips. The movement just made his muscles flex. Made his abs stand out in all their glory even more. Wide shoulders. An eight pack. Maybe a ten when it came to his abs. Powerful arms and thighs. Giant cock.

Stop noticing everything about his body!

"Ahem." Alice cleared her throat. "I'll walk you to the door."

He smiled at her and closed in. There was something about his smile that gave Alice a very, very bad feeling. "Sweetheart." Saint stopped when he was right in front of her. His gaze seemed—dammit—tender as it rested on her. "What makes you think I'm going anywhere?"

CHAPTER SEVEN

Alice lifted her brows. "Well, I'm afraid you're wrong on that point." He needed clothing. "You can't stay here all day. As much fun as our bout was, round two will have to wait."

"Ah, so you're already planning for next time? Me, too. I can hardly wait."

Crap.

"And did you just say 'fun' when you described what we did?" Saint scratched his chin. Didn't seem to notice that he had on zero clothing. "Is that the word you want to use?"

Do not look down. "What word do you prefer?" Alice asked him politely.

"Oh, I don't know. Primal."

It had been.

"Consuming."

She'd felt consumed.

He nodded. "Addictive."

That gave her pause. "You think you're addicted to me?"

"I think it could be very easy to get addicted to someone like you."

She stiffened. "Well, all the more reason for you to be on your merry way." She skirted around him. Made her way to the bathroom. Ah, yes, there were his jeans. She grabbed them and turned to toss them back to Saint.

Only to find him frowning at her. "I hurt you."

"No, you made sure I was quite ready for you." Pain had been the last thing she felt. Primitive, consuming pleasure? Double check.

"No, something I just said hurt you." His head tilted to the right. "What was it?"

She tossed the jeans his way. Of course, he caught them with one hand. Lifting it casually at the last minute. "I have no idea what you mean." She looked at her wrist. No watch, of course. She'd taken it off before hopping in the shower. "I do have a lot on my plate today so..."

"Do you always kick out your lovers after they give you two orgasms?" He pulled on the jeans. Left the top unbuttoned.

"Kicking out is better than killing them, isn't it?" Earlier, lust had fogged her brain. He'd been right. It *had* been a very long time for her. She'd given in, and now she had to get her footing back, fast.

Saint stalked toward her with that lazy grace of his. "Why are you afraid of me?"

"Maybe I'm afraid for you." *No.* She had not just said that. Alice barely stopped herself from slapping a hand over her mouth. What? Did good sex make her chatty? Was this some new, horrible character trait that was emerging?

Or...her heart twisted...was this part of Saint's plan? "Why did you have sex with me?"

A hard shake of his head. The intensity of his stare strengthened. "Let's get back to why you're afraid."

"I'm not afraid." Her spine stiffened. "Of anything or anyone. Haven't you heard? I'm the—"

His fingers curled under her chin. "Let me in."

His touch sent a surge of need through her. A bad thing. "Didn't you notice before? Would have thought it was hard to miss. I already *did* let you in."

His lips twitched. "You are dangerous."

"So I've been warning you."

He leaned closer. "I also think you were right."

"I'm always right." Except when she was wrong. Then she was very, very wrong.

His gaze drifted over her face. "If I'm not careful, I might fall for you."

Her breath froze. She kind of choked, and Saint frowned in concern. "Alice?"

"Don't," Alice bit out. "That would be your funeral."

He kept touching her. "I can't help you if you don't tell me what's scaring you."

"You were almost killed this morning. Did you forget that big event? You, not me. *You.* Maybe it's time for you to look at this scene and realize that men who get too close to me have unfortunate things happen to them." Which was why... "One and done." Absolutely. "This was a fun interlude."

His jaw hardened. Such a delectable jaw, and she hadn't even had the opportunity to lick it. Pity.

"We already covered that we went beyond fun," Saint reminded her, voice low.

Yes, they had. "Be smart, Saint. Get away from me. Get out of town. Because if you stay with me, more trouble is going to come your way. It is only a matter of time." Trouble always followed her. Ever since she'd been a teen.

"I don't run."

Of course, he'd say something like that. Typical.

He leaned toward her. Brushed his lips over hers. "But I will leave."

He'd leave town. Right. Good. He'd be safe then and—

"I'll leave your house because that's what you want, for the moment. And I need to go find Tracy Eldridge."

Her stomach twisted hard at the name.

"How often do you run through that park?" Saint asked.

Why did that matter? Frowning, she replied, "Pretty much every day."

"You should alter your habits. I told you that before. It's not safe to repeat the same pattern."

Since when was anything in her life safe? And maybe he should consider that she made her path the same deliberately. But, no, now wasn't the time for that talk. "Why do you care about where I run?"

"Because Tracy cares. When she's in town, she always books a room that overlooks the park. And she leaves early—she was gone out early today. I think she's been watching you." His nostrils flared as he released her and stepped back. "Didn't get a good look at the shooter. At first, I assumed it was a male, but it very well could have been her."

"But the attacker shot at *you.* Not me." Alice injected mild surprise into her voice. "Have you managed to piss off your client?"

"The shooter didn't fire until you barreled into me. That shot could have been meant for you *or* for me."

Well, damn. Alice did a quick replay of the scene in her mind. He could be right.

"I'm going to find her. I *will* be seeing you again."

The cop on scene hadn't held out much hope of finding the shooter. But Saint was going to get the job done? Good for him.

"Where are you going today?" he asked.

"Keeping tabs on me already? How very controlling of you."

"Alice..."

"I'm going wherever I want. That's where I always go."

"I'll find you," he said with a nod.

Her eyes narrowed. "That a threat? Or a promise?" With him, she'd discovered it was hard to tell.

"It's both, baby." Saint kissed her again. Slowly, thoroughly. She might have leaned toward him a little bit because if this was going to be their last kiss—she *should* make it the last—then she needed to enjoy it. Savor it. And this kiss seemed different than the others they'd shared. Softer, yes, but, also more possessive.

His head lifted. "Watch that sweet ass of yours today."

"Watch yours," she returned without missing a beat. "It's quite a find to discover one as good as yours."

He winked at her. *Winked.* And something funny happened to her chest.

"Thanks for noticing," he said, "it is one of my better assets."

He had *not* said—

"That and my hunting skills. They're top-notch, too. I never stop until I get my prey."

Now she did feel like that was a threat.

Before she could say anything else, he continued dressing. Headed down her hallway. Scooped up one or two other random items of clothing along the way. And a few moments later, he was gone.

She locked up after him. Peeked out of the window to watch Saint walk away. He waved, as if he knew she was watching. Cocky Saint.

Alice let the curtain fall. She backed away. And when she realized that her fingers were trembling, she balled them into a fist. There wasn't time to waste. Alice knew she had a lot of work to do.

Or rather, a lot of enemies to eliminate.

And she knew exactly which enemy was number one on her list. Saint might be looking for Tracy, but Alice was way past the point of playing *nicely* with that woman any longer.

You've been watching me? You've been stalking me?

Time to turn the tables.

***

Marcel waited for her at three p.m. He stood in front of the speakeasy, his hands shoved into his pockets.

She smiled when she saw him. "Thanks so much for meeting me."

"You said it was important." He glanced around. "This about the guy from last night? Want me to make sure he stays away?"

Ah, Saint. "No, not about him at all." She headed toward the back, aware that he followed her. Her car had been removed earlier, and the lovely red paint was on its way to being cleaned off. Alice didn't even spare a glance for the security cameras, though she knew her movements were being recorded. "I wanted to talk about your new position."

"My position?"

She unlocked the back door. Frowned when the security system didn't beep. Odd.

"Alice?"

She realized she'd frozen.

"What position do you mean?" Marcel pushed.

"Oh, yes. I told you last night that I thought you had management written all over you." Alice glanced back at Marcel. Maybe Logan had forgotten to set the alarm before he closed up. A mistake that couldn't be repeated. She'd talk to him as soon as possible. "I want you to start shadowing Logan. He'll train you so that you can take over the floor."

Marcel's eyes widened. "Are you serious?"

"Absolutely." She faced forward and made her way through the back room and toward the bar. "He has been wanting a partner for a while, so this move will be perfect to—"

Pounding interrupted her words. Very hard, very determined pounding that seemed to be coming from the front of the building. Except, it certainly wasn't opening time. The speakeasy never got going until well after dark. And they had *just* been in front of Abracadabra, and no one had been out there.

So who is at my door now?

The pounding continued, and a quiver of unease pulsed through her. If it had been night and the music had been blasting, she never would have heard that pounding. As it was, the sound should have been muted because of the small corridor that led from the entrance to the bar area. But whoever was outside was doing one hell of a pummeling routine on her door.

Obviously, it's someone who does not want to be ignored.

"I'll take care of it," Marcel said immediately. He marched toward the pounding. "I'll send whoever it is packing, don't you worry."

She slid a glance toward her office, then back at him. "Wait. I'll come with you." Because that pounding was particularly fierce and she'd already had enough unpleasant surprises, thank you very much.

There was one of those old-fashioned peepholes set in the main door. Not one of those tiny little circles that were installed in so many current doors. This one was more like a mini-grill. Reminiscent of castles and days long gone by. The grill had amused her when Alice had first seen it in a catalog, so she'd made sure it was included in her door.

Before he unlocked the front door, Marcel opened that grill. "We're closed," he snapped.

"Open the damn door!" Saint barked right back.

"Him, again." Marcel was less than pleased.

"Alice, I can see you," Saint added grimly. "She's here, and I need you to let me inside."

"She?" Alice edged closer to the door. "Just which 'she' would you be talking about?"

"Tracy. I think she's in the building." Intensity roughened each word. "I tracked her here, and I need to get inside."

Alice bit her lip. "How did you track her?"

"Not exactly by legal means, so let's just discuss that shit, later, okay? Because I'm scared she's in there so she can take another shot at you. Just like this morning."

Marcel's head turned toward her. "What's going on?"

"The alarm didn't go off," Alice said softly. Goose bumps rose on her arms. "Open the door."

Marcel had those locks and the door open in record time. Saint surged inside. He immediately went to Alice. Curled his hands around her arms. "You're okay?"

She was perfectly fine. "Careful," she warned. "That sounds like real worry in your voice."

"It fucking is real worry. I think she's lying in wait for you."

"Who are we looking for?" Marcel demanded. His hands had fisted at his sides.

"Tracy Eldridge." Saint didn't let her go. "Blond hair. Five-foot-ten. Possibly armed so we need to be extremely careful." He pushed Alice toward the door. "My ride is outside. Take my keys and wait in—"

"No." She didn't plan to wait anywhere outside. "I'll search, too. But I think you're wrong." Words that needed to be said. "Marcel and I just came in the back door. She wasn't in the storage area. She wasn't in the bar. She's not here."

None of the hard tension left his face. "I got intel that says otherwise."

Intel? Her goose bumps got worse.

"She could have been hiding when you came in. When she saw that you weren't alone, she kept out of sight." He looked over at Marcel. "You take the back room. Alice and I will search her office."

Her heart raced faster.

"You didn't mention your office in that little list you just ticked off." He released her. "Stands to reason that's the one place she's most likely to be. Especially if she was waiting for you."

He had a point. Alice turned down the small corridor that would take her back to the bar. "This has gone on long enough."

"Damn straight." He caught her wrist. Pulled her back. "So, we need to understand the rules."

Rules? She wasn't much for rules. How could Saint have missed that about her personality?

Marcel lingered. Listened.

"I get that you don't want to wait in the car. Fine, poor choice of words from me," Saint admitted.

"Yes," she agreed. "Poor. You don't ever stash me in a car."

"But *you* don't get to go charging in first. You stay behind me."

"Why?" A mocking glance at him. "Because you just can't stand the thought of anything happening to me? The idea makes you absolutely crazy?"

"Yes." No hesitation.

Well...Alice swallowed. She didn't have a ready response for his admission.

"And I'm the one with the gun," he pointed out grimly. "So, unless you've gotten one hidden somewhere under that skin-tight dress of yours..."

"Thanks for noticing." It was tight.

"Then you stay back. I'm not about to let her hurt you." His eyes glittered. "*No one* will hurt you."

How very protecting. And if that was the way he wanted to play it...Alice stepped back and motioned for him to go forward. She was highly conscious of Marcel watching them.

"So that's how it is," Marcel muttered. "Even with my warning?"

"We'll have a lovely chat later," Saint promised him silkily. "For now, let's go make sure someone isn't waiting to attack Alice, shall we?" Saint didn't give Marcel a chance to respond. He curled his fingers around Alice's and headed down the corridor.

When they reached the bar area, Marcel turned toward the back. Saint and Alice kept heading for her office. It was still dark in the bar. Alice hadn't even gotten the opportunity to turn on the lights. Illumination trickled through her high windows and chased away some of the shadows. Glancing around, she saw that nothing appeared disturbed. "Maybe you're wrong," she told Saint.

"One way to find out." He let go of her hand and pulled a gun from beneath the back waistband of his jeans. The gun had been hidden behind the fall of his shirt until that moment.

His left hand went to the doorknob of her office.

That was when she realized the door was open. Just an inch. Maybe two. Normally, she had to enter her security code to enter the office.

But the door is open.

"Did you secure the door last night?" Saint wanted to know.

Last night? "Absolutely," she replied honestly. She remembered that distinctly. Shutting it and locking it the previous night. "That was all right before Marcel and I had a wonderful discussion about how you were going to wickedly seduce me and steal all my secrets."

His shoulders tensed. "Really not the time for that."

No, she didn't suppose it was. Her hand reached out and pressed to his side. "Be careful."

"Now you're making me think you care," he whispered back.

Her hand dropped away.

"Stay out here." A flat order from Saint. He shoved open the door. Rushed inside. And..."*Fucking hell.*" Shock. Alarm.

She inched forward. "Saint?"

"*Fucking hell.*" Another exclamation. Same words. Rougher. Angrier.

She took another inch forward—

Saint appeared in her doorway. "Don't go inside."

"But it's my office." Of course, she could go inside. Alice pressed up onto her toes and tried to crane around him. "I'm assuming Tracy is not inside since you just rushed right back to—"

"She's inside."

Alice stopped standing on her toes. "You just left her in there?" Her lips pressed together. "Enough of this. I will handle her." She shoved forward.

He didn't move out of her path. "No, Alice. *No.*"

"No?" Her own voice rose. "No? How about once—just once—maybe I could get someone to be on my side? If she broke into my office, if she is in there because she wants to hurt me,

I'm not walking away. I'm getting that bitch arrested. She can rot in a jail cell. She can—"

"She's dead."

Her mouth hung open. "What?"

"And you don't want to see her. Shit, no one wants to see that."

The drumming of her heartbeat was even louder. She *had* to get into the office. "Okay." Soft. Uncertain. "Okay." Alice spun away, sure he would follow. "We'll call the cops. We'll get them here."

She heard the faint pad of his steps as Saint moved to follow her. After waiting half a beat, Alice did a fast turn to the right. She shot past him even as he swore and grabbed for her.

She made it to the door. His arms curled around her stomach and hauled her back, but her hands slapped out and touched the edges of the doorframe because she had to see for herself if—

OhmyGod.

Alice sagged back against Saint.

"Sweetheart, I tried to warn you."

Her body shuddered.

She could see Tracy. See her perfectly. The other woman *was* in Alice's office. In Alice's office...in her prized magical prop, the water torture chamber. Only the chamber wasn't empty. Someone had hooked up a hose and run it from Alice's bathroom sink all the way to the chamber. The water had overflowed from the cell. Soaked the carpet.

Tracy floated in that torture chamber. Her hair drifted around her, and her bound hands—and feet—were clear to see through the glass.

Alice's knees gave way. She would have fallen right then, but Saint's grip held her upright.

"It's okay," he whispered. He was more hugging her than holding her. "I've got you."

He was so wrong. She wasn't okay. He wasn't okay. *Nothing* was okay.

CHAPTER EIGHT

They'd separated him from Alice. A move that Saint understood, but it still pissed him off when he found himself cooling his heels in an interrogation room at the police station. After finding Tracy, he'd called the cops. Alice hadn't said a word. She'd looked shell-shocked. Too pale. Too brittle. He'd wanted to wrap her up in his arms and keep her safe from everything and everyone...

But there was the little matter of a gruesome murder to handle. A murder that had been committed in Alice's office.

Fuck.

"So, let me see if we have this straight." The detective in front of Saint gave him a tired smile. Heidi. Heidi Lockett. Fairly fresh-faced, but her eyes were sharp. Her partner, Jamal Preacher, looked older, and his eyes said he'd seen too much depravity during his time on the force.

Both seemed competent. And suspicious as hell.

Heidi tapped the table. "You and Alice Shephard entered the office together and discovered the body."

"Not one hundred percent correct." They'd been through this before. "I entered first, saw the body, and asked her to stay outside. Figured the less contamination of the crime scene, the better." And he just hadn't wanted Alice to see the other woman that way. There were some images you didn't need in your head.

"But Alice didn't listen to you. She pushed her way inside?" From Jamal.

More like blasted past him in a flash. He'd have to remember she could be very, very quick on her feet. "She looked inside. Not so much a push as a dodge." He hadn't seen it coming because he'd been too busy trying to figure out who the hell had killed Tracy.

"Tracy Eldridge was your client?" Now Heidi was talking again. She and Jamal kept swapping turns with questions. They had a smooth partner relationship going, he'd give them points for that. A nice, fast pace of rapid-fire questioning to keep the suspect off balance.

And Saint did think he might just be a suspect. For the moment. He also damn well knew Alice was at the top of their list. "Tracy came to my office because she wanted help in solving a cold case." He didn't glance at the one-way mirror to his right, though he did wonder who might be in there, watching him.

"Her brother's case?" Jamal asked.

"That would be the one." A cold cup of coffee sat in front of him. He hadn't touched it. Didn't intend to do it. The cops would always keep the coffee coming because the caffeine would hype up perps and make them need to use the restroom. Anything to get a perp nervous or unbalanced.

Jamal shared a look with Heidi before querying, "And how much did Tracy pay you to take the case?"

No sense lying. "She offered two hundred grand for me to find conclusive proof that Alice killed Donovan."

Jamal whistled.

"I never cashed the check. It's still in my desk, back in Florida. The Ice Breakers work pro bono."

"Uh, huh." Heidi's doubt was clear. "But you *took* the check. What did you do, just put it in your desk for fun?"

"No, I did it to calm her down." And he stayed perfectly calm as he kept answering questions. "I got the feeling that if I didn't take the case, she'd go to someone else. Someone who might be willing to do just about anything for two hundred grand."

Jamal leaned forward. "And you wouldn't? Do just about anything, that is?"

He didn't take the bait that Jamal offered. No way was he going to lose his cool. "I have plenty of money. I'm not desperate these days."

Jamal rubbed a hand over his carefully shaven jaw. "Sometimes, it's not really about money, though, is it? Lots of other things can motivate a man. Not just greed. Plenty of other sins out there." He frowned at Heidi. "I might be called

Preacher, but you're the one in church all the time. Remind me, what were those seven deadly sins? Greed and gluttony..."

"The cardinal sins." Heidi's focus on Saint hadn't faltered. "Greed, pride, wrath, envy, gluttony, sloth, and, of course...lust."

Saint couldn't help it. A slow smile spread over his lips. "That the best you've got?" A disappointed shake of his head. "And here I was, being impressed. Thinking that the two of you were more than marginally competent. Then you had to go and shatter my hopes and dreams." He released a despondent sigh. "If you're saying I killed Tracy due to some insane lover's quarrel—"

"That's not what I'm saying at all." Heidi leaned forward. "Tracy was after Alice Shephard. The same Alice Shephard that you have been seen with on multiple occasions."

"Because I was investigating her."

"Just this morning," she continued, as if he hadn't spoken, "a uniform reported that you and Alice were together in Forsyth Park. That someone tried to shoot you...or perhaps tried to shoot Alice."

"Yes. That happened."

"The uniform noted that you and Alice seemed quite...friendly."

He lifted a brow. "Odd detail to note."

"Not really." Jamal rose from his chair. Began to leisurely pace around the small room. "Pretty sure Alice has a history of getting men to fall for her at the drop of a hat. You'd just be the latest in a long line. And maybe you got pissed when you realized Tracy had gone over the edge. That she was targeting Alice, so you decided to eliminate a problem for your new girlfriend."

They were seriously suggesting that he'd killed Tracy for Alice?

Saint couldn't help it. Laughter spilled from him.

Not surprisingly, the two detectives did not look amused.

He laughed a little longer then asked, "Got any proof to go along with that suspicion?"

Silence.

"Didn't think so." His smile had completely faded. "Now I'm done having my time wasted. Either charge me with something or open the door for me while I walk out."

***

"Another murder, and another day when you're right in the middle of things."

Alice sat with her spine perfectly straight, her legs crossed, and one ankle swinging lazily. The chair in the interrogation room was horribly hard and uncomfortable, but she made sure to act as if she was sitting on a plush throne. Appearances had to be maintained, after all. And there was no way—not even for a second—that she would allow herself to appear rattled in front of the two cops.

Heidi Lockett and Jamal Preacher. She'd met them before. They made a habit of dropping by Abracadabra just to make her life extra stressful. It had come as no big surprise to discover that they were going to be the homicide detectives working this case. Also, no surprise? They were already biased against her. "This is actually my first murder," Alice reminded them. Her eyes widened. "What others do you know about?"

Jamal's lips tightened. "I think my partner was referring to the three missing men in your past."

Alice put a hand to her chest. "They still haunt me, and I still hope they will come home soon to end this nightmare." Part of that statement was true. Part was false. They'd never know, though. They would just think she mocked them.

"One of those *missing* men...his sister was just found murdered in your office." Jamal hauled out the chair across from her. The legs screeched, sounding like nails on a chalkboard.

"Are we sure it was murder?" Alice queried.

Heidi gaped at her. "You think she tied herself up and jumped in the tank?"

"Stranger things have happened. Besides, magicians do that routine all the time."

Heidi stopped gaping and glared. "This isn't funny."

"No, and I'm not laughing. I am telling you that Tracy Eldridge was unstable. I told you that for a very long time. She'd been stalking me. Harassing me. Last night, she sprayed paint on my car and me, and she—"

"She attacked you last night," Jamal cut through her words to say. "And she's dead today. Dead in *your* torture chamber. Dead in *your* office. So I'm thinking you got pissed, and you decided to get vengeance on her because she wouldn't stop messing with you. She even hired that guy Saint to poke into your life. You thought he was really interested in you, but he's just been working to send you to jail where you—"

Her hand rose to her chest. Waved in the air. "Please." Soft. Breathless. "You're hurting my feelings."

"The hell I am," Jamal snapped.

He was right. The hell he was. "I think you're getting ahead of yourselves." Her gaze swept between them. "You don't even have a time of death yet. You haven't finished searching my office for clues. And by the way, just have at it. Search to your heart's content."

"Thanks. We will." A clipped response from Heidi. "That's what we do at *crime scenes*."

Should she try applying reason? Maybe. "How would I have lifted her body into the tank? She was bigger than me. And shouldn't she have left some sort of defensive wounds on me?" Alice held out both unmarked arms. Made sure she left them up long enough for the cops to take a good, long look. "If you check my security camera—I have one at the back of Abracadabra— you'll see me arrive with Marcel Taylor. We entered together. I wasn't at the speakeasy until that point. Then Saint arrived. We discovered the body—a sight that will fill my nightmares—and then we immediately called the police." A delicate pause. "You."

And you hauled me into an interrogation room even though I was cooperating fully because, sure, I have to be guilty. Why not?

Jamal's sharp gaze studied her. "We have our ME working on the body. We'll have time of death soon. And we'll have plenty of evidence."

Wonderful for you. Alice didn't say that. "I don't know how it is with bodies that have been submerged in water," Alice mused as she lowered her arms. Her brow furrowed. "Does that interfere with the body's temperature? The decomposition rate? Wash away evidence?"

Their glares got darker.

"You'll have to let me know." She uncrossed her legs and pushed back her chair. The screech was a softer slide of nails on a chalkboard. Alice smoothed down her dress as she rose. "Or rather, let my lawyer know, will you? Because I won't be talking to you again without her. I came to you today as a courtesy. This was a shocking, terrible act. One I had nothing to do with. Someone very dangerous is out there, and instead of viewing me as the aggressor, perhaps you need to take another look at the case."

They didn't try to stop her as she walked calmly for the door. How could they stop her? Not like she was under arrest.

"You want us to believe you're the victim?" Heidi's mocking question grated almost as much as those roughly sliding chair legs.

Alice opened the door. She stiffened a bit when she saw Saint lounging nearby. Close enough that he could have overheard the interrogation? Sneaky Saint. He straightened when he saw her. She dipped her head toward him, but spoke back to the cops as she replied, "Goodness, no. I'm no one's victim. But in this particular case," her gaze held Saint's, "I'm not a killer, either." She stepped toward Saint.

He offered his hand to her.

"Maybe the new boyfriend is!" Heidi called out. "You considered that? Do you know where *he* was when Tracy was being stuffed in that water tank? We know he was pissed at her. We know he thought she fired that shot this morning. Maybe he wanted to make sure she didn't hurt you, so he took her out."

She took Saint's hand. "One moment, you're seducing me so you can bring me down. The next, you're supposedly killing for me." Her fingers linked with his. "I do wish they'd pick one scenario and go with it. Flipping back and forth makes me dizzy."

"I didn't kill her." All growly. That sexy, growly voice she liked.

"I didn't, either." She was sure the cops were watching them. Maybe she should give them a show. "But I did seduce you."

He smiled at her. "Wrong. I seduced you." His head lowered over hers. His lips brushed against her mouth. A tantalizing, all too brief touch. "Ready to go?"

More than ready.

Smiling when a woman had been murdered. She knew they both looked cold-blooded. Suspicious. Innocent people probably wouldn't be smiling. They'd cooperate more. Talk and talk to the cops but...

Alice had never claimed full innocence, and she knew her Saint was a long way from innocent, too. You couldn't live the kind of lives that they had and keep your innocence.

They walked away still holding hands. He was steering her toward the front of the station, but... "Based on personal experience, it's going to be a feeding frenzy." She was sure reporters would be lined up already. Some helpful tip from a cop, no doubt. "If you don't want your image all over the news, you should let me go out first." Low, for his ears alone. "I'll give them a statement, and you can slip away."

He stopped.

So did she.

His head had turned toward her, so she did the same. She enjoyed looking into his eyes. So deep and dark.

"You trying to protect me?" A quiet question from Saint.

She shook her head but...*yes.* Maybe. "Just giving you an out."

He lifted their linked hands. Kissed her knuckles. "I don't need one." Then he turned to face the front. Saint took a step forward.

Squaring her shoulders, she did the same. As soon as those glass doors opened...

"Alice! Alice, is it true that your missing lover's sister was found murdered in your—"

"Alice, were you enraged because Tracy Eldridge knew you had killed—"

"Alice, is this your new lover?"

She looked at the male reporter who'd just fired that loud question. Tyler McQuinn. His brown hair, as always, had been carefully styled. His suit held zero wrinkles. And his bright green eyes? They were avid with intent. Before she could answer the question—any of them—Tyler turned his attention to Saint.

"Are you afraid to be with Alice?" Tyler demanded. "Aren't you worried you'll be next?"

"Next for what?" Saint asked lazily. His fingers gently squeezed hers.

He was putting himself straight into the line of fire. An unnecessary move. He hadn't needed to do that. She could have easily distracted the reporters. Tossed a wee bit of blood into the water, and they would have been thrilled with the chum. While they were busy with her, Saint could have slipped away.

Instead...

"The next to vanish." Tyler pressed closer.

Saint laughed. "I don't plan on vanishing." Confident. Cold. "What I do plan on doing..." He let go of her fingers, but only so he could wrap his arm around her and pull her even closer to him. "I plan on staying beside Alice." His gaze slid over her face. "I'll be between her and any threat that will come."

"Did you view Tracy Eldridge as a threat?" A random shout. "Did you—"

"*Alice!*" The familiar voice broke through the din.

She eased back from Saint so that she could see Logan as he stood behind the crowd of reporters. He jumped into the air. Waved at her.

"Got the car waiting!" Logan blasted.

Sure enough, he did. Now it was just a matter of getting *to* him. But Saint solved that problem. He—

"Get the fuck out of our way," Saint ordered. Then he started forward, with her sheltered against his chest. One strong arm wrapped around her shoulders. The other cleared a path. The reporters leapt out of his way, and she didn't blame them. There was an intense, focused ferocity emanating from him.

Logan yanked open the back door of his SUV.

Alice slid inside. Logan immediately tried to shove that door closed—

Saint caught it. "No, asshole. I'm coming, too. Just get in the front and *drive*." He jumped in and moved beside Alice. His thigh brushed against hers.

The door slammed shut. Logan stomped around the vehicle and had the engine growling to life moments later. He checked the rearview. "The ride was just for Alice."

"Yeah, well, it saved my ass from having to hail a taxi. My rental is still at the speakeasy."

Because the cops had, ah, escorted them in patrol cars. Separate patrol cars. Probably because they hadn't wanted her and Saint to talk privately before getting to the station.

The SUV pulled away from the curb. "Alice," Logan sighed her name. "What in the hell is happening?"

That was the big question. The question that had haunted her for a very long time. She slanted a glance at Saint. Was he ready to hear what she had to say? Maybe. Would he believe her? *Probably not.* "I think it's obvious." Even to her own ears, her voice sounded incredibly tired. "He's back."

Tension filled the vehicle. Tension that she knew came from Saint. "Who is?" he demanded.

"Oh, just, you know..." Weary to her soul, Alice shoved her hair back from the side of her face. "Just my friendly neighborhood stalker and, apparently...*murderer*."

CHAPTER NINE

She wasn't joking. No smile curved Alice's full lips, and her voice had been dead serious.

"You have a stalker?" Saint asked her carefully. "And you're telling me this *now?*"

Her head angled toward him. "Technically, I had more than one. But seeing as how Tracy Eldridge has been removed from the equation..." She swallowed and brushed back her hair once more. He caught the faint tremble in her fingers before her hand dropped to her lap. "I think I'm down to one. One very dangerous stalker."

"You should get out of town," Logan said from the front seat. "Immediately."

"Running isn't the answer," Saint fired back. "She can't just leave. If some SOB is locked and loaded on her, then he will—"

"Logan didn't mean me. I'm generally quite safe. Though I suppose safe is a relative term." A careful exhale from Alice. "He meant that you should leave town."

The SUV braked at a light. "Yep. Meant you," Logan clarified from the front. "Provided, you know, that you want to keep living. Shouldn't have fucked him, Alice. Bad idea."

A deadly stillness swept over Saint. "She can fuck me all night long and every damn day." Low. Lethal. "None of your affair."

He saw Logan throw up his hands. "Hey, take it easy! I'm not the enemy! You know yourself that men who get involved with Alice disappear. You chose the life, man. Hope it was worth it."

Alice leaned forward and grabbed the seat in front of her. "How about you drive? Could you do that? The light changed like, a whole minute ago." Her cheeks had flushed. And had that been hurt in Alice's voice?

He didn't like Alice in pain. "Worth it."

She looked back at him even as Logan gunned the SUV. It lurched forward. Alice swayed a little, and Saint curled his hand over her shoulder to steady her.

"Worth it," he repeated.

She licked her lips.

"Easy to say now. Let's see how long that lasts," Logan announced. "I'm guessing when he comes for you, you won't still feel that way. You'll be wishing you'd kept your hands *off* her."

Alice rolled her eyes. "You are not helping matters *any*. When I called for a ride, I thought you'd do the friend bit. Show up. Get us out of there. And *not* provide some sort of extremely depressing discourse on my life—"

"Uh, there was a dead woman floating in your office. Things *are* depressing. Pretty damn dangerous, too. I'll say again...he should get out of town."

"I'm not going anywhere." Saint kept touching Alice. "How long have you had this stalker?"

She swallowed once more. "Hard to say. Potentially since...I was eighteen?"

What. The. Fuck?

"Not like it was obvious at first. Only later did I start to put things together. He's, um, possessive. Doesn't like for others to get too close." Her long lashes swept down to conceal her gaze. "When they do, he eliminates them."

The three missing exes. "Sonofabitch."

"Yes, that's typically how I think of him, too."

"He's talked to you? Made contact?"

Her lashes lifted. Her gaze darted toward the front of the vehicle. Toward Logan? "It's rather complicated," Alice explained.

"Murder often is." Saint was tired of the bullshit. Rage pulsed through him. "If you had a stalker, if you knew someone else was behind all these crimes, why the hell didn't you tell me from day one?" Instead, she'd kept him in the dark. Now Tracy was dead. He'd assumed Tracy had been the shooter that morning, but what if it hadn't been her? What if it had been Alice's stalker?

Fuck me. Tracy was stalking her, too. I've been dodging Alice's steps and...this guy, too? This fucking sonofabitch who—

That proud chin of Alice's angled higher even as her head swung back toward him. "If I had told you back then, would *you* have believed me?"

"I—" Dammit. He wasn't going to lie. "No."

Her lips pulled down. "Exactly." Sadness. She settled back against the seat. "You don't even know if you believe me now, do you?"

He let the question hang in the air between them.

Her shoulders hunched. "Thanks."

He was hurting her. Hurting her seemed to hurt *him*. "I don't know what to believe." An absolute truth. "You've been keeping secrets from me."

"Don't feel bad about that, man!" Logan called from the front, voice oddly cheery compared to Alice's. Compared to Saint's. "She keeps secrets from everyone, even me, and I'm the closest thing to family she's got."

"She has me now." Not that he was family but...he was something. He did not know what the hell they were to each other, but Alice was linked to him.

He was linked to Alice.

Logan laughed. "Sure. You're here with her, until you're done with the case and you either lock her away or clear her name. Then you're out of town, and she's left behind."

Leave Alice? He rubbed his chest. He wasn't gonna think about that. "I don't plan for the future."

"And I try not to look at the past," she whispered.

He could see why, considering her past. "Yeah, mine's pretty shitty, too."

Alice's stare darted his way.

"You will tell me everything," he vowed.

Logan braked again. "And what are you gonna do, hero? Save the day for her?"

"No." He was far from a hero. He needed Alice to see him for what he was. "But maybe I'll just put some deserving bastard in the ground for her. Will that work?"

***

Alice didn't let her shoulders slump. Iron will kept her upright. They'd finally made it to her house. Surprise, surprise, there had been some reporters hanging around outside, too. They'd had plenty of lights with them to combat the darkness of the night.

Good thing she didn't have close neighbors. They would have been pissed.

Logan insisted on coming inside. He kept glaring at her and Saint. Saint, for his part, seemed incredibly cool. Almost too calm. She feared it might be one of those calm before the storm situations. When the storm hit, Alice had a feeling it would certainly be a sight to see.

"The speakeasy is a crime scene. Cops won't let anyone in or out." Logan stomped around her den as tension rolled off him. "They want to interview all the employees. Want every bit of security footage we have." A bitter laugh. "They don't get that we only had cameras in the back."

That wasn't exactly true, but she didn't speak.

"Clusterfuck." Logan swiped a hand over his face. "What the hell are we gonna do now?"

"Hire more staff." She could be as cool as Saint. More so. Her voice had sounded perfectly undisturbed.

Logan whirled toward her. "Excuse me?"

"When the cops are done and we're given the all clear, the line to get inside Abracadabra will stretch for blocks." She could use a drink. Would that help her throbbing temples or make them worse? "Everyone will want to see the murder scene. We'll have to open up my office. Change it into a real VIP room. People will pay extra to get inside."

Logan's eyes widened. Then... "Hell, yes!" A grin split his face. "Hell, yes, they will. We thought traffic was heavy when they just wanted to get a peek at you. But if they are at an actual murder scene..." He shook his head. "Shit, we can even let those paranormal tours book private visits. They'll try to contact Tracy from beyond the grave. Maybe they can even get her ghost to tell them who shoved her into that—"

"Is that shit supposed to be a joke?" Saint's voice cracked like a whip.

Uh, oh. The storm is coming.

"I—" Logan snapped his lips closed. "It's business."

"Exploiting a dead woman? That's your business?" His burning gaze landed on Alice.

She shrugged. "It will pay the bills." Oh, but she sounded like a cold bitch. *I am what I have to be.*

"Yep. Yep, it will." Logan slapped his thigh. "Okay, I'll hire more staff. On it. And do you need me to call your lawyer? Get Raven ready to roll in case you're arrested?"

"They never arrest me. No evidence." A drink was definitely in order, but first... "I'll talk to her. Don't worry." It never hurt to make sure your lawyer was at the ready.

Logan crossed to stand in front of her, seemingly ignoring Saint. A lie, of course. Saint was a hard man to ignore.

"At first..." Logan's voice had dropped. She knew he only wanted her to hear this part. "When I heard a body had been found in your office, I was afraid it was you. That the freak had finally crossed the line and gone after *you*." He wasn't joking any longer. No more dark plans for their business. Suddenly, he seemed deadly serious.

But his concern wasn't necessary. "He never hurts me. That's not the point."

Logan's expression hardened. "He just hasn't hurt you *yet*. Your luck will run out one day."

Her luck had run out long ago.

Logan dragged her into a bear hug. "Call if you need me. I'm always just a phone call away."

She nodded, knowing he felt the movement.

When Logan eased back, he spared a glance for Saint. "Guessing you plan on staying?"

"I'll be moving in."

Her brows rose. Alice didn't quite remember issuing an invitation for him to do that. Someone was being quite presumptuous. But now wasn't the time for an argument. That could wait until Logan was gone.

Saint was the one to see Logan to the door. "Thanks for the ride," he drawled.

Yes, they'd have to be sure and get Saint's car from the speakeasy soon...maybe after—

Logan spun and jabbed a finger into Saint's chest. "I don't like you."

Saint peered down at the offending finger. "I can absolutely assure you that the feeling is mutual."

"*She* likes you, though."

Alice did not move.

"Or else you wouldn't be in this house right now," Logan added. "So you take care of her. If someone tries to hurt her, you fucking take the bastard *out*. Got me?"

"I think you've made yourself quite clear."

Grunting, Logan stormed away. Saint watched him go. There were a few shouts from reporters that drifted through the open door. Then he closed it. Very, very softly. Flipped the locks.

In all the commotion of the day, she hadn't gotten her window fixed. The boards were still in place. She should go ahead and send out a text about that to her repair—

"Ever consider that maybe Logan is your stalker?"

She'd known the question would come. "Of course."

Surprise rippled across Saint's face. Surprise, then a flash of anger as he stalked toward her. "And yet you still let the bastard near you?"

The storm is getting closer. "Would you like a drink?" Then, not waiting for an answer, she turned away and strolled toward the kitchen. "I would like a drink. A big, delicious glass of wine." She didn't *run* away from him. She walked—at a normal speed— toward her kitchen. In the kitchen, she pulled down two wine glasses and opened the bottle of wine that she'd left chilling. "It's sweet. That's the only kind of wine I like, so if that's not to your taste, then I'll just drink both glasses." She filled the glasses nearly to overflowing because it *had* been a day. Her fingers curled around one stem. Lifting the glass, she saluted a grim-faced Saint. "Cheers."

His hand flew out and curved around her wrist. The sudden move made her shake the wine glass, and a few droplets spilled on her white marble countertop.

"What a waste," she said, exhaling despondently. "Now if you would release me so I can finish my drink?"

His hold tightened. Not in a hurting way. He'd always been incredibly conscious of his strength when he touched her, something she found oddly sexy. But him stopping her from the drink? Not sexy in the least.

"Alice." Her name held so much tension. "You think Logan might be your fucking stalker and you let him into your home? You work with him every damn day? What in the hell are you doing?"

"First, if you don't let go of my hand so I can have this drink, I will be flinging wine all over you. You've been warned."

They had a stand-off that lasted for...

One.

Two.

Three.

F—

His eyes narrowed. He let her go.

Delicately because she wasn't there to guzzle, Alice sipped her drink. Sweet goodness. "Second, I didn't say I thought he was my stalker. I told you that I had considered the possibility. I would be a fool not to have done so since Logan has been in my life since I was a teen."

"And?"

"And...are you going to drink your wine or not?"

"*Alice.*"

"You have a muscle jerking near your jaw. Is that a nervous tic or rage?"

"You are playing with me."

No, she was pushing him. There was a difference. She intended to push and push to see just how far she could go until his storm broke over her. "Logan cried for a week when we found a stray dog that had been run over near Abracadabra, so I don't think he exactly has the killer instinct that my stalker would need." She sipped. Swirled the wine in her glass. Sipped again. "Do *you* have a killer instinct, Saint? Something tells me that you do." In the SUV, he'd offered to put her stalker in the ground.

Had he meant those words? Doubtful. He could hardly be at the point where he was ready to kill for her. In order to do that, he'd really need to love her.

He didn't.

That muscle ticked again along his jaw. "Maybe Logan didn't think the dog deserved to die. Maybe he thinks the men in your life do."

Ah. Well, that was one way to look at things. "You didn't answer my question." She lowered her wine glass back onto the counter. "Do you have a killer—"

His hands closed around her waist. In a blink, he'd lifted her onto the counter. My, my, he could certainly move fast, and she did enjoy seeing his strength in action. He stood between her legs, and her dress had hiked up to a wonderful degree. Maybe enough to tempt him and...

He lowered his head toward her mouth. She parted her lips for him.

"No, baby," he rumbled. "I'm not fucking kissing you."

How very disappointing.

"You want me to give you oblivion again?"

A little oblivion would be wonderful.

"That's not happening. Not until I get my answers."

In his fast movements, he'd somehow managed to not even touch the wine glasses. Since he wasn't kissing her, she reached over. Lifted his. Sipped it. "Tease."

He took the glass from her. Turned it and lifted it to his mouth. She noticed that he put his lips in the exact spot where she'd had hers. He drew in a long pull of that wine. "Yes," he said, holding her stare as he lowered the glass back to the counter. "You are."

She curled her hands behind his head and pulled him toward her. Her mouth crashed onto his, and Alice kissed him with all the passion she felt. She wanted his storm. She wanted it to break over her and sweep them both away. Out of control. Running on need and lust. Obliterating everything else that had come before. Wiping away the horrible images and taking away the pain and—

Alice caught herself. Stopped. Instead of hauling him closer, she pushed him back. Her breath came out in quick bursts. Her fingers trembled. "Sorry." Since when did she apologize? "Bad impulse control. You called me a tease, so I wanted to show you I wasn't." She licked her lips. Alice could taste him and the wine. After a moment of contemplation, she realized that she liked his taste better than even her favorite Prosecco. "When it comes to you, I don't tease."

"Don't you?"

Her own storm began to swell. "No, I don't." Hadn't he realized that yet? He should have, damn him. "From the beginning, I told you to stay away. I warned you it was dangerous to be close to me." He hadn't listened to her warning.

"You neglected to say it was because you had a crazed stalker taking out the men in your life!"

Her lashes flickered. "Not all the men." *Dammit.* She could have slapped a hand over her mouth. "Look, Tracy wasn't a man. And I'm pretty sure he took her out, too."

"Why?"

Why? "Because she was hurting me. Because he thinks he knows what's best. Because he thought it would make me *happy.* I don't know, pick a reason." Saint was still between her legs. Way too close. "Look, if you aren't going to do something fun with this position, can you move?"

He looked down at her legs. "You don't have your knife on you."

"A good thing, or else the cops would have taken it at the station."

"But you told me that you wore it all the time."

Whoops. Did he remember *everything* she'd ever said to him? "Not all the time, clearly. I didn't wear it when I went jogging. I don't have it on now."

His head lifted. "Did you know you were going to be taken to the police station?"

"How would I have known that?" Breezy. "I'm not psychic. Not like I knew we'd be finding a dead body in my office."

The expression in his eyes chilled her. "Did you know she was dead before I got there?"

"You're the one who found the body, remember?"

"I can't fucking help you if you won't tell me the truth!" A snarl. Not loud and angry. Low. Deadly for its softness.

And her response was the same as something broke inside of her. *"And I can't tell you the truth if I don't trust you! If I don't know that you will take my side no matter what happens."* Alice gasped as she heard the words she'd just uttered. Overstep. Way, big, major overstep. She wished that she could pull those words back but wishes never did anything. She knew. Once upon a time, she'd made a thousand wishes. None of them had ever come true.

She wanted off that counter.

"Before you told me…" His voice was still low. "You said that you didn't like to sleep with men you didn't trust."

Yes, she had told him that.

"Yet you fucked me anyway."

Alice flinched.

He noted the movement. A faint furrow appeared between his brows. "Want to tell me why?"

"Because I felt like fucking." That sounded good. Heartless. "So I broke my rule. Silly me. Now if you could give a lady some space—"

"Want to tell me why my words just hurt you? Because I really don't like it when you hurt. Makes me feel pretty savage if you want the truth. And the fact that *I* just hurt you…" A grim nod. "Makes me fucking mad at myself."

This was…more honesty than she'd expected. But it was just her and Saint. No one else to hear. No one else to see…Maybe it was time to be honest. To be raw. "Maybe I wanted it to be more than fucking. So if I didn't *fuck* you, if it was something more, then I didn't break any rules, did I?"

"Alice…"

"Donovan Eldridge was so charming to everyone he met. He knew how to work a room. How to have everyone eating out of the palm of his hand." *Too much honesty.* But it was too late to stop. "He knew how to charm a dumb nineteen-year-old who'd never been to public school and who was so desperate to have someone love her. He knew all the right things to say and do, and before she knew it, he was controlling her life. Telling her what to wear. How to act. Telling her that she would only belong to him. Telling her that no matter what, she would never, ever get away."

In her mind, Alice could suddenly see the ravine that haunted her. Her feet skirted near the edge. The rocks slid over. Fell below. If she stepped much closer to the edge, she'd go over, too. She'd fall and fall...

Like Donovan had fallen?

"Alice?"

Her eyes squeezed shut, but that just made the image of the ravine stronger. Sharper. "That girl thought he wanted to love her, but he really wanted to own her, and she realized that—that she didn't want to be owned by anyone. Definitely not someone who liked to hurt her a little too much."

She knew why she was talking. Why she was telling him this when she'd held back from everyone else for so long. Because Saint had picked up on her weakness without realizing it. He'd said...said he didn't want to hurt her...

Saint's words played through her mind once more. *"Want to tell me why my words just hurt you? Because I really don't like it when you hurt. Makes me feel pretty savage if you want the truth. And the fact that I just hurt you...Makes me fucking mad at myself."*

Her mouth had gone dry. Maybe she did need more wine. "Donovan didn't get mad when he hurt me. I think he liked it."

"Alice, are you telling me that sonofabitch was abusing you?" Rage burned in each word.

"Tracy was disturbed." *Was.* Past tense. Because Tracy was dead. "So was Donovan." *Was.* Past tense. Because no one got to enjoy hurting her. No one laughed while she cried. No one.

Because she would be no one's victim. *Not ever again.*

"I will fucking kill him." Guttural.

Oh, such a lovely sentiment but...

Too late, I already did. But she managed to hold that part back. It was too much. If she said the words, there would be no taking them back. If he learned her deep, dark secret, Saint could destroy her.

Sharing session—over. Besides, Saint wouldn't understand. Or...would he?

I need him to choose me. I need him to say screw it to everything else and just choose me. No matter what I've done.

Why in the world was she still making desperate wishes? Almost as if she was a scared teen again.

"You think he's the stalker?" Saint asked, voice rough and growling with his rage. "You think he's been hiding all these years, watching you, waiting? Making sure you don't get close to anyone else?"

She shook her head. No, she did not think that Donovan was stalking her.

The faint lines near Saint's mouth tightened. "You think your stalker eliminated him, too?"

Again, a small shake of her head. She knew for a fact that her stalker hadn't killed Donovan.

"*Talk to me.*" His hand rose. His fingers slid under her jaw. "I want to keep you safe. I have to know what I'm up against."

"I'm not a serial killer." He'd called her that, once.

A furrow appeared between his brows. "Baby..."

"Maybe Logan was right. Maybe you should go. Maybe you should get far away from me."

He didn't move. The rough calluses on the edges of his fingertips slid over her cheek. "I'm not going any place."

Wasn't that one of the reasons she'd given in to her need for him? Because he knew how to fight back? "I agree to the deal."

Now he looked confused. "What deal?"

"You wanted us to work together to find out who the real killer is. The person who—who took out the others. I'll do it. I'll take the deal. We can work together." Her words came too fast. But they had to do this. *No more.* "I don't like this game. I've played it too long. I want it to stop."

His hand fell away from her face. He took a step back. One, then another.

Not the reaction she'd wanted. Dammit, she'd have to lay herself bare for him. "Please," Alice said.

A hard shake of his head. "No."

Her heart dropped.

"No, you don't fucking beg anyone for anything, understand? Not you, Alice. That's just not *you.*"

"You...that means you'll work with me?"

He reached out—

She tensed.

But he just lifted a wine glass. Downed the wine in an instant. "I'm not just working with you. We're stopping the bastard." His eyes promised hell. "I meant what I said before. If I have to put him in the ground for you, I will. That's a promise."

CHAPTER TEN

He'd just offered to kill for her.

Saint grabbed the edges of the counter and held tightly to them. Rage boiled inside of him. He'd held his control in place all freaking day. Maintained it through the interrogation, through the pack of reporters but now...

He was about to break, and he knew it.

It was a danger he'd sensed the first time he'd met Alice. A danger and a temptation. The urge had always been there, the desire to just drop the chains that he kept in place.

To let his darkness out.

"Don't say things you don't mean," Alice murmured.

Fucking Alice. Fucking beautiful Alice. With her secrets and her pain. The pain that she tried so hard to keep hidden, but it would still slip into her incredible eyes. Whisper through her voice.

Donovan had hurt her. The knowledge had been growing with every bit of intel Saint uncovered. Not some golden boy. Not some perfect boyfriend.

A monster.

"Why didn't you go to the cops?" Saint bit off from between clenched teeth.

Her lashes flickered. "Which time are you referring to? You need to be a little more specific."

"When Donovan hurt you," he said deliberately, "why didn't you go to the cops?"

Her tongue slid over her lower lip. "What makes you think I didn't?"

Fucking fuck.

"Nineteen. That's how old I was. My parents were both dead then. I'd grown up bouncing from town to town with my dad's shows. That meant I was always an outsider, no matter where I went." There was no sorrow in her voice. She wasn't looking for pity. Not Alice. Just stating facts. "Donovan was very much not an outsider. If I told one story and he told another...well, who do you think the local law would believe?"

And records had been erased. Or else no records had ever been created because he hadn't found them when he'd dug deep on Alice. He *had* made her life his priority. He'd wanted to learn every detail about her. Getting to unravel the mystery that was Alice—that had been his mission.

He could feel the warmth from her body. She still wore that tight and tempting dress, and it had hiked way up when he'd put her on the counter. The bottom of the dress barely covered her panties. It would be so easy to reach up and touch her. To take what he wanted.

I want her. "If we're working together, you have to tell me everything." Each word hit heavily into the silence that had stretched between them. "No lies. No half-truths."

"But I'm really good at lies." Her tongue slid over her bottom lip.

I have no doubt that you are.

His gaze had fallen to her mouth. He didn't think she'd licked her lip to be sexy though, yes, that sensual motion of her tongue made his aching dick all the harder. No, he thought she was nervous. Afraid. But still throwing up her defenses because that was just Alice.

I'm really good at lies.

"So am I," he told her. His gaze rose to pin hers.

"I guess that's something we have in common."

They had a lot in common. Too much. His hands released the counter. Slid a little closer to her. Stopped on the outside of her thighs. Her scent—so light—teased him. "Just what all do you think we have in common?"

"We're both fighters," she replied. "We don't just stand there and take it when people try to hurt us." Her lips pressed together. "Tried that once. Didn't work so well for me."

You fought back against Donovan. You fought and...did you kill him, my Alice? He wanted to ask. The question burned through him. But if he asked...and if she didn't lie...

"We know what it's like to be predators," Alice continued carefully. That his fingers had started to caress the outsides of her thighs. "We weren't meant to be prey."

No, they weren't. But someone was making a terrible mistake by thinking they were. That someone would pay.

"We also know what it's like when the people around us think that we're monsters." Softer. Maybe a little sad.

Alice shouldn't be sad.

She was right, though. They did both know what it was like when the world looked at you with hate and fear. When he'd been wanted for those crimes...when he'd been hunted, and his own brother had tracked him down and locked him away...

Everyone thought I was guilty. No matter what I said, they wouldn't believe me. His brow furrowed as he stared at her. "If I told you that the stories were wrong, that I *had* killed those people years ago, that I got away with murder..." He kept stroking her silky skin. "What would you say?"

Her breath caught.

He didn't know what drove him. Maybe because so many had looked at him back in those days with suspicion and anger. Maybe he wanted to know just how far he could push Alice. Maybe...

"*Did* you kill them?" Alice whispered.

"Did you?" he returned without missing a beat.

She swallowed. "If you told me that..." Her hand rose. Pressed to his cheek. "I'd say...what were your reasons? Why did you do it?"

"For the hell of it."

Her head shook. "That would be a lie."

He could feel his heart racing.

"You wouldn't kill for fun. You wouldn't kill just to do it. That's not who you are. Taking a life isn't some easy choice. It rips you apart and shatters you on the inside. When you get put back together, you're never the same."

She'd given him a confession. One he could hear in the echo of her words.

"You didn't kill them," she added.

But, Alice, did you?

Her fingers trailed down his cheek. "If I told you that I had killed before...what would you say?"

She *had* told him. In her way. And he still fucking wanted her. She'd all but confessed, and he still stood between her thighs. His hands had curled *around* her thighs. He should be backing away. He should be putting space between them. He should be... "I'd ask you why."

Her lower lip trembled. "And would you lock me away?"

"Alice—"

Her fingers flew to press against his mouth. "No. Forget it. Don't answer. I don't want you to answer." Fast, tumbling words. "Kiss me." Her fingers fell away. "Just kiss me one more time. Just pretend that everything I said—just pretend it didn't happen." Almost pleading.

Hadn't he told her not to beg for anything?

Saint knew Alice was trying to distract him. She'd opened a door, let him see a glimpse inside. The real Alice. Afraid, determined. A victim...a killer?

She wanted to pull back. To regroup. To find a way to get back in control.

Too late. There would be no control. Not for him. Not for her. He would strip her bare. Destroy every defense that she had, and he would know every part of her. No more hiding. No more manipulation.

He wanted the real Alice. He was going to get her.

"I'll kiss you, sweetheart."

Her lips started to curl. Relief and pleasure gleamed in her eyes.

Oh, no, my Alice, you aren't taking back control. You're going to lose it.

His hands rose up higher. Pushed between her legs. Found the edge of her soft panties.

"Wh-what are you doing?"

"Getting ready to kiss you." He yanked hard and tore the panties.

"Saint!"

He eased down in front of her. Moving so he could be at just the right height as he spread her legs and dragged her forward.

Then he kissed her. He put his mouth on her hot core, and he tasted her.

Her hips surged toward him. "This...ah, th-this wasn't what I meant."

It was what he wanted. He licked her clit. Felt her shudder. "Want me to stop?" A growl against her.

A shiver slid over her. "*No.*"

He hadn't thought so. Saint feasted on her. Drove his tongue into her even as his fingers began to tease and stroke her clit. Over and over again. He wasn't being careful or slow. He licked hard and deep, then went back to her clit and strummed her relentlessly because he wanted her to come apart for him.

He heard glass shatter, and Saint jerked back. Rose. His gaze flew around because he wanted to make sure Alice hadn't been hurt—

"Just the wine glass," she panted out. "Saint, don't stop!" Her whole body quivered, and he realized she'd been close to coming for him. So close.

Now she was on the edge.

He'd push her over.

Staring into her eyes, he stroked her. Her breath caught as her eyes flared wide. Deliberately, he pushed one finger into her.

So damn tight.

And a second. He pushed those fingers inside, stretched her. Kept his eyes on her. She was the most beautiful thing he'd ever seen in his life.

She's mine.

His fingers were in her. His eyes *on* her. She arched into his touch, rocked against his hand, rode him, and he had to lean forward. Had to drive his tongue into her mouth. He hadn't gotten drunk from the wine, but she could make him drunk. Drunk with need and desire. A lust that raged so hot he thought it might burn them both, but he didn't care.

He wanted her. Nothing in this world would have stopped him from taking her.

Her mouth tore from his. "*Saint!*" Her inner muscles squeezed tightly to his fingers. He heard the pleasure break in her voice.

The first orgasm.

Good, but not enough.

He didn't let her ease out of that release. He scooped her into his arms, carried her to the bedroom, and lowered her onto the bed.

She still had on the dress. No shoes. He had no clue where her shoes had gone. Didn't really care. He grabbed for the condoms in her nightstand drawer. Actually managed to *not* drop the drawer this time. He unhooked his jeans and started to—

Alice was touching him. Sliding her fingers around his dick. Stroking him. Pushing him closer and closer to that tempting precipice. "Alice…"

She leaned forward and closed her mouth around him.

Fuck.

Her tongue licked. She sucked him. Her hair slid forward and teased his abdomen as she took him in deeper.

His hand clenched around the wrapper in his hand. His jaw had clenched, too. Every muscle felt as if it had clenched, and she kept stroking him with her wicked tongue and sensual lips. Oblivion called, and he fucking damn well wanted to answer—

"Alice."

Her head lifted. She smiled at him. "Was I doing something wrong?"

He tumbled her back on the bed.

Her soft laughter just fueled him on. Alice thought she was taking back control. Not happening. He sheathed his dick in the condom. Caught her wrists. Pinned them above her head and held them there with one hand. Her legs were open for him. His dick pushed at the entrance to her body.

"How much can you take?" Saint half-snarled.

"Everything."

That was what he gave her. No restraint. No control. He drove into her and let go completely. Her hips shoved back against him, and she cried out—in pleasure. The same wild, reckless pleasure he felt as they wrecked the bed. As he thrust into her again and again, and he could feel her second orgasm coming. Her hands twisted in his grasp, but he didn't let her go. His mouth pressed to her neck. Licked and nipped because he knew just how sensitive she was in that spot—he'd figured it out last time.

She shuddered beneath him. Arched. Undulated.

Took more of him.

Her legs locked around his hips, and his free hand pushed between their bodies. He squeezed her clit as he drove hard—

She screamed. A quick, choked cry as she came for him.

Her orgasm squeezed his dick, tight ripples that sent him hurtling after her as his climax slammed into him. Hard. Fucking powerful. Sweeping through him and wiping out all thoughts but—

Her.

Only Alice mattered. Only Alice.

***

"You're...not gonna stay in the bed."

Alice's voice. A little disgruntled.

Saint sprawled beside her—in the bed—and didn't bother to open his eyes. He'd been enjoying himself. He'd ditched the condom moments before in the bathroom and returned to her. He *might* have been about to slip into sleep, but then she'd spoken. "Wasn't planning on moving." He had stripped.

She hadn't. She still wore the dress. Minus her panties, of course.

"There's a perfectly good couch in the other room."

His eyes opened. Saint rolled onto his side. "I just gave you two orgasms."

She stared back at him. The lamp from her bedside cast plenty of illumination onto them, so he could see her quite clearly.

"Were you counting?" she asked. "That's not very gentlemanly."

"Don't remember saying I would be gentlemanly." Her lips were slightly swollen. He loved her lips. Loved her mouth. Loved the things she could do with her mouth.

Yep, definitely *not* gentlemanly.

"Won't you sleep better on the couch?" Alice pushed.

"Nope."

"You're not taking a hint."

"You're not hinting, sweetheart. You're trying to kick me out of bed. So cold."

She sucked her lower lip between her teeth. "I...don't mean to be cold." Her voice was different. A little uncertain. "I'm not a very good sleeper. I toss and turn a lot. Have the occasional nightmare."

"We all have nightmares." Gentle.

"Not like mine."

He wondered just what scared her when she slept.

"I didn't want to—to disturb you, so I thought you might want to take the couch."

Before he could reply, she rolled away. Climbed from the bed. "But it's your choice. I warned you. If you wake up, and I've pulled a knife on you in my sleep, you can't say I didn't give you fair notice."

He sat up, slowly, and watched her march for the bathroom. "Do you often pull knives on the men who sleep with you?"

His words stopped her at the bathroom door. "Thought you'd researched and discovered that I hadn't been with a lover in a very long time." She looked over her shoulder. "Not until you came along."

He had. But it was still nice to hear her confirm it. When it came to Alice, he'd discovered a core of jealousy that unnerved him.

"I fall out of bed sometimes." A shrug of one delicate shoulder. "Strike out. You might find yourself being attacked in the middle of the night. Hardly the scene most men would enjoy."

The sheets curled around his hips. "I can handle myself." He inclined his head toward her. "But if you don't want me here, I'll go sleep on the couch." His hand rasped over his jaw. "I'm just trying to understand our relationship."

"Relationship?"

"Um. Do you just want to have sex with me so that you can release all the tension and fear that you keep wound so tightly beneath your surface?"

She stiffened. "I'm not afraid."

Yes, sweetheart, you are. I can see it now.

"Or do you want more from me?" A deliberate question.

"What might that more be?" Alice returned with one brow rising.

"Oh, you know, someone who *isn't* afraid of what might happen in the middle of the night. Someone who can keep you safe, even from yourself."

She swallowed. "A hero. How...cute."

"Nah, baby. That's not what you want. You want someone who can handle the dark. Who isn't going to run if things go to hell. And that would be me. You know it, deep inside. It's the reason you let *me* inside."

"You're saying the reason I had sex with you is because—"

His rumbling laughter cut her off. "Not meaning that kind of inside, though I enjoy the hell out of sinking deep into you. My new favorite thing in the world, in fact."

She gripped the edge of the door.

"You let me see you, my Alice."

Her chin lifted. "I have no idea what you're talking about."

"Yeah, you do." He did not take his gaze from her. "You thought I was worth saving, remember?"

Her lashes fluttered. "You're talking about...what I said at the fountain. Look, I—"

"I happen to think you are, too."

She turned her head away from him. "Stay in the bed. Go to the couch. Do whatever you want. Doesn't matter at all to me."

Yes, he thought it did.

The door shut behind her. Saint turned off the lamp and settled back in the bed. And waited for Alice to come back to him.

CHAPTER ELEVEN

"I couldn't get in the shower." Alice's low voice came after she crept out of the bathroom and slipped toward the bed. She didn't know why she was telling this to Saint. She should just shut her mouth and get into the bed with him.

Shadows and darkness filled the room, but she knew he was there. He hadn't left to take a spot on the couch.

"I stepped inside," she continued, "and I turned the water on, and I just kept seeing her." Tracy. Floating in that chamber. Her hands bound. Her feet bound.

The shower had seemed far too similar to the water torture chamber.

"I didn't like her. I didn't like what she'd done to my life," Alice continued quietly. "But I didn't want that to happen to her. It wasn't part of my plan."

His fingers curled around her wrist. "Get into bed."

"I took a bath instead of a shower." But she'd been so tense in that claw-footed tub. "Do you think she was alive when she went into the water? I-I hope she wasn't. I've heard drowning can be a terrible way to die. It's not fast. You struggle to breathe, to catch a breath, to get out and—"

"Get in bed." An order. Harder. Rougher.

She let the towel fall—the towel she'd wrapped around her body—and she took a step toward—

He pulled her into the bed. Rolled her. Tucked her against him and tugged the covers up over her. Saint also kept one arm wrapped around her stomach.

"I don't want to die that way." Why could she not stop talking? "I don't want it to be slow and painful."

"You're not fucking dying."

His arm was strong around her. He was warm. She could almost feel safe. Not that safety was something she sought.

It wasn't.

His dick was heavy and long behind her. It pressed against her, but he wasn't making any sexual moves toward her. Saint just held her. Kept her tucked against him like she was...something that mattered. She didn't, of course. His plan had been to take her down. But the way he held her...

"I'm not nice, Alice."

Quiet. Low.

"I didn't think you were," she said. Just as quiet. Just as low.

"I didn't kill those people back when I was eighteen. I was a suspect because the first victim—a bastard named Ronnie Watts—I had fought with him. Hell, not just fought, I beat the shit out of him."

She didn't flinch. Didn't try to pull away. She did ask, "Why?"

"Because I had a friend named Bo. Small guy, always getting picked on, but he was fast. The kid could pick a pocket and be two blocks over before anyone knew it. Bo ran with me. I watched out for him. Back then, my life was the streets. Didn't have much else. My dad was always a piece of shit. In jail. Trouble. My mom...she did the best she could but...she OD'd when I was seventeen."

"I'm sorry." Even softer.

"Ronnie was her dealer. I knew it, everyone did. I kept telling him to stay away. To stop giving her the drugs, but he wouldn't listen. He didn't care. Then she died and Bo—Bo took something that belonged to Ronnie. So Ronnie sliced him. Cut him deep and sent Bo to the hospital."

She was almost afraid to move. Alice didn't want to do anything to stop Saint from talking.

"Bo was part of my crew. Ronnie had taken my mother from me. He wasn't going to take anything—anyone—else. So I hunted him. I confronted him. And when he came swinging at me with his knife, I fought him. I kept fighting him until he wasn't moving, and three guys had to drag me *off* him." Calm words. Vicious violence.

Her heart raced, but her words were just as calm as his had been as she noted, "He was still alive."

"Yeah, he was. Beaten to hell and back, but alive. *Then*. Two days later, Ronnie was found with a knife shoved in his throat."

Again, she didn't flinch. But he couldn't see her face, so she let her eyes squeeze shut.

"He was the first. Others followed. People who I'd fought with. Some that I barely even spoke to on the streets. Didn't matter, though. Because the cops knew I'd had trouble with Ronnie, so they were quick to point the blame at me. When I realized I was being suspected of multiple murders—a dumbass kid who already had a rap sheet—I knew I would have to prove my own innocence." His hold remained steady on her. "I also knew I had to run because I didn't want to get locked away."

"You ran, and your brother Memphis chased you." A part of the story she already knew.

"Memphis doesn't chase. He hunts. He hunted me. At the time, I think he believed I was just like our piece-of-shit dad. Memphis and I are half-brothers. Don't think he even knew who I was, not until he started the hunt. He was good, still *is* good. The best when it comes to hunting."

"Even better than you?" A careful question.

"You don't want Memphis to come for you. If he does, you might as well be locked up already."

She opened her eyes. Stared straight ahead. "He locked you up."

"I kept telling him I was innocent. I knew things looked bad, but I hadn't done it. Seemed like no one believed me, though, especially not Memphis. The day he turned me in, he just looked at me. Stared hard then walked away."

Bastard. She didn't exactly like Memphis.

"When you're young and you're the new one in jail, you have to fight hard. I tried telling the cops and guards I was innocent and—"

"Saint." His new name. This part had been in the reports Logan gave her.

"Yeah, they mocked me. Said they were sure I was a fucking Saint who'd been locked up by mistake."

He had been, though.

"When the other inmates came for me, I fought back. Harder and more viciously than they expected. I kept fighting, every single day, until I looked up and Memphis was back."

Memphis. They kept returning to him.

"He hadn't given up on me. He found proof I was innocent. Would you believe it...*Bo* did it. Bo. The one I wanted to protect. The one I thought needed me."

Oh, damn. I do not like this plot twist.

"He was tired of being picked on. So he started by getting even with Ronnie. Then every other person that had ever wronged him. Guess he got a taste for it. Some do, you know. Get a taste for the violence. For killing."

"Why are you telling me this story?" At first, she'd thought...Alice wasn't sure what she'd thought. That maybe he was telling her he would protect the people who belonged to him. That he would help those who needed him. But, nope. Not the moral of this particular tale.

"I didn't need to get a taste for violence. I always had one."

She sucked in a breath.

"You can feel the darkness in me, can't you, Alice?"

Maybe. *Yes.*

"I think Memphis felt it, too. That's why he tried to get me focused. Trained me to hunt criminals. Wanted me to understand that there was a right and wrong way to live in this world. I had been in jail. I knew I didn't want to go back. I knew I had to stick to the *right* side. So I blended. I did all the things Memphis told me. I've been good at hunting. It's natural for me."

She released the breath she'd been holding. A careful exhale. "I feel the darkness." Why deny it?

"I would not hurt you." Rasped. Almost...torn from him?

"Saint...*Sebastian.* Don't you understand? I don't fear your darkness." She turned in his arms. Faced him. Brought her forehead to rest against his. "I like it."

He didn't speak again.

Neither did she. But his arms wrapped around her, and he pulled her even closer.

***

"I'm not going to marry you." Alice took off the engagement ring. Got caught by the bright sparkle. Such a pretty ring. Such a big diamond.

"Of course, you are." Unconcerned. No, amused.

She put the ring on the table near the door. "I don't love you."

Corey laughed as he rose from the couch and headed toward her with his easy grace. "That's not required." He smiled at her. The same smile he always had. The one that never seemed to reach his eyes. "You're perfect for me."

No. She wasn't. "I can't be what you need."

"You're *exactly* what I need." He stopped before her. "You will never be afraid when I'm close. I can keep you safe from *everything*. I can make every bit of trouble or pain you've felt vanish."

Perhaps he could. But he couldn't make her love him. She wasn't sure that she could love anyone. "You're not as bad as you pretend to be."

His eyelids flickered. "Alice..."

"You should be happy. I want you to be happy." And he would not be happy with her. Because one day, he would want more. He would want love.

She didn't know if she could ever give that to him or to anyone.

Alice turned away.

"Alice, don't you leave me!" His voice thundered after her. "Don't you walk away!"

Her hand reached for the doorknob. "I'm sorry."

"Alice!"

***

Alice jerked, and her eyes flew open.

Still in bed. Still with Saint.

She'd warned him that she wasn't an easy sleeper but...Alice squinted to try and see in the dark. Saint didn't seem to have felt her jolt in the bed. His breathing came deeply, easily, as he continued to sleep.

Being as careful as possible, Alice eased away from him. A bit tricky because he had one arm wrapped around her stomach, but she managed the task. Her feet sank into the lush carpet, and she crept toward her closet. Once inside, she shut the door, dressed quickly and quietly in the dark, then prepared to slip away. If her luck held, Saint would never know that she'd left the house—or the bed. She'd be back long before he awoke.

Alice opened the closet door and nearly slammed straight into the big, muscled chest that belonged to Saint.

His hands came up and clamped around her arms. "Hey, sweetheart," he murmured, voice tender. "Going somewhere?"

"You were faking." She should have expected that from him.

"I was sleeping. Then your elbow rammed into my ribs, it sounded like you were hyperventilating, and you dove out of the bed and ran to the closet. Being the good boyfriend that I am, I came to check on you."

Had she rammed her elbow into his ribs? She— "Boyfriend?" That word pierced straight through her.

"Um. Yes. I know, I'm hardly a boy. But calling myself your manfriend just doesn't have the same ring, does it? I suppose we could go with lover but, again, not really the way you introduce someone." His thumbs lightly rubbed her arms. "You don't walk up to someone and say, 'Oh, by the way, this is my lover, Saint.' Just not the way most people do things."

She didn't pay attention to what most people did.

"We've had sex twice now. You've had four orgasms."

"You need to stop counting." She was way, way off balance.

"No, I don't think I will. At least not until you come at least one hundred times for me."

One hundred— "Stop playing with me."

"I'm not. Wouldn't dream of it." But he released her. "Nightmare, my Alice?"

"Why do you do that?" She skirted around his big, shadowy form. She didn't turn on any lights. A deliberate move. If someone was watching her house, a light would alert any onlooker.

"Do what? Be sexy? Sorry, it's just the way I am. Twenty-four, seven."

He was making a joke? At that particular moment? "I mean why do you say 'my Alice' when you talk to me?"

"Oh." A rustle. Had he just grabbed his jeans? "Didn't realize I was doing that."

"You do it a lot." So much that she'd even tried tossing it back at him and saying 'my Saint' but he hadn't seemed to notice. "Why?"

"Because..." But he seemed to flounder. As if he didn't know himself.

Hmm. Perhaps she should help him out. "Is it because you're falling for me, and you want me to belong to you?" A sigh. A despondent one. "Sorry, but that's just not meant to be. I don't belong to anyone." Alice maneuvered for the door. She made sure not to bump into any furniture.

His fingers closed around her wrist. "He left a mark on you."

"Excuse me?"

"Donovan made you fear belonging to someone. Because he wanted to control you so completely."

"I belong to myself."

"You do and always will."

She wished she could see his face. Read his expression. But in order to do that, she would need to turn on the lights. Not something she could do.

"Why are you sorry?" Saint asked.

Her eyebrows jerked up. "You are losing me, Saint. I have no idea what you're—"

"Before you elbowed me in the ribs, you said you were sorry."

Hell. Her feet seemed rooted to the floor. Suspicious, she asked, "Did you sleep at all? Or did you just hold me and watch me and try to figure out my weaknesses?"

"I already know your weaknesses. No need to figure them out."

She backed up, caught herself, and surged forward instead. "I don't have weaknesses."

"Oh, yes, you do. I'm your main one."

Her mouth opened, but the denial didn't come.

"If I weren't, you wouldn't have saved me at the fountain. If you were the cold-blooded killer described by reporters and cops, you would have just stood in the shadows and let the shooter fire at me. You knew I was investigating you. You knew I wanted to find proof you were guilty. All you had to do was stay quiet and your problems would have gone away."

"I've never been good at staying quiet."

"Instead of watching me get killed, you risked your life to save me. Bad, bad mistake."

It depended on how you looked at things.

"Because you showed your feelings," Saint added. He felt so close.

"You have no idea what you're talking about." She needed to stop wasting time. She had a narrow window of opportunity to accomplish her goals. She'd already glanced at her bedside clock. It was three-thirty in the morning. "Why don't you just go back to bed, and I will—"

"You said I'd fall for you. But, Alice, I think you fell for me."

She should laugh. Tell him that was ever so adorable. Mock him for his cute confidence. Instead, she said, "Wrong." She was sad about this part. "I can't love, Saint. So don't go thinking that I do—or that I ever will." The mistake Corey had made. "I'm not wired like everyone else."

Alice reached out for her door.

Saint caught her fingers. Brought them up. Kissed her knuckles. "Oh, baby, whoever told you that?"

Dammit. Why did his touch always seem to burn straight through her? "No one had to tell me. I *know* how I am."

"Wired differently. Sure, so am I. But why think you can't love?"

Because she hadn't before. Because she'd always felt frozen and isolated. Because—

"Because you fake a lot of your reactions, so you don't know how to be real anymore?" he murmured. "I can help with that. I've found that if you let that careful control shatter, things can get real. You might find yourself feeling one hell of a lot."

She didn't want to feel a lot. She'd felt a lot growing up. Felt the devastation when she *watched* her mother die. Pneumonia. People got pneumonia all the time and were *fine*. But not her mother. Not her fragile, beautiful mother. She'd withered. Been so pale in that hospital bed even as she'd tried to smile and tell Alice that she would get better.

You didn't get better.

Then Alice had been gutted when she found her father after his heart attack. Been lost and alone when the show closed, and she'd been kicked out of the little trailer she shared with her father. She had been in so much pain that it had nearly ripped her apart. The grief had suffocated her. Smothered her voice. Taken everything.

Then Donovan had appeared...

Promising fucking *love*.

"Love is a lie," she said, voice hushed. "Don't ever believe it." Her hand pulled from his. She grabbed once more for the door and yanked it open. Alice stepped into the hall.

Only to find Saint dodging her steps. "Where are we going?"

"*I'm* going to Abracadabra."

His arm curled around her stomach. He pulled her back against him. "Did you forget it was a crime scene?" His breath blew lightly against the shell of her ear.

She fought a shiver. "Hard to forget."

"But you're going there anyway, in the dead of night."

"I like to think of it as the early morning." He *had* dressed. She could feel his clothes behind her.

"Why?"

"Why do I call it early morning—"

"Why are we crashing a crime scene?"

We. "Don't remember inviting you to tag along."

Soft laughter. Mocking. "We're working together, remember? Where you go, I go."

Alice had feared that might be his reaction. She'd hoped to slip out while he slept, but, no such luck. Now she'd have a sidekick. But that didn't have to be a bad thing. With Tracy's murder, Alice could admit that she felt a bit...nervous. In the back of her mind, hadn't she always realized...*It's only a matter of time until he comes after me.* Because her stalker had an obsession. Eventually, all obsessions ended.

"If the cops see us, we'll get hauled back to the station," Saint warned her. "Cops get territorial about things like their crime scenes and, you know, interfering with murder investigations."

"I'm not interfering." She was. One hundred percent. "I'm looking for clues." She also needed to pick up something. "I would have searched when we found Tracy, but you wouldn't let me go back inside." He'd held her too tightly. Just as he held her tightly now. "The cops don't know him. I do. And I think he might have left a message for me."

Saint released her. "Now why would you think that?"

Sadness pulled at Alice. "Because he always does."

CHAPTER TWELVE

Getting away from the reporters had been easy. There had only been one news van still on Alice's street, and there had been no sign of anyone near it. They'd slipped out the back door of her home, though, just in case. And Saint had discovered that Alice had a car stashed in a small garage a bit down the road. *Still* on her property, as she'd informed him. But the driveway to that little garage hadn't led to the main street. It had snaked back and been perfect for escaping.

When they arrived at Abracadabra, the building sat, dark and empty. Alice had parked several blocks away and as they hurried to her speakeasy, Saint caught sight of his own ride. He would be leaving in it, and if any cops should appear and question them, he could always say that he'd come to pick up his rental. A fairly decent cover story.

"They put up crime scene tape." Alice seemed annoyed.

He didn't point out to her that a murder *had* occurred, so crime scene tape would be required. Instead, he rubbed his chin and said, "What's the game plan here? Are you gonna tell me you have some secret passage that will allow us entrance so that anyone watching the building will never know we've been here?"

"Uh, no, I was just going to use my key and go in the rear door." She looked back at him. "Let's just stay toward the shadows, okay? The alarms are all disengaged, I took care of that before we arrived."

Sure, she had.

"So it's just a matter of getting in and out quickly. And *not* being seen."

He inclined his head politely. "Thanks for the instruction. Probably should tell you that this is far from my first B&E."

A cop sat in a patrol car across the street from her building, but his head was down, his eyes seemingly glued to the glowing phone screen in front of him. *Way to watch out for trouble.*

She crept toward the back of the building, barely giving the cop a glance. "It's not a B&E. I own the building, remember?"

Crime scene, sweetheart. That means you are not supposed to be here. But he wanted to see exactly what it was that Alice thought might be inside. Something she believed the detectives had overlooked? Or something she feared they would find?

Either way, he'd known from the moment he felt her trying to slip out of bed that she would not be escaping him. He hadn't been kidding when he said that wherever she went, he'd go. As far as he was concerned, Alice was in danger. She needed protection. He'd be giving it to her. Moving silently, he stayed right with her. "Are you worried about the cop out front?"

"Only if he stops being hooked to his phone. Don't really think he's supposed to have that out while he's on a shift, do you?" She didn't reach for the back door. Instead, Alice looked to the left and right. Glanced *down*, as if searching for something.

"He probably has a partner. Usually there are two in situations like this one. The partner might be far more attentive."

"Well, maybe the partner is on a bathroom break because I didn't see anyone else." She kept peering at the ground.

He lightly tapped her shoulder.

Her head whipped up.

"Can I help you find something?" he asked politely. "Something *out* here? Because I thought we were going in the building. The longer we stay outside, the more risk we put on ourselves." He was already risking plenty by being there. If they got caught, they'd both be hauled to the station again. Except...

Saint realized he hadn't even hesitated to follow her to Abracadabra.

"No, no, there's nothing out here." A little too rushed. But Alice was finally moving. She unlocked the door. And, sure enough, there was no beep of an alarm. She darted inside the back room and didn't turn on any overhead lights as he followed her.

She pulled a small penlight from her bag and shone it before her. The darkness around them seemed particularly thick as they advanced.

"Why aren't there more security cameras here?" he asked when they entered the bar area.

Her light darted to the thick, black curtains that lined the right wall.

For a moment, Saint could have sworn that he saw one of the curtains flutter. His body tensed.

"There is another camera. It's in my office."

What the fuck? Saint curled his hand around her shoulder. "There's a security camera in the room where Tracy was killed? And you're mentioning this *now*?"

She swung back toward him. The pencil light bounced off his chest. "Yes, I'm telling you now. I brought you along with me to find it. I'm trying to trust you. You might have missed it, but trust is exceedingly hard for me."

"Why do we need to find the camera? Don't you have it set up online? Shouldn't you be able to access it from your phone?" Everything was a click away these days. She *should* have been able to pull up the security feed with a few taps of her fingers. Then they should have been able to see everything that had happened.

Her breath rustled out. "No one but me knew about the camera in that office."

"Not even Logan?"

"No."

Interesting.

"It went down yesterday. I didn't even notice at first, not like I check it all the time. I just...I had a few groupies try to break in before, so I wanted to keep tabs on the room. Some of the things in there have great value to me. I installed the camera myself, told no one else. But..."

But someone had found it. From the sound of things, it had been found and disabled. "Let's go." The sooner they searched her office and got out of there, the better.

Before she could move, though, he took the pen light from her and flashed it toward the curtains on the right.

No more flutters of the fabric. Just stillness.

"What is it?" Alice pressed closer.

Oh, just his instincts screaming at him. "Your office. Now."

She darted toward her office. He followed right with her, and in one hand, he gripped the light. In the other, he'd pulled out his gun.

The door to her office was wide open. She slipped inside and hesitated, then flipped the light switch on the wall.

The sudden illumination had him blinking. "Alice..."

"No one can see the light but us. The windows have a special glass on them—something I requested. No one can see inside." The windows were also up damn high, an odd architectural issue he'd noticed before. "The light will help me work faster," she said as she hurried across the room.

The water torture chamber had been removed. He figured the cops had decided to take the whole thing in as evidence. Probably a good idea.

Alice didn't even glance toward where the chamber had been. Instead, she went to the left, toward the top hat that still rested on the round table. She put her hand inside the hat.

"Uh, don't you think the cops glanced in your hat?"

"There's a false bottom. They wouldn't have known how to open it."

Sure, a false bottom. He should have thought of that. *Magic tricks.*

"The security camera is inside. The fabric is actually extremely thin at the bottom, think like mesh, so I could put the camera in—it's tiny—and it could record everything that happened in front of the hat."

So the camera had recorded them the other day when they'd had their make-out session. Good to know.

"I don't know why it stopped transmitting," Alice said. "I—" She broke off. Shuddered.

He bounded toward her. "Alice?"

"The camera isn't here any longer." She still had her hand in the hat.

He swung the penlight inside the hat so he could get a better view. Her hand rose. She'd fisted her fingers around something. Something very small.

"He *did* leave me a message." Her hand uncurled.

A diamond ring rested in the middle of her palm. Bright. Sparkling.

"This was my engagement ring." Her fingers closed around the diamond ring once more. "Corey gave it to me, and I gave it back to him the night he—he vanished." A faint hesitation.

Saint knew she was holding one extremely expensive ring. The diamond was massive.

"I haven't seen the ring since Corey disappeared. I thought he'd taken it with him." Her words were hushed, but fast. "No, no, that's not true. I'm supposed to tell *you* the truth, right?"

He wanted the truth. He also wanted the fear in her voice to vanish.

"I thought his killer took it. I left it on the table near Corey's front door. He shouted after me. Told me I couldn't leave him, but I did. I left, and he vanished, and he didn't come back." She looked down at her fisted hand. "He's not ever coming back."

Or maybe he *had* come back. Alice didn't seem to be considering that possibility. Maybe the ring was a sign that her ex had come back, after all. Maybe he'd been there all along. Something they would talk about. *After* they finished the search and got the hell out of there. "We should give the ring to the cops."

She tucked it into her bag. "Why?"

He paced around the room. "Because it's evidence, sweetheart."

"The camera is gone. He knew it was there. How did he know?"

Because he's been watching you. Very, very closely. Saint didn't touch anything as he searched. He already knew his prints were spread out in the room and over Alice's desk. But there was no sense in more contamination.

More contamination. Right. She's taking things from the crime scene. That's plenty of contamination—and tampering. He paused in front of the bathroom door. "Where did he get the hose?" The bastard had been prepared. The hose. The chamber. And Tracy.

How did he get Tracy here? Had he brought her from another location or...

"The spray paint isn't here."

Saint looked back at Alice. She'd opened her desk drawer.

"I put it inside, but it's gone." Alice bit her lower lip. "Think the cops have it?"

He thought of the brick that had been tossed through her window. The paint on it. And the SUV that had barreled down the street. "Sweetheart, we both know that's not the case. I thought you were going to start giving me the truth." Anger hummed through him. "If you're trying to set up a scene so I will—"

Thump.

He and Alice both stilled. Then in the next instant, he ran for her open door. That sound had been faint, but he *knew* he'd heard it. Someone else was inside the speakeasy.

"Saint, wait!" Alice's cry.

He didn't wait. He rushed back toward the darkened bar, and when the penlight swept around...Saint saw that a chair had fallen to the floor. As if someone had bumped into it in the dark and sent it tumbling down.

Fuck me.

"Saint, what are you—"

"We are not alone."

She stopped. Alice stood just a foot or two behind him. He swept the light to the fallen chair so that she could see it, then he darted it around the bar. He trekked over those curtains slowly. One section of the wall at a time.

"Be careful." Alice inched closer. Her hands pressed to his back. "Old magician's trick. You wear black and you can blend in with the curtains. It's how they used to make the woman in the box disappear, old-school style. She'd be wearing black, she just pulled up a mask and she vanished—the crowd wasn't close enough to see clearly, so she blended with the black inside the box—"

Yeah, he didn't know what damn trick Alice was talking about—what *effect*—she meant, and he didn't really care right then. Because he'd just seen the curtain flutter again.

To the right.

And was that...Yes, it was...His light hit a black ski mask. He saw the bastard's eyes in the small holes, glaring back at him. "Get back, Alice," Saint growled.

"Saint—"

The figure screamed and barreled forward, leaping straight from the black curtains and coming hard at Saint with his arms raised. Saint aimed his weapon. He got ready to—

Alice slammed into him. "Saint, no!"

Was she fucking kidding?

Footsteps rushed past him as the figure ran toward the back room—toward the back door. Saint pulled away from Alice. "Stay here!"

"No, Saint, wait, you don't—"

He was already giving chase. He caught the figure in the back room and shoved him into the wall. Hard enough to shake the bastard's body. The penlight had dropped from Saint's hand when Alice slammed into him, but he damn well still had his gun. He whirled the SOB around—

The fool tried to headbutt him. A move Saint easily dodged. He brought his weapon up to fire—

"Saint, *don't!*" Alice's plea. Because, of course, she hadn't stayed behind. Not her. "Don't shoot, it's—"

"I know it's fucking Logan," he snarled back. "And that makes me want to shoot all the more."

The figure in black cried out. Scared. Angry. He swung at Saint once more.

An attack Saint dodged. Then he shoved the barrel of his gun against the other man's head. "You freeze or I will pull the trigger."

And...

Laughter.

From the man in black. From Logan. "The hell you will," Logan snapped back. "That's not what you do. You hunt down criminals. You turn them in. You don't kill—"

"You don't know me," Saint said, words ice cold and lethal. "You have no idea what I am capable of doing."

"Saint..." Alice's low voice.

"Call him off, Alice," Logan barked. "Tell him to get his hands off me, now!"

"Go get the cops out front, Alice," Saint ordered, never moving his gun and keeping it dead center on Logan's forehead. "Tell them we were checking the property and saw someone breaking in. We caught the perp. They'll want to take him in to custody."

"Alice!" A desperate cry—no, a plea—from Logan. "Don't! They'll lock me up!"

"Yeah," Saint snarled right back. "That's the point."

Alice didn't leave. *"Saint, do not shoot him. Please, move the gun."*

She couldn't be serious. "If he doesn't get twitchy, I won't have to shoot. How about getting those cops, sweetheart? Now?"

She still didn't move to leave. Instead, she crept closer. Her hand rose and pressed to his arm. The arm that was extended as he held the gun on Logan. "I'm asking you—for me—to lower the gun."

"What kind of game are you playing?" Saint rasped.

"Why does everyone always think I'm playing?" Sad. Then, "Please."

He knew what she was doing. She knew it, too. Begging. They'd talked about this issue.

Logan didn't seem to even be breathing. He'd gone statue still. Jaw locking, Saint lifted the gun away, and he took a step—

Logan yelled and surged forward. He drove his fist toward Saint's jaw, but he missed, and that swinging hand slammed toward Alice and—

The fuck, no. A roar seemed to rip from Saint. He kicked Logan in the gut, sent the jerk barreling back and crashing into the wall. Alice didn't want him to use a gun? Fine, Saint had always preferred to work with his hands. "Hold this." He pushed the gun toward Alice.

"I—" She took the gun.

He drove his fist into Logan's mask-covered jaw. "You don't ever swing at her."

"I wasn't!" Logan shook his head, seemingly dazed by the blow, but his hands fisted. "I was swinging at *you!*"

"Because you hate me? Because I'm taking her from you?" Saint taunted. "Yeah, I am."

Logan swung out with his fist again, a fairly decent hook.

Saint didn't let the blow land. Instead, he ducked, then fired out with an upper cut that clipped Logan under the chin and had his teeth rattling together. Logan weaved, stumbled, and Saint's fist thudded into his cheek in the next instant. Logan's feet seemed to give out beneath him, and he slammed onto the floor.

"Enough." From Alice.

Saint glanced toward her. She'd grabbed the pen light and angled it into his eyes. "We need to calm down," Alice continued as she clutched the gun in her right hand. Gun in the right. Penlight in her left. "I'm sure he can explain if you let—"

A guttural yell broke from Logan right before his arms locked around Saint's waist and he threw Saint to the ground.

Thanks for distracting me, sweetheart.

Saint pounded his fists into Logan's side. Hit the vulnerable kidney area. Enjoyed the howl of pain that came as—

An annoyed voice demanded, "Are you through playing?" Not Alice. A masculine voice. A familiar voice. A voice that should not be there. "I swear I taught you better than this. You don't play with the prey."

Saint kneed Logan in the groin. Logan groaned and rolled to the side.

Before Saint could reply to the man who'd just burst in the back door, Alice jumped in front of him. Alice and her light and her gun. She shone the light on the figure, and she pointed her gun at him. "Don't you dare take another step!"

The man held up his hands, showing he was unarmed. Right. Like that meant he wasn't a threat. He didn't seem bothered by the light shining on him. Instead, his gaze flickered from Alice to Saint.

Saint rose to his feet.

Alice moved her body slightly, angling so that she was fully in front of Saint. And never lowering her gun.

The man frowned. "Are you...trying to protect him?"

"I'm just wanting to make sure he doesn't accidentally get hit when I fire this gun. Saint is out of the way now so..." Alice let her words trail off.

"So you'd shoot his brother? That what you're saying? If so, you are certainly as cold as they say." A drawl that *might* have been admiring.

But, no, Memphis—and it was Memphis in the doorway, even though his brother should *not* be there—had it wrong. Alice wasn't cold at all. Saint thought she might just burn too hot.

"Brother?" Alice repeated. Then she nodded. "Oh, I see."

Logan groaned again. "My balls..."

Alice ignored Logan. She seemed completely focused on Memphis.

"Yep, I'm his brother." Memphis began to lower his hands.

"All the more reason to shoot," Alice said. "*You* are the one who dumped Saint in jail."

Uh, oh. "Alice." Now it was Saint's turn to put his hand on her shoulder. "Do not shoot him."

Still, she kept the weapon pointed.

Memphis's brow furrowed. "What's happening here?"

"Alice holds grudges," Saint explained. Obviously. "Alice..." He moved his hand toward her arm—the extended arm—and gently applied pressure. "If I don't get to shoot Logan, you sure as hell can't fire at my brother."

Her head turned toward him. "Are you going to say 'please' to me? Are you going to plead the way I did?"

He heard a shout from outside.

"Didn't think so," she murmured.

"The cops are coming." He didn't wait. He took the gun. The last thing he wanted was for Alice to be found holding a weapon when the cops stormed inside.

Memphis looked over his shoulder. Whistled. "Finally. Didn't it take them long enough to join the party?"

Saint put the gun on the floor. And he was already raising his hands even as the uniforms appeared and blasted, *"Freeze!"*

CHAPTER THIRTEEN

What a clusterfuck of a situation. *This* was why she didn't normally work with partners. If she'd just come to Abracadabra on her own, then she would have avoided all this unnecessary drama.

Alice stood behind Abracadabra and tried to look innocent. A bit hard considering the situation, but she thought she might be able to pull this scene off. Now, if fate could just help her out a wee bit...

"Alice..." Heidi sighed her name. "Do you know what happens when you break into a crime scene?"

A still-groaning Logan had been taken and put in the back of a patrol car. Another serious disaster. For the moment, though, Alice had to handle the fire right in front of her. "I didn't break into my own building, detective."

"No? According to the responding officers..."

The officer who had been playing on his phone and the buddy who'd been missing when she first arrived?

"They found you *inside* the building."

Alice opened her mouth to reply—

"I told you already, detective," Saint interjected, voice smooth as silk. "We heard someone inside. When we went to investigate, we found Logan, wearing a ski mask. He jumped at me. I had to defend myself."

Some of that statement was true. Some was false. Alice could respect the blend of both. She could also respect that Saint was trying to cover her ass. The trip had been her idea.

Heidi swung toward him. Her partner was on scene, too. Jamal was currently having a very animated talk with Memphis Camden about fifteen feet away. Lots of hand gestures were occurring.

The lights had been turned on behind her building. Behind it, in it. Everywhere.

Alice cleared her throat. "Is there any chance that I'll be getting my bag back?"

"You're not getting the bag or your car," Heidi informed her with more than a hint of smug satisfaction. "We're searching both to make sure you didn't take any evidence from the scene."

She could argue about the legality of that search, but why look extra guilty? Sighing, Alice lifted her hands into the air. She turned around slowly. "Feel free to search me, too, if necessary. I have nothing to hide." The light hit the diamond ring she wore—on her right-hand ring finger. No, she wasn't hiding anything. She was displaying it in plain sight. For all the cops knew, she'd arrived with that ring. She would be leaving with it, too.

Saint's gaze fell to the ring. His jaw hardened.

Don't say a word. She sure hoped he would not say—

"Meow."

Relief nearly staggered her. "My darling!" Alice called out dramatically.

Both Saint and Heidi looked at her as if she'd lost what last bit of sanity she'd originally possessed. Whatever. Alice rushed toward a dumpster.

"Meow."

The black cat crept from behind the dumpster. Alice grabbed it, ignored the way its claws scratched over her arm, and brought the precious beast in for a tight hug. "I was so afraid I wouldn't find you."

"What in the hell is that?" Heidi's voice notched even higher than normal.

Alice turned back toward her. "It's my cat. Clearly." She held up the cat. Didn't even flinch when more claws cut into her arm.

Heidi squinted. "Does that cat only have three legs?"

"Yes, very astute of you to notice. He does. I was so worried about him." She stroked the scraggly fur on the top of the cat's head. "I convinced Saint that we must come and search for him. Normally, I bring him food each night, but with my dear speakeasy shut down and turned into a crime scene..."

Despondently, she glanced toward the rear door of Abracadabra. "I worried that he would go hungry." Her stare returned to Heidi. "So we came here to find the cat. And we heard the sounds inside. The door was open, we went in and..." Her shoulders hunched. "The rest you know."

Heidi stomped toward her. Anger seemed to burn in her wake. "Do I look like a fool to you?"

"*Meow.*"

Alice was pretty sure the cat had just said...yes. He had also stopped raking her with his claws and almost seemed to be cuddling against her. "Why would you ask that?"

"You...Alice Shephard...you expect me to believe that *you* came rushing out in the middle of the night to save a cat?" Bitter laughter. "Right. If you were so worried about the stray, why not come sooner? Why wait until four a.m. to come for the mangy—"

"His name is Houdini," Alice said, lifting her chin. "I don't refer to him as 'The Stray' because he doesn't like that."

Heidi's jaw sagged open. After a moment, she managed to snap it closed. "You are shitting me right now."

Alice almost expected to see smoke rising from Heidi's form. Almost. "No, I'm not. And I didn't come to get him sooner because I was at the police station for most of the day. You know that. You were with me. When I got home, reporters had surrounded my place. I collapsed in bed...and woke up from a terrible nightmare, knowing I had to find my cat."

"Uh, huh. You raced out to find the stray—"

"His name is—"

Heidi threw up a hand. "Spare me! I don't want to hear this crap. You were found *inside* a secured crime scene. You're getting locked up, lady. Your cat can go to the shelter. I'm sure they'll take much better care of him there than you ever would!" She tried to take the cat.

His claws raked over her hand, drawing blood.

Good kitty.

"I'd suggest that you stop wasting time with Alice," Saint directed rather calmly, in spite of the tension. "And instead go focus on Logan."

Alice cast him a quick, searching glance. He stood a few feet away, with his arms crossed over his broad chest.

"He was the one wearing the ski mask," Saint noted. "Which, you know, obviously, I'm not a detective, but, damn, doesn't that seem suspicious?"

Jamal and Memphis strode toward them.

"And I would *strongly* suggest that you take a look inside the back of Logan's SUV," Saint added.

"Oh? And why is that?" Heidi asked.

"Because I think you'll find the spray paint can he used on the brick that he *threw* into Alice's window. Pretty sure I caught sight of his SUV fleeing down the road after the attack. Uniforms took down details about the attack, so I'm sure it's on file back at the station."

Heidi tensed. She also crept closer to Jamal.

"Why would Logan throw a brick in Alice's window?" Jamal shook his head. "That doesn't make a bit of sense to me."

Saint didn't change his casual pose in the middle of the chaotic scene. "Sure it does, and you know it. It makes perfect sense if he's been obsessed with her for years, and he can't stand the idea of anyone getting close to her. Don't really think the brick—and the lovely message of 'Die' that was painted on it—were for Alice, though. Think he was telling me what would happen if I didn't get away from her."

Alice pulled the cat closer. His head bobbed against her chin.

"The brick came hurling through the window when I was with Alice, and then the next thing I knew, I was being shot at in a park." His tone remained steady as Saint continued his tale, "Shot at by someone who happened to be dressed all in black and wearing a ski mask, just like Logan was wearing when we found him in Abracadabra."

Goose bumps rose onto her arms.

Jamal seemed to consider Saint's words. After a few moments of silence, he nodded. "It fits."

He—"What?" Alice questioned. All her employees had black uniforms. She had a black uniform. And you could get a ski mask anywhere—

"Fits with the security footage we retrieved," Jamal explained.

Her hold tightened on the cat. His head turned, and he licked her. "What footage?" There was no footage.

"Footage taken from the building across the street. You know they've been doing some construction over there."

Yes, certainly she knew. But the tenants hadn't moved in yet. They were a very long way from—

"They put up a few exterior cams. We got the footage, and we saw Tracy Eldridge when she arrived at Abracadabra. Was around nine a.m."

Nine a.m. She didn't look at Saint.

That was the first time we had sex. Roughly around that time, anyway. After they'd finished talking to the cops in Forsyth Park—a situation that had taken forever—then they'd gone back to her place and had the best sex she'd enjoyed in...forever.

"Didn't see the person who opened the door for her, but Tracy was escorted right inside." Jamal nodded. "Like she was going in for a meeting or something."

The blood seemed to pound harder in her veins. Alice could hear the drumming echo of her heartbeat in her ears.

Jamal's badge had been clipped to his hip, and his hand moved to his side, brushing over it. "That timeline sure seems to indicate that Logan could have fired the shot at Saint—that attack in the park was around—"

"Six thirty," Saint supplied.

"Yeah, he could have shot at Saint, then easily been here to meet with Tracy. Must have lured her here." Jamal's stare raked her. "Maybe he promised to tell her something about you, Alice. Something she could use to hurt you."

"I'm cold. Tired. I'd like to go home." Her voice was clipped.

"But it was a lie, of course. He got her here, killed her, and left her for you."

The drumming was louder. The cat's head bobbed against her once more.

"Maybe he thought she'd be a present." Heidi was giving her opinion now. How wonderful. "He shoved her in your favorite magic trick and thought you'd be happy. *Were* you happy?"

Alice turned her head toward the female detective. "Not a trick, and I don't remember telling you it was my favorite." The cat squirmed in her arms. "I need to take Houdini home. I want to go h—" *Stop it.* She sounded weak. That couldn't happen. Alice pulled in a slow breath. "You don't have a reason to hold me. Other than, well, the fact that you don't like me." But what they were saying...the camera footage, the fact that Tracy had been at the speakeasy to meet someone...

Someone opened the door for her and took her right inside. Logan? *Logan?* No, this was...

He'd been hiding in Abracadabra. And someone had let Tracy inside... Let her inside and killed her.

Alice swallowed. "Should I be calling my lawyer?"

"Probably," Memphis said. It was the first time he'd spoken since he and Jamal had stopped their private chat and joined their little group.

Her gaze cut to him. Narrowed. While he'd been having that heated discussion with Jamal, had Memphis mentioned that she'd pointed a gun at him?

"Probably a good idea," Memphis clarified. "Given everything that's happening."

"We're taking Logan in for questioning." Jamal squared his shoulders. "I'm quite interested to see what all he has to say." He stepped toward Alice. "Sometimes when people feel pressured, feel cornered, all kinds of secrets come spilling out."

Logan doesn't know my secrets.

"You should stop acting like Alice is guilty of something." Saint positioned his body at her side. He reached out. Scratched the cat behind its ears.

The cat's purr rumbled through his little body.

"From where I'm standing..." Saint began.

He's standing at my side.

"Looks to me like Alice has been the victim. She's had a stalker for years. Someone who eliminates the men who get close to her. Someone who takes out people who hurt her. If Logan has secrets, they are his own. In addition to searching his ride, I'd be tearing apart his place if I were you. Serials do like to keep trophies. A little tidbit I picked up over the years."

Serial killer. He kept going back to that. He was wrong.

"Take her home," Jamal directed grudgingly. "But don't even *think* of leaving the city."

"Wouldn't dream of it," Alice said as she turned and began walking away. Back toward the front of Abracadabra. "Why would I leave my home?" She held the cat close to her chest. His little body felt oddly warm against her.

Saint kept pace with her. His brother fell into step on her other side. She didn't look at either man. Just stared straight ahead, and when she reached the front of Abracadabra...

More lights.

Bright, flashing police lights that swept the area. And, of course, a news van. The same van that had been parked at her house.

"There she is!" A cameraman surged toward her.

Tyler McQuinn sprang in front of him. "Alice! Alice, please tell me what brought you to the crime scene at such a late—"

"She was picking up her cat," Saint groused. "Out of the way."

"Why is Logan Becker in a police car?" Tyler fired his questions as fast as possible. "Is he being arrested? Did he kill Tracy Eldridge?"

"No comment." Memphis shook his head. "Back off, buddy. Give us space. *Now*."

"But, but—"

Memphis and Saint stepped even closer to Alice. Both were big, strong. Walked with a dangerous kind of grace. Both also gave off serious *don't-fuck-with-me* vibes. Vibes that obviously intimidated Tyler because he scampered back.

His cameraman kept filming. She hoped he got some great footage. Footage of her protectively holding her precious three-legged cat and looking suitably distraught.

They strode past the patrol car. Through the back window, she saw Logan. Her gaze met his.

"When they search his SUV, they'll find the spray paint can." Saint seemed confident. "That will give them something to hold him on."

Logan's head turned to follow their movements. When his stare darted to Saint...

Fury.

She looked away from him. "How do you know they'll find the can?" They'd reached Saint's rental car, the vehicle he'd left when they'd been hauled in for questioning about Tracy's murder.

"Because I heard it rolling around in the back when he picked us up from the police station. When you were talking to him, I glanced over and saw it."

Her gut clenched. He'd known...since then? "You didn't say anything."

He held the door open for her.

Memphis just watched them.

Saint smiled. "Neither did you, sweetheart."

"Excuse me?"

"You knew from the instant we saw the SUV rushing away from your house that it was him. You recognized his car, but you didn't say a word to me."

No, she hadn't.

"Then you did the whole routine of searching for the spray can in your drawer a bit ago." He kept holding the passenger side door for her. "Want to tell me what that was about?"

Her gaze darted down the road. Tyler and his cameraman were watching them. Jamal had stopped near the patrol car. No, she didn't want to tell him what that had been about. At least, not there. Alice slipped inside the vehicle. It didn't quite seem fair that her car got impounded, but he was free to leave in his rental. The cops definitely liked him better.

Saint leaned in toward her. Pulled the seat belt over her and snapped it. But she thought he only did that so Saint could edge in close to her ear and whisper, *"This fucking ends. You are going to tell me everything."* He eased back. Smiled tenderly down at her. "Don't worry, my Alice. You're safe now." He slammed the door.

Saint walked a few feet away so he could talk to his brother.

Memphis...

She remembered, all too well, what Saint had told her about Memphis.

You don't want Memphis to come for you. If he does, you might as well be locked up already.

Alice felt something run down her cheek. She reached up to brush away what had to be a loose cat hair or a piece of dust or...

The tear touched her finger.

Saint opened the door. Slid inside the car. "Memphis is going to meet us at your place so we can all talk." He frowned. "You're bringing the cat?"

"I came for him." Wasn't that what she'd told the cops?

"Rescuing cats from burning buildings?" His hand turned the key, and the engine flared to life. "You warned me that might be next."

Not understanding, her head turned toward him. The glow from the instrument panel sent a flare of illumination through the front of the car. "What in the world are you talking about?"

"When you saved me." His hand lifted. "You said the next thing I knew, you'd be saving a cat from a burning building. Didn't realize you meant this guy. Got to tell you, he looks scary as hell."

"I like scary."

"I know." His fingers brushed over her cheek. He tensed. "Alice, what the fuck is happening?"

"I think the police are going to arrest my best friend for multiple murders."

"No. I mean, why are you crying?"

She looked away. *Because I can't let them do that.* Because Logan wasn't the killer. And because, in the end, she wasn't going to be as wicked as she wanted to be. "I want to go home."

Unfortunately, though, she'd never really had a home.

Saint drove them away.

CHAPTER FOURTEEN

"Saint...Brother...Friend..." Memphis sent him a shark's smile. "What the actual fuck are you thinking?"

Saint glared at his older brother. "She can hear us, you know."

"Why? Whatever do you mean? Surely you're not suggesting that your new *psychotic* girlfriend is possibly eavesdropping on our conversation?"

Oh, he was sure she was. Alice had said something about getting her cat settled—*a cat, seriously?*—and she'd disappeared into the kitchen. Saint had dragged his brother into the den. "She's not psychotic."

"How certain are you of that fact? Because the woman held a gun on me—"

"And you missed the part..." By moments. "When I held a gun dead-center on Logan's forehead."

Memphis's eyes widened. "Christ."

"I don't think *he* missed it."

Memphis surged toward him. "This isn't funny."

Saint looked over his shoulder, didn't see Alice, and he jerked a hand through his already disheveled hair as he peered back at his brother. "I'm not laughing. *You* shouldn't be here."

"Why? Because without me, you're free to crash and burn?"

"No, because she doesn't like you."

Memphis widened his eyes. "I'm supposed to care because...?"

"Because she's going to close down when you're nearby. I've been working hard to get her trust, making real progress, then you had to show up." Hell. "Tell me you came alone."

Memphis rolled one shoulder in a shrug.

Dammit. "Who else is here? Did you call in more Ice Breakers? Or is it Eliza? Did you drag her with you?"

"I didn't drag Eliza with me. I snuck away when she wasn't looking."

That sounded right.

"Didn't know what I was walking into," Memphis added grimly. "The last I heard, my brother had been *shot at* so I got my ass here as fast as I could, and yes, I called in reinforcements. Clearly, your impartiality has been blown to hell and back, so you need some fresh eyes on Alice."

"I don't need other eyes on her. I've got Alice."

Another step toward him. "Do you?" Memphis clearly doubted that fact. "Or does she have you? From where I stand, it looks like she's got you jumping to her defense. *Lying* to cops for her. No, man, don't even try to deny it," he said when Saint opened his mouth. "I was there, remember? You backed up her story when you could have thrown her to the wolves. *I* could have done the same thing. She had the gun on me, remember?"

"I didn't know who you were." Alice's cool voice. Coming from a few feet away. Saint had known she was there. Not because she'd made a sound. She hadn't. Alice had moved silently, and a glance down showed him why—no shoes. But he'd known she was there because he'd caught the faintest hint of her scent.

Both men focused fully on her.

"For all I knew," Alice sent Memphis a sweet smile, "you were the killer, returning to the scene of the crime."

"Oh, yeah," Memphis drawled. "I hear they do that sometimes." He snapped his fingers. "Quick question for you, why were you at Abracadabra tonight? Want to tell me again about how you love rescuing strays? Totally missed that part when I read your bio."

Alice met Saint's stare. "He is not growing on me." Gracefully, she made her way into the den. Settled onto the couch. Swung one bare foot lazily. "I thought perhaps he would—you grew on me, after all, Saint. But, no. I still feel an intense dislike for your brother."

Saint walked toward her. He towered over her. "Baby, that's just because you're still pissed that he locked me up in the first place. Why do you keep ignoring the fact that he got me out, too?"

"What?" Memphis's surprise was clear. "That's why she doesn't like me?"

"I'm sure there are any number of reasons not to like you," Alice allowed with a careless wave of one hand. "But, yes, that is currently at the top of my list." She didn't take her eyes off Saint. "I know he got you out, but if he'd trusted you, if he hadn't turned you over to the cops in the first place, you'd still be Sebastian. Not Saint."

Silence. He actually...felt those words go through him.

Her gaze bore into him. "You wouldn't have needed to fight so hard. Wouldn't have needed to face the darkness inside over and over until it became such a strong part of you. You would have still had the chance to be a different man. He took that all away." Now her gaze flickered to Memphis. "So, yes, I do have a bit of a grudge against you. Consider yourself warned."

Memphis cleared his throat. "I was warned the minute you pointed the gun at me."

A dip of her head. "Again, I didn't realize who you were then. I thought you were the killer, returning to the crime scene. I feared you'd hurt Saint, and I couldn't let that happen."

"Why not?" Curiosity filled Memphis's voice.

"Because I collect strays?" A question. Then a shake of her head. "No. No. That's not it." Once more, she returned her stare to Saint. "I told him why before. Saint knows."

Because she thinks I'm someone worth saving.

He stared hard at her. Easily saw the beauty that was on the outside. The delicate chin, the sharp cheekbones. Lush lips. Beautiful eyes. All on the *outside*. Surface didn't matter, he knew that. The surface could lie and twist and deceive.

What was Alice like beneath the surface?

She pulled in a breath as he watched her. Squared her shoulders with a gentle determination. Nodded. "The cat is settled with some milk and blankets. He will be fine for a while, but, ah, when I don't come back, can someone make sure he's taken care of?"

Was she asking him to watch her *cat?* And...wait... "Why won't you be coming back?"

A faint tightening of her lush lips. "Because I'll be in jail."

The world seemed to shift hard beneath Saint's feet.

"Would one of you mind taking me to the station? Actually, Saint, this is probably your dream come true, so how about you do the honors?"

He slapped his hands down on the cushions behind her and leaned in close. *Not a fucking dream.* "What in the hell are you doing?"

"Confessing." A wan smile. "Do you think it will be good for my soul? I hope so, or else all those stories are straight lies."

"Alice..."

"The detectives think Logan killed them all. I don't have many friends in this world. He has stood by me when no one else did."

"He might be fucking *stalking* you—"

"No." She was adamant. "You're wrong. It's not him."

"The spray paint can was in his ride! He threw that brick through your window."

"Yes." A nod. "But I knew that. I'd already talked to him about that. He thought you were a threat to me. He's protective, and he wanted—"

"To eliminate threats?" Memphis cut in to say. "The way Tracy Eldridge was eliminated?"

She didn't look his way. "Logan would never kill anyone. He doesn't have that instinct."

She was wrong. No, she was blind. Because she thought the guy was her *friend?* "Alice..."

"I have to confess." Lower. Softer.

He leaned even closer to her.

"I have to confess because I can't just toss away someone I care about." Her gaze cut toward Memphis. "I can't let someone else suffer..." She bit her lip. Returned her stare to Saint. "For something that I—"

"*Memphis!*" Saint snarled as he straightened. "Get the hell out!"

Alice's eyes widened. "What? Saint—"

He spun toward his brother. Pointed for the door. "Get the hell out. I need to talk to Alice alone."

Memphis didn't move. He did look at Saint as if he'd lost his mind. "We both know what she's about to say."

"You don't know jack about Alice. Leave." Saint marched toward his brother even as his body vibrated with barely contained fury.

Still, Memphis maintained his position. "She wants a ride to jail. You need to give her that ride."

No, no, no. Once, yes, once that had been the plan. If she'd been guilty, he'd planned to lock her away...

If.

And Alice, dammit, she was trying to confess. He knew that was what she was doing. Confessing to him and Memphis. Going to the cops to confess. All to protect Logan.

Fuck that. "She's not going anywhere."

Memphis's jaw hardened. "Saint, you're not thinking clearly."

He was crystal clear. "She's not going anywhere."

"Uh, Saint?" From Alice. "Perhaps you should listen to you brother on this one. I do believe your thinking might be impaired. Maybe you didn't get enough sleep."

"Alice, don't fucking push me right now." His hands fisted and released. Fisted and released.

Memphis shook his head. "This is what happens when you get personally involved with a mark."

"She's not a damn mark." His teeth snapped together. "She's *my* Alice."

Memphis's brow furrowed. "Saint?"

"Get out, Memphis." The last time he'd give the order. "I need to talk to her, alone."

Memphis glanced over Saint's shoulder. *He's looking at Alice.* "You know what she's going to say."

"I can throw your ass out," Saint offered.

Memphis blinked. His attention jerked back to Saint.

"I don't want to do that." His control was cracking. "I need to talk to Alice."

Once more, Memphis studied him. An intent look. What could have been sympathy flashed in Memphis's eyes. His hand rose. Clamped around Saint's shoulder. "I didn't want to turn you in, either," he muttered. "One of the hardest fucking things

I've ever done. When you care about someone..." An exhale. "It tore me apart. I couldn't even sleep, not until I cleared you."

When you care about someone...

Care? Is that what Memphis thought was happening? That Saint *cared* about Alice? "You're wrong," he said bluntly.

A swift inhale from behind him. From Alice.

Memphis just sent him a twisted, half-smile. "I'm dead right. But there's a big difference between our situations."

Yes, there was.

"*You* were innocent."

"No." A shake of Saint's head. "I just hadn't killed those people."

Memphis opened his mouth, then stopped. His gaze sharpened, and he...gave in. "I need to go make some phone calls. I think I'll go step out back for a few minutes. Can't exactly go out front. You got a ton of reporters there."

Yes, the reporters had come flocking back.

Memphis scraped his hand along his stubble-covered jaw. "Ten minutes. I'm sure that's how long my calls will take." He backed up a step. "And in ten minutes, you better be sane again, Saint." With those words, he turned on his heel and headed toward the rear of the house.

Saint stood there, watching him leave, and he didn't move, not until he heard the faint click of the back door closing.

"Saint..." Alice sighed his name. "What are you doing?"

What he had to do. He swung toward her. "You don't get to—"

"I killed him."

Saint froze. His legs seemed to lock in place.

Her smile broke his heart. "But you already knew that, didn't you? You knew I was a killer from the moment you met me." She bit her lower lip. As she huddled on the couch, Alice seemed smaller. More fragile than ever before.

The surface is a lie.

"Tracy was right about me. I killed her brother. I killed Donovan Eldridge, then I lied about it for years. The grief ripped her up. Tore her apart. And in the end, she died, too." Alice wrapped her arms around her stomach. "I did that. I *did* that.

Not Logan. I'm not going to let him be punished for my sins. I'm going to the cops. I'll tell them what happened."

He closed in on her. Each step felt heavy. Cold. He seemed to be freezing. A cold that burned hotter than any rage. When he was close to her once more, his hand lifted and curled around her chin. His fingers stroked her so carefully. "My Alice..."

Her lashes lifted. She turned into his touch.

He curled his body toward her. "What in the hell..." Saint whispered. "Makes you think I would ever let you do that?"

"I—"

His mouth took hers. With fury. With need. With absolute desperation.

***

Memphis huffed out a breath, then put the phone to his ear. The sun had just started to rise, shooting gold and red streaks across the sky. He had a bad feeling in his gut. A feeling that told him this day would be just as shitty as the night.

"Hello?" A woman's sleepy voice.

"Tony, we have a code freaking thirteen." As in...bad. Something very, very bad.

"Memphis?" Instant alertness. "Has something happened to Saint?"

Sure, you could say something had. His brother had lost his mind. That was what had happened. "You searched Providence Canyon State Park, right?"

"You know I've looked into Donovan Eldridge's disappearance before."

"And you're *sure* there was no body out there?"

"It's over a thousand acres," she reminded him. "Banshee and I did our best, but the terrain isn't exactly what I'd call the easiest to navigate. We looked, yes, but am I sure no body had been dumped out there? Of course, not. I'm not perfect, you know."

But when it came to finding the dead, she was damn close. "You made it to town?"

"Yes. I checked in my hotel, and I had *just* gone to sleep. Then you called with this crazy code-thirteen talk. How about you be a whole lot more specific and tell me what's happening?"

He'd contacted Tony, Dr. Antonia Rossi, on his way to Savannah. He'd wanted another Ice Breaker on the case, and Tony tended to get along fairly well with Saint. Not everyone did because, yeah, his brother could be an asshole.

So can I. A family trait.

"Memphis?" she prompted. "Look, I'm here. I found a dog-friendly hotel for Banshee. We are ready to go, but you know I can't stand working in the dark."

"I think the Black Widow is about to confess." *Think?* More like, he knew. She would have spilled all right in front of him if Saint hadn't stopped her.

What had his brother been thinking? *That's the problem. He isn't thinking. Not with his head. His dick? Yeah, definitely.*

"You are not serious," Tony breathed.

"Dead serious." He glanced back toward the house. "Don't know if you heard yet, but Tracy Eldridge was murdered."

"Oh, I heard all right. Caught the news story with Tyler McQuinn."

He was pretty certain that reporter was currently camped out with his crew on the road in front of Alice's house. "Shane Madison disappeared from Savannah."

"So did Corey Abbott."

"Their bodies could be close." Donovan's remains were a different matter. But vics two and three... "If she talks to the cops, I want you and Banshee on the scene. If Alice gives up general locations, then you'll find the bodies before anyone else can."

"That can only happen if the cops want to cooperate with us."

About that... "I already spoke to one of the lead detectives. I told Jamal Preacher you were coming, and he said he'd like your help." Tony had a reputation among law enforcement.

She can find the dead.

"You said *if* she talks to the cops."

Yes. "Alice Shephard just asked for a ride to the police station."

Stunned silence. Then... "Why aren't you driving her right now?"

Because Saint has lost his mind.

CHAPTER FIFTEEN

Alice locked her hands around Saint's shoulders. All she wanted to do was hold tight and never let go. This was the man she wanted. This was the man she—

Alice pushed him back. "No." Ragged. *Get it together, woman.* But nothing was together any longer. Everything was falling apart. Hadn't she always feared it would? "When a woman tells you that she killed a man, you don't kiss her."

His dark eyes narrowed.

"You take her to jail." Softer, but less ragged. She wet her lips and wanted his mouth again. But she couldn't have it, just like she couldn't have him. "Like I said, dream come true, am I right?"

"You killed a man."

"Yes." She'd done it. Confessed for the first time in her life. Was it supposed to make her feel better? It didn't. There was no magical lifting of a burden from her shoulders. She didn't suddenly feel all guilt free. Alice just felt tired.

Saint smiled at her.

That is not the right reaction. But, then, perhaps he was happy because now he could finish his case. Cross her name off his list and move on to another big Ice Breaker challenge.

"You're not a serial killer."

"Excuse me?"

He laughed. "You told me from the beginning, didn't you?"

Her fingers pressed into his shoulders. "I don't think you're responding just right."

"Baby, what's been right about us?"

Everything. Her mouth opened, but closed before she could mess up and say something she shouldn't. Instead of replying, Alice shrugged.

"You told me on day one, didn't you?"

"I told you a lot of things. Unlike you, however, I don't have perfect recall of every conversation."

"Don't remember every conversation. Just remember *you*."

Good to know she'd left such a strong impression on him. Alice jumped from the couch and tried to put some distance between them.

"The first night, I said you were a serial killer. You told me you weren't."

I'm not. She squared off to face him.

"It's because a serial kills multiple people." He smiled again and closed the distance she'd just put between them.

"You should stop doing that. It's weird when you smile and you talk about killing."

He leaned in close again, as if to kiss her.

But he didn't kiss her. Saint murmured, "You only killed Donovan, didn't you, sweetheart?"

Her lower lip trembled. She nodded. "Yes." A breath. "I killed Donovan." Still, no relief. No magical sense that she was doing the right thing by confessing. Instead, now, in addition to her tiredness, Alice felt sad.

She wouldn't be seeing Saint again.

"And the others?" Saint waited.

Her head cocked. "Isn't one murder enough for you?"

"In your case, no."

"Saint..."

"Alice."

Her arms curled around her stomach. "What do you want from me?"

"I'm starting to realize that I want everything. Pretty sure that's what I'll be taking."

What was that even supposed to mean? "Look, you came rushing into town, being the big, bad hunter that you are. You wanted to find proof that I was guilty of murder. Well, you have it. I just confessed." She paced away from him. Stopped. Turned back and held her arms out to him, with her wrists up. "I'm sure you or your brother have cuffs around some place. Turn me in. Lock me up. Go celebrate for days."

His nostrils flared. "You know that shit is not happening."

"You're not going to celebrate." She could buy that. Alice nodded. "Fine. Murder is a bad thing to celebrate, but at least you—"

"You're not fucking going to jail."

She was. "I *killed*—"

He caught her wrists. Curled his fingers around them. "Tell me everything. Every single moment that led up to Donovan's death."

She didn't like reliving every single moment. In fact, she tried not to think about that day at all, and because she tried to block the memories, they slipped into her dreams. "We were out hiking. It was hot. We were both sweating. And I stopped to take a drink of water."

She *hated* this memory.

"And?" His thumbs brushed along her wrists.

"And Donovan snatched the water bottle out of my hands. He told me that I could drink when he said I could drink." She didn't like the hollow sound of her voice. Didn't like anything about this memory. "So I killed him. There. Done."

Saint shook his head.

Her breath shuddered out. *Fine.* "I tried to get the drink back from him. I was really, really thirsty." In that instant, her throat felt parched. "He...he threw it into the ravine. Told me that I'd have to suffer. He laughed." She could still hear his laughter. "That's how he was, you see. Controlling. More and more every day until I almost couldn't even speak any longer. But *that* day, when he threw down my drink and it was so hot, I just...*Enough*," Alice snapped. The same word she'd yelled at Donovan.

Saint kept stroking her wrists.

"I turned away. I walked away. Told him we were done. I wasn't living that way any longer. I couldn't be with *him* any longer. But he grabbed me."

"He wasn't letting you go."

She looked at him but saw Donovan. "He had these really bright blue eyes. They'd crinkle at the edges when he smiled, and he would look so harmless. So friendly. So *charming*." Such a lie. She'd learned to lie from Donovan. "But he wasn't smiling. He was screaming. He hit me. I fell, and I slammed my head on a rock." She still carried the scar from that fall, hidden beneath her hair. "He kicked me while I was down." Her ribs had been battered. One broken. She'd told the cops she'd gotten that broken rib from her fall.

Saint glanced at a point over her shoulder. Shook his head slightly. Looked back at her.

Alice continued, voice flat, "I don't know how many times he kicked me, but I was really close to the edge, and I was afraid I'd go over. So I-I grabbed him. Wrapped my hands around his ankle. He didn't expect that. It, uh, knocked him off balance, and *he* fell. He sort of shot forward, and the next thing I knew, Donovan had gone over the edge and into the ravine." She tugged on Saint's hold.

He let her go.

"It was supposed to be such a pretty view. That was why we'd gone up there. A pretty view. And...he was gone. I stood up, and I inched closer. I needed to see over the edge. I needed to see him. I..." Alice stopped.

"He was dead," Saint said.

"No." She wanted to close her eyes for this part, but that would be cowardly. She should look right at Saint when she told him exactly what she'd done. "Donovan had managed to catch himself. When I got to the edge, his hand flew up and curled around my ankle."

Surprise flashed on Saint's face.

"He jerked hard, and I knew I was going to fall. I *did* fall. I landed on my ass, and he started dragging me forward. Screaming at me. Telling me I'd be sorry. And I—I kicked him. I kicked him with my free foot, trying to make him let go." She swallowed. "It was so hot that day, did I tell you that? Who goes hiking out there in the middle of July? But Donovan wanted to go. And what Donovan wanted, he had a way of getting. "

"He didn't let you go."

"Oh, yes, he did. He had to let go because I kicked so hard. He let go and he fell, and the last thing he did was scream my name." A scream she could still hear.

Saint remained standing in front of her. Waiting.

What did he want? *More?* "I didn't climb down to help him. Didn't even try to get down there. I could see him. His leg was at an odd angle. And his head..." *No, not now. Don't go there now.* "I sat on the edge of that ravine. I don't even know how long. It got dark, and then it got sunny again, and I realized that I needed to move. So I walked and walked and I didn't go to check on Donovan." She could feel a headache behind her right eye. "Why check on the dead?"

Saint's lashes flickered. "Alice..."

"It rained after the sun rose. Did I tell you that? I was walking in the rain, and I drank some of it because I was so thirsty. And, um...I kept walking. I didn't have the keys to the truck. Donovan had them. So I walked and walked and eventually..." A shrug. "I met a ranger on a trail. I said Donovan had wandered off during the night. Everyone started hunting for him. No one found him." Her hands fell back to her sides. "I told the authorities we were in Providence Canyon State Park, but I gave them the wrong area in that park. I thought, eventually, Donovan might be found, but I knew the animals would get to him first. They'd help destroy evidence. And maybe everyone would believe that he'd just slipped and fallen in the dark. Such a tragic accident."

"It wasn't an accident." Saint's expression seemed so savage.

"No, I killed him."

"Baby..." Torn from him. His eyes blazed. "You defended yourself. He was *hurting you*. The bastard would have killed you! You had to save yourself. You—"

"My God." She blinked, stunned. "You...fell for me."

"Alice..."

"I warned you about that." Alice stepped closer to him. She rose up and pressed a soft kiss to his cheek. "I told you that would happen."

His hands settled around her waist. Warm. Strong. She'd never feared that he would physically hurt her. Not Saint. But...

She had been worried he'd break her heart. Turned out, surprise, surprise, she had one.

Maybe he did, too.

Alice kissed his cheek once more. "If you can't do it..." She stepped back, as much as his hold would allow, and glanced over her shoulder at Memphis. He stood near the wall. While he was certainly silent on his feet, she'd noticed when Saint had sent a fast glance in that direction.

She'd been aware of their audience. But she'd kept making her confession.

"If Saint can't do the dirty deed," she said to Memphis, "I'm sure you can." She forced a smile. "Ready to lock me up and throw away the key?"

***

"Over my dead body." Saint stood in front of his brother and tried to fight the rage that twisted and churned within him. "You're not taking her in, you understand me? It will be—"

"Yeah, yeah, I got it." Memphis glanced down the hallway. Alice had just disappeared that way moments before. "Over your dead body. I heard you the first time."

Alice had left, saying she was going to change and get ready for her big trip to jail. Saint would have liked to have thought she was just being dramatic. Being *Alice*. But this time...

The woman truly believed she was getting locked up. "Not happening."

A furrow lodged between Memphis's brows. "Did you ever see a pic of Alice when she came out of that park?"

"What?"

"I read about her injuries. Got a copy of the report from the ranger's office."

Saint had, too.

"But there was no picture included. There have never been any pictures of a bruised and bloody Alice anywhere."

"She's *not* lying," Saint snapped.

"Like Alice Shephard never lies."

Saint's hands flew out and grabbed Memphis's shirtfront. "She's not lying about this."

Memphis glanced down. "You're wrinkling my already wrinkled t-shirt." He looked back up. "I'd advise you to take a few deep breaths."

Deep breaths weren't going to do jackshit for him. Because he'd had a bad feeling...all along... "I knew he hurt her." He jerked his hands back from Memphis. "The pieces started filling in almost immediately. Little tells. Donovan was controlling. Too possessive. She was afraid to belong to me because—" Saint stopped. Sucked in a stupid deep breath. Right. It did *nothing.* "Self-defense. That's all it was. Open and shut."

"Maybe, but she covered it up. Lied to authorities. Probably even destroyed evidence. And you're conveniently forgetting the other missing lovers."

"She didn't kill them."

"I'm not so sure—"

"Alice didn't kill them!"

"Bro, you need to calm the hell down. I get that things are stressful for you, but—"

"Stressful?" Saint's laugh was bitter. "Nothing is stressful for me. The woman I—" *Don't. Stop.* "The woman I want—*my Alice*—is trying to be a martyr. That's a terrible look for her."

Alice appeared in the doorway. She'd dressed in black. Pants. Shirt. Heels.

"Terrible," he repeated as he glared at her. "You don't carry the martyr look well at all. So how about you go back to being my favorite villain instead?" He stalked toward her. "Your confession isn't going to clear Logan. The bastard probably killed Tracy, you get that, don't you? And are you so conveniently forgetting Corey and Shane? The two men who—"

"I haven't forgotten them, and I'm trying to make sure *you* don't wind up like them."

What the ever-loving-fucking-fuck was she talking—

Her gaze jumped to Memphis. "Are you taking me? Or am I going to have to steal your car and do this bit myself?" She huffed out a breath and tapped her right foot. "The paint should have been removed from my convertible by now. If I had it back, I could drive myself. But, no, the convertible's not here, the cops have my backup car, and either one of you glaring gentleman escort me or I will have to—"

Saint stepped in her path. Towered over her. Smiled down at her.

"I don't like your smile." Her eyes narrowed in suspicion. "It worries me."

"No? You once told me you thought it was quite dangerous."

Alice cleared her throat. "I stand by that assessment."

"*I'm* quite dangerous." Something she should have realized by this point. "So you don't need to worry that I can't handle myself. You don't need to worry that some bastard in the dark is going to come and take me out the way he did Corey and Shane. You don't have to turn yourself in because you think if you're locked away—if you're locked away from *me*—that he won't focus his attention on me any longer. That he won't come for me. That I'll be safe." Saint smiled at her.

"Stop doing that," she whispered.

"Stop understanding you? Never." Not when he'd worked so freaking hard to do it in the first place. "Because I do understand now. You're not turning yourself in for Logan. Hell, I think part of you *is* scared he might have killed Tracy. That why you went to your office? To see if he'd screwed up and left evidence behind?"

She pushed a lock of hair over her shoulder and didn't answer.

I know you, sweetheart. "You're not making the big sacrifice of your freedom for him."

Her chin lifted. "Then why would I do it?"

His fingers rose to drift over her cheek. "Because, sweetheart, you made a fatal mistake."

"Confessing all to you?"

"Nah." He brushed his mouth against her lips. "Falling in love with me."

CHAPTER SIXTEEN

"For the last time, I didn't kill Tracy!" Logan glared at the detectives. "I shouldn't even be in here—"

"You were found with a can of red spray paint in the back of your SUV," the female detective pointed out. Heidi something. He couldn't remember her last name. Pretty woman, but her voice grated because she kept yelling at him. "Did you spray paint the word 'Die' on a brick and throw it into Alice Shephard's front window?"

Shit but it was hot in there. He swiped at the coffee cup in front of him. Drained it. That was his third? Maybe fourth. Logan didn't know for sure. "Look, Tracy is the one who had the spray paint. She tagged Alice's car. We showed you the video of that—Tracy probably threw the brick, too." His jaw ached like a mother. Saint was such a bastard.

But he had a killer hook.

"Why were you inside Abracadabra tonight?" The guy was asking the question now. Preacher. Jamal Preacher. Easy to remember that last name.

"Uh, because I work there? Because I wanted to check on my business and make sure the cops didn't trash the place too much?" He could not stay in this tiny room much longer. No way, no day. "It's hot in here. Can't you turn up the air?"

"We'll get right on that," Heidi murmured. He noticed she didn't rise, so it had to be hard for her to *get right on that*. "What is the nature of your relationship with Alice?"

"She's my boss. I'm her friend. And why are you asking all these questions? Look, Saint and I had a little fight. No big deal. I won't press charges if he won't." Logan smiled. He also fiddled with the empty coffee cup. He was starting to get the jitters.

"This isn't about Saint pressing charges." Jamal leaned forward. "Have you ever had a romantic relationship with Alice?"

"Alice? Nah. She's like a kid sister. Known her forever."

Jamal and Heidi exchanged another look. They kept doing that. So annoying. "I'm not hot for Alice, okay? She's not my type." He liked women who laughed a lot. Were carefree and casual. *So* not Alice.

Heidi raked him with her stare. "Then why were you and Saint fighting? If, as you say, there's nothing between you and Alice..."

He could hardly say...*Saint attacked because he found my ass hiding in Abracadabra.* "This isn't what you think..."

"We *think* you murdered Tracy Eldridge because you didn't like the way she was harassing Alice." Heidi's words came out in that grating, shrill tone again. "We *think* you're obsessed with Alice. Have been for a long time. Ever since you worked in her father's show. You've been watching her for years. You want her for yourself."

"No. A big *no*. I'm not interested in her that way. I *told* you that already. Aren't you listening to me?"

"When she gets close to men, you eliminate them."

Logan tapped the bottom of the cup on the table. "I think I need to use the restroom."

"Did you kill Corey Abbott?" Jamal questioned, voice soft but eyes hard.

"No. Absolutely not." He was sweating bullets.

"Did you kill Shane Madison?" Heidi fired.

"No! Listen, I liked Shane. I wouldn't have hurt him!"

Jamal waited a beat. "Did you help Alice hide their bodies?"

He blanched. "What? Wait...hold on. *Hold on.*"

But Jamal smiled and his nostrils flared, like he'd just caught some kind of scent. "You and Alice both like magic, don't you? Bet you're pretty good at making things—people—disappear."

Oh, God. Logan crushed the coffee cup in his hand.

Jamal noted the movement. Nodded. "Now I'm gonna ask you again, did you help Alice hide their bodies?"

"I—"

The door swung open.

"Not another word," Raven Scott said as she appeared in the doorway. "My client is not talking to you any longer. You need to book him or let him go. *Now.*"

Logan fell back against his chair.

"Your client?" Heidi rose. "Since when?"

"Since his employer texted me about twenty minutes ago and paid his fees."

Alice. She didn't leave me hanging out to dry.

"Now, stop dicking around," Raven announced. "I haven't had coffee, and it is way too early for bullshit."

***

"Bullshit," Alice whispered.

Saint just smiled that sexy, dangerous smile of his. She gripped the phone in her hand. She'd gotten a text a few moments ago—Raven had been arriving at the police station. In her message, Raven had assured Alice that she'd be taking care of Logan *and* that she'd stick around for Alice to arrive.

Because I am definitely going to need my lawyer when I go in. Sure, she technically *had* killed Donovan in self-defense, provided anyone actually believed that story, but there were a few other pesky details that had to be sorted out. Like...

Lying to the cops. Hiding evidence. And that time she went out to make sure the body was well and truly covered up.

Pesky, bothersome details.

Saint was still doing some featherlight-touch thing on her cheek and her stomach kept twisting harder and his *brother* was watching this entire scene with a frown on his handsome face. Memphis *did* somewhat resemble Saint. In her mind, Memphis was a less attractive version of Saint, but she supposed some would find him fairly handsome.

He didn't have a hard enough edge for her.

Saint did.

Saint...*thinks I love him.*

Alice exhaled and tucked her phone into the back pocket of her pants. Then she patted his cheek. "We have fantastic sex together. That's not love."

"Nope," he assured her, not even missing a beat. "But this is."

"*This?*"

"This. You trying to act like you don't care because you want me to walk away. You turning yourself in to the cops because you're worried someone is going to hurt me. Cute."

Her eyes narrowed.

"Really sweet," he added.

Her eyes narrowed more. She'd been freaking *crying* in the other room, but she'd fixed her makeup and come back with her game face on and now this jerk was mocking her? This jerk who—

"You love me so much. Thanks, Alice. Don't think I've ever been loved like this before."

Damn right, you haven't. And you never will be again. "You are obviously of no use to me." Cold, cruel words.

Saint laughed.

Her gaze leapt to Memphis. "You hate me. I'm tempting your brother and leading him down a path of darkness and despair."

Memphis rubbed his chin. "You are a dramatic one, aren't you?"

You have no idea. "Take me to the police station."

But Memphis didn't move. Saint was just standing there, too—being all delusional and saying she *loved* him, and this just could not continue. "Fine. I'll handle this myself." Not like it would be the first time she'd had to take care of things herself. Alice spun and rushed for the door.

"Alice..." Saint called after her.

She'd poured out her soul for the man. Revealed her deep, dark past, and he should have been gloating because he'd gotten what he wanted. Proof of her guilt.

She grabbed for the door handle.

"Alice, *don't!*" Saint's sharp warning.

Screw him. She did what she wanted. She hurried onto her porch. The reporters at the edge of her yard all immediately seemed to surge closer. Questions were thrown at her. She darted down the steps, and her feet practically flew over the sidewalk. Who would be her lucky driver? "Tyler!" Alice shouted when she saw him. He was always hungry for a story. "Give me a ride to the police station, and I'll give you an exclusive that you won't ever for—*ooh!*"

She'd been grabbed from behind. Grabbed and *lifted* and was now being carried over Saint's wide shoulder.

Oh, the hell, no. "*Saint,*" she thundered. "Put me down, *now.*"

His hold just tightened. "I'll put you down when I have you where I want you."

The reporters were getting this. They were filming. And no one was doing a single thing to stop the insane man who was carrying her back into her house.

"I don't want to hurt you," Alice warned. But she was pretty sure she could deliver an unforgettable kick to his groin from this angle. He'd be on the ground. She'd be free. She could—

"Then don't leave me, sweetheart. Because I'm pretty sure that would wreck me." He was already on the steps again.

Alice slapped her hands against Saint's broad back and heaved herself upward. The vantage point gave her a perfect view of all the reporters. She glared at them. Such assholes. Did they regularly just watch while a woman was carried away?

Saint took her inside her house, past the open door, and past a gaping Memphis.

"Way to be a helper there, Nashville," she said, deliberately changing his name just for spite. Just for—whatever.

He laughed. "It's Memphis."

She was done with him. Alice heaved her body. "Saint! Put me down or I will be kicking you so hard in your dick that—"

"Baby, why would you want to injure something you adore?"

He was such a bastard. *He's also right.* She did adore his dick. Sue her.

"Yeah, I'm gonna head out for a bit," Memphis announced, and it sounded as if he choked down a laugh. "Think you two need to clear some things up. I'll, uh, go meet with Tony. She's in town because she wanted to dig up some bodies with us. I'll let her know that might be happening very, very soon. Don't worry, I'll lock up on my way out." The door closed.

She fisted the back of Saint's shirt. "I am not amused."

His hand rose. Pressed to her ass. "Neither the fuck am I." He began stalking down the hallway.

"Saint?" A little worried. Vaguely worried.

He carried her into her room. Strode forward and dropped her on the bed.

The phone jabbed her in the ass, so Alice yanked it from her pocket and tossed it aside. "Listen—"

He pounced. No other way to describe it. One minute, he stood near the bed. The next, he was over her, with his powerful body caging hers. "You're not getting locked into a cell."

"I told you." Her voice sounded way too breathless. "I said you wouldn't be that heartless when the time came." She did enjoy being right.

"Fuck heartless. You don't belong in a cell. You belong with me."

Alice blinked quickly because she was not about to cry. Not again. It had been bad enough the first time. "Saint, I am not a good person."

"What happened to Corey Abbott?"

"What?"

He caught her right hand. Held up her fingers and the gleaming ring. "What happened to him?"

Her breath came faster.

"I don't like the ring on you, Alice."

"I don't, either." But she didn't know what to do with it.

Saint pulled it off. Glared at it. Then frowned. "There's an inscription inside."

No, there wasn't. "That's wrong." There had never been an inscription in the ring.

Saint had already hopped off the bed. Moved toward her nightstand and was holding the ring beneath the light. He squinted as he stared at the inside portion of the band. "Alice." Rough. "What happened to Corey?"

"*I don't know!*" Okay. She needed to lower that edge of panic. "Look, Corey...he wasn't perfect, all right?"

"I know all about the fucking wannabe-mob-boss boyfriend, Alice. I know he had a record. I know he'd been busted half a dozen times, but he kept seeming to get out of jail as if by magic. I know he met you when you were waiting tables at one of his clubs, and within weeks, you were *running* that club."

"That's how I learned to make Abracadabra a success." Slowly, she sat up on the bed. "Corey taught me. He...he wasn't nearly as bad as he wanted the world to think."

"What happened to him?"

Her breath chilled her lungs as she gave him the truth. "I don't know."

His hand closed around the ring. Made a fist. "Thought you weren't going to lie to me anymore."

"Whatever gave you that impression?" An instant response. More instinct than anything. A defense. A distraction.

"Alice, I can't help you if you don't tell me the truth."

She practically ran to him as something seemed to snap inside of her. A taunt line, breaking apart. A trapeze that would send the performer hurtling to the ground. *I'm falling, and I can't stop.* "I broke up with him because I couldn't love him! Corey wanted me to love him, he'd done nothing but be *good* to me even though the world kept screaming he was a criminal." The words were too fast. Too hard. "The *good* boy had treated me like he was a monster. He'd hurt me. Nearly dragged me down with him, but everyone praised Donovan like he was the second coming. Even after he vanished."

Saint's grip tightened even more around the ring.

"I couldn't love Corey. I told him that I couldn't. It just wasn't there. Maybe I was too broken inside. Maybe I just never knew how to love. Maybe it was too soon after Donovan and I was still scared..." Too scared to let go completely. "But I left the ring. Even when he called after me, even when he screamed after me, I walked out the door. The last thing I heard was him telling me not to walk away. Corey yelled my name. I could hear the pain in his voice. I said I was sorry, and I shut the door." A shuddering breath. "The next day, I learned that when his housekeeper arrived, his place looked as if it had been hit by a tornado. Everything was smashed and destroyed. One hell of a fight scene. There was even blood spatter on the floor. And Corey was gone."

Saint's eyes narrowed. "You never saw him again."

"No one has seen him again." Her breath heaved in and out. "Give me the ring."

"Why?"

"Because there was no inscription. I put it on his table when I left him, and I haven't seen it since that night. The stalker left it for me. He's sending me a message."

Saint still didn't open his fist. "You said he always leaves you messages."

Her head moved in a jerky nod. The flood gates had opened, and there was no turning back. Saint wanted to hear every detail? Fine. She'd tell him. In the end, he might use what she told him to burn down her world.

Too late, it already feels like I'm surrounded by ashes.

"What has he left before?"

"I've gotten gifts from him since my dad died." Not really gifts, but what else could she call them? Creepy calling cards? Weary, she raked back her hair.

Saint stepped toward her. "You dad died of a heart attack."

"Sure. Yeah. That's what the cops said. No signs of foul play. Just a sudden heart attack. Those things happen." That was what she'd been told. The cops on scene had patted her shoulder. Mumbled to her that they were sorry. Asked if they should call someone.

There had been no one to call.

Alice hated the memories. "The day after I buried him, I found a broken wand under his pillow. I was cleaning out his room, and it was waiting for me."

"I don't understand, Alice. Walk me through this."

She *was*.

"What's the deal about a broken wand? Your dad was a magician. Probably had a ton of wands around his place."

Alice shook her head even as her stomach twisted. "The Broken Wand Ceremony," she whispered. "It started with Houdini. You break the wand, and it's supposed to be like—like losing magical power. It's a sign when a magician passes."

A heavy stillness settled over Saint. He watched her with the intense gaze of a predator. "Did you think someone killed your dad?"

"*Did* I? Do I? Maybe. Yes. No. I can't say." The question had ripped her apart. Wrecked her world. Then she'd met Donovan. *Hello, wreck, times two.* "I just know it was a message. I also know that after Corey's disappearance, I got another one."

"Corey." His lashes flickered. "*Not* Donovan. You didn't get anything after Donovan—"

"He didn't hurt Donovan. *I* did that."

A muscle flexed along Saint's jaw.

"After Corey vanished, I went to his club. I found an open pack of playing cards in the top drawer of his desk."

Saint didn't look particularly impressed. "So there were cards there, big deal. I'm sure the guy played poker all the time."

"Oh, he did." A faint smile. "He could beat you out of your life's savings in two hands. But those were trick cards. A marked deck. He'd never used cards like that in his games. Only a magician uses those."

Saint nodded. "So you found cards, and you thought they were a message to you." A very careful tone.

Her spine stiffened. "Don't mock me."

"I'm not. I'm trying to understand, but, baby, the cards could have just been there. Your father's wand could have broken, and he tossed it aside. This isn't proof that someone has been after you all this time." His voice deepened. "We need proof. We need real, actual proof that someone committed the crimes. Something that we can use to hunt the bastard."

"Fine." Frigid. "Does the fact that I saw him help?"

"What?" Sharp. Snarled.

"The fact that I saw him," Alice repeated doggedly, "does it help? Because I did, you see. I walked in when he was attacking Shane. I followed the trail of blood that had been left behind. *I saw him.* Dressed all in black. Wearing his mask. Standing in Shane's home. Holding a bloody knife. *I saw him.*" Her breath heaved in and out. "Is that good enough for you?"

CHAPTER SEVENTEEN

Her pain beat at him. Saint *hated* Alice's pain. "Fuck." He dropped the ring. Let it fall to the lush carpeting even as he grabbed for Alice. But her eyes widened. She looked down and sank to her knees.

"Alice?"

She grabbed the ring. Jumped right back up and shoved the ring under her lamp. "Conjure," she read. A shiver worked over her body. "*OhmyGod.*"

"Alice." He locked his hands around her shoulders. "Tell me what happened after you saw the man with the knife." Why hadn't she told the police about him? How had she gotten away from him? *What happened?* The questions blasted through Saint's mind, even as growing fear—for her—seemed to numb his blood.

"I went into the kitchen." She gazed at the ring, turning it slowly over in her fingers. "I followed the trail of blood. I had a bottle of champagne in my hands because Shane and I were going to celebrate. I'd signed the contract, got the building for Abracadabra. Everything was working out." She looked up, a little furrow between her eyes. "I was happy."

The numbing cold spread even more within him.

"We weren't lovers. That part was always wrong. I...maybe we would have been. But we were...friends. He didn't judge me. Shane just wanted to help. He helped me to get the building. Taught me everything I needed to know so I could work out the best deal on the property. He was—everyone said he was cutthroat. That he would do anything for a deal, even sell his own mother. So many stories circulated about him, but..." She glanced back at the ring. "Stories circulated about me, too. Not all were true."

"Alice." Deliberately, Saint sharpened his tone. He had to break through the pain he could feel surrounding her. "Tell me what happened when you followed the trail of blood."

Her eyes squeezed closed. "I went into the kitchen. I rounded the corner, and he was there."

"Shane?"

"No, the man in the mask. He had a knife. Blood smeared the end." Soft. Emotionless. "I had the champagne bottle in my hand, and I swung it at him as hard as I could. I swung it three times, and he fell back." A swallow. "I ran. I was going to get help, I-I was. But I didn't make it to the door."

Keep your voice steady. But fear and rage just churned sharply within him. "Why not?"

She bit her lower lip. "Do you believe me?"

"Yes." No hesitation.

Her eyes opened. "Why?"

"*Because I fucking love you. Now tell me why you didn't make it to the door.*"

Her lips parted. Surprise—shock—slid over her face. "Saint?"

He kissed her. Deep and hard and possessively. With passion and fierce intent. Alice was his. There was nothing he would not do to protect her. He would be eliminating this threat, no matter what it took. He would make the bastard pay for hurting her. "Tell me," he breathed against her lips.

"You don't really love me." A careful denial.

"My Alice." So tender. "Yes, I do. I love every single part of you."

Tears filled her gaze. Made the topaz shine even more. "Don't lie to me."

"Not to you, baby. We can lie to the rest of the world, but not to each other. Understand? Going forward, never that. Never to each other."

Her lower lip trembled.

"Tell me," he ordered. Harder now.

"He caught me before I could get out the front door. He grabbed me by the nape of my neck. Slammed me into a wall."

Fucking sonofabitch. I will rip you apart.

"I don't remember anything after that, not until I woke up. I was on Shane's couch, and I-I could smell bleach."

Shit. The killer had cleaned up. Saint knew it even before Alice said—

"The blood was gone, wiped off the marble tiles. Everything was perfectly in place. The champagne bottle was chilling in a bucket of ice next to me, and there was a bright, blood-red scarf next to the bottle. The kind of scarf that a magician uses all the time in his act. The color always catches the audience's attention and can be used as a great distraction."

Saint was sure the blood-red color had been a deliberate choice. "You didn't tell the cops about him."

"I had a giant bruise from where my forehead had hit the wall. It looked like I had been in a fight, and the man everyone thought I was intimately involved with me—he had just vanished. Victim number three." A bitter smile curled her lips. "Would you have believed me? Before you answer, let me tell you, I *looked* around that house. I searched for any clue I could find. There wasn't even a drop of blood there any longer. If I had told the detectives that someone attacked me—that the same person killed Shane—would you have thought I was telling the truth, or just trying to cover my own ass?"

"How did you know he killed Shane?"

Her lashes fluttered. "Because in my nightmares, I see Shane's body slumped behind the man in the mask. He's on the floor of the kitchen."

Sonofabitch. "Did that really happen or is it just a dream?"

"I don't know," Alice whispered. Her hand rose. She unfurled her fingers. Stared at the ring. "I'm not a completely heartless bitch, you know."

"Never said you were." *You have a heart, baby. It belongs to me.*

"I left Shane's house after I searched the place." Her lips curled down. "I lifted a phone from a stranger's purse on the way home, and I put in a call to nine-one-one. Told them that I'd heard shouting at Shane's address. That I worried there was a fight. I wanted to get the cops involved. I knew that if they went to his place and no one could find him, they'd start investigating." She kept looking at the ring. "By the time the cops made it to *my* house—because, of course, they'd show up to question me sooner or later—I'd given myself a quick new haircut and bangs. The bangs hid the bruise on my forehead. I told them everything I could..."

"But you never mentioned the man you'd seen. Or the fact that Shane might have been stabbed."

"*Might* have been?" Anger whipped in her words. "I thought you believed me. I thought you were going to take my side. I thought—"

His hand closed over hers and that fucking ring. "I do." A pause. "I am."

"What?"

"I do believe you, baby. I believe you were attacked at his place. I think you were probably scared as hell. And I am taking your side. From here on out, that's the only side I do take."

Her breath shuddered from her.

"Tell me why," Saint pushed. Even though he suspected...

"Why—what?"

"Why you got so scared when I told you that 'Conjure' was inscribed in the ring." He waited. Saw the flash of fear come and go in her eyes. Saint nodded. "Say it."

"Because they disappeared."

He didn't speak, not yet.

"Conjure," Alice said the word with anger beating in her voice. "It's when you make something suddenly appear. The freaking opposite of what happened when Corey and Shane vanished."

To him, the inscription was a message of intent. He knew Alice feared the same thing. "The stalker isn't gonna hide in the shadows any longer. He's ready to appear, and you know it."

"I don't want him to hurt you."

Aw. That was sweet. Really. He sank his left hand into the silken weight of her hair and pulled Alice forward. His mouth took hers once more. Harder. Deeper. With a desire that she couldn't miss.

She kissed him back with the same wild ferocity, but there was a desperation in her that he could feel. As if she was afraid that if she didn't hold on tightly enough, he'd vanish.

Never fucking happening.

His mouth lifted. "I'll put him in the ground before he hurts you."

Alice shook her head. "Saint..."

"You think I would even hesitate to kill if it meant protecting you?" They should be clear. "I'm a hunter, Alice, and I enjoy the hunt. This bastard is out there, and he's my prey now. I'm not stopping until I have him."

"It's not Logan," she denied. "I know you think it's him, but it isn't. Logan might do some shady things, but he's not a killer."

He wasn't about to jump into the Logan fan club. But he had other suspicions. "How do you know they're dead?"

Her lashes fluttered. "Excuse me?"

"If we don't have bodies, then how do you know they died?"

"I told you—I-I...in my dreams, Shane is dead..." But her words trailed away.

Saint nodded. "Dreams. What about reality? Without a body, you don't have proof." It was the reason she'd never been charged with any crimes. Because there was no proof the men *were* dead. "For all you know, sweetheart, one—or both—of your exes could still be alive." Not Donovan, Saint had marked him off the list. But Corey or Shane...

Which one of you bastards has been playing a game with Alice?

"You're wrong." A sharp bite of anger. "They're *dead*."

He stared at her and waited to see if she'd show doubt.

"They have to be..."

"Maybe, but maybe they're fucking not. Lucky for you, I have a friend in town, and when it comes to finding the dead, no one beats her. *No one.*"

***

"We need a search parameter. I can't just spread out a map of the city and slam my finger down on a magic spot. That's not how this works and you know it, Saint." The woman with the long, dark braid glared at Saint.

He glared back.

Beside the woman, a beautiful German Shephard waited at careful attention.

"If we *knew* where the bodies were, we wouldn't be here," Saint snapped back. "This is your department. Your *specialty*."

"Maybe if your new girlfriend would be a wee bit more forthcoming then I could start to locate the bodies—"

"For the last time, Alice had nothing to do with the disappearances!"

Alice's phone beeped. She glanced down at the screen and read the message from Raven. *Logan is good. They're keeping him as long as they can, but he's done talking to the cops. I'll have him out before you know it.*

She tapped out a quick response. *Thanks. Add it to my bill.*

Three dots appeared and then...*You still coming to the station?*

"Alice?"

Her name seemed to hang in the air. Her head whipped up, and Alice realized that everyone else in the room—the woman who'd been introduced as Tony, Memphis, Saint, and even the dog—had eyes on her. She'd obviously missed something important. But her mind had been elsewhere. Not even on the text that Raven had sent but on the fact that...*Is it even possible that Corey or Shane could be alive?* After all this time?

Memphis cleared his throat. "Do you have an opinion on that?"

Yes, I think it's impossible. There's no way they're alive. If they'd been alive, they would have contacted her. They wouldn't have just vanished and left her alone. "Sorry." Her lips stretched into her cool and controlled smile. "What was the question?"

"Do you think the bodies are even in the city?"

She blinked.

"What about Donovan Eldridge?" Tony asked. *Dr.* Antonia Rossi. Memphis had rattled on about her degrees. Lots of degrees. Super sharp. Someone Alice knew she had to be very, very careful around. "If we had more details on his body, then we might be able to track him. From everything I've gathered, it's likely he was killed at Providence Canyon State Park."

Oh, that was certainly likely.

"Maybe we can find his remains and get evidence to tie to his killer." Tony nodded all enthusiastically. As if she'd just had the best idea ever.

Yes, let's not do that. Alice met Saint's stare.

"Donovan isn't important," he said without any hesitation. "Our focus needs to be on Corey and Shane. They're the most likely suspects."

Memphis rose from the edge of the bed. They were in a hotel room on the outskirts of town. Tony's room. At Saint's words, Memphis had snapped to attention. "Did you just say 'suspects,' bro? Because I thought we were looking for victims."

Alice had thought the men were victims, too. She *still* thought that.

Her phone beeped and vibrated again. She peeked down at it. Another text from Raven. *Are you coming down here?*

Alice fired off her reply. *Not now. If things change, I will let you know.* Because her big confession to the cops was on hold, for the moment. The whole point of turning herself in was to protect Saint. To draw the killer's attention *off* him. But if Saint insisted on hunting the bastard, then she had to stay close to Saint.

I won't lose anyone else.

She hadn't loved Corey. She'd felt frozen back in those days. As for Shane, he'd been good to her. An asshole to the rest of the world, but good to her. They'd been friends. Maybe they could have been more. But Saint…

It's been more, from the beginning. They'd never been friends. Maybe enemies? No, that wasn't quite right, either. There had been something between them. An awareness that cut far past the surface and seemed to sink straight to her core.

Another text appeared. *Just so you know, the cops seem awful excited about something. They rushed out a while ago while I was handling paperwork.*

Wonderful. Just what she needed. Excited cops.

Before they'd left for this meet and greet with Memphis and Tony, Alice had taken the time to change. *Dress for success.* A look that was more damsel than cat burglar. Until she made an actual confession, she could do with some news footage of herself looking soft and tragic. With that in mind, she'd switched into a rather demure skirt and a flowing top. She wore strappy sandals, and, yes, she'd strapped a knife to her thigh, too. If she decided to go in for a confession with the cops, she'd be sure to leave that lovely weapon behind. But until then, she'd felt more secure having it on her.

After all, she needed something to help her protect Saint.

"If we find both bodies—Shane's and Corey's—then they will be victims. But if only one is in the ground, then I'm thinking we know exactly who we are after." Saint's growling voice had her attention jumping back to him.

Memphis hurried toward Saint. "You're telling me that you think one of her dead exes is to blame?"

"Not dead," Saint corrected. "Missing. Unless you have a body, there's no crime."

Tony gave her dog's head a light pat. "That's not entirely true."

The dog seemed incredibly well-behaved, and the canine's sharp, rather judgmental gaze kept coming back to Alice.

"Good boy," she murmured as she rose.

The dog tensed.

Yes, obviously, the dog didn't like her. Good thing she was more of a cat person. Alice casually strolled for the door. "Saint, I think we're wasting our time."

"Yeah," Memphis drawled. "Because you're looking for the dead."

"*Missing*," Saint snapped back. "And my money is on Corey Abbott."

She froze, about a foot away from the door. Alice turned her head to look at Saint. "Why?"

"Because I smell blood, baby."

She didn't smell a damn thing. Well, perhaps the dog.

"You broke up with him. You left *him*. The last thing he said to you was don't leave, but you left anyway."

She'd had to leave him. "I couldn't..." No, she would not say this in front of their audience. Her confession was for Saint alone. *I couldn't give Corey what he needed.*

Saint surged away from his brother and moved to stand beside her. "I know," he said, voice soft. "And I think that pissed him the hell off. I think he got even angrier when he believed that you were falling for Shane later. So mad that he broke in, and he stabbed Shane to death."

Alice sucked in a deep breath.

Memphis cleared his throat. A loud and probably unnecessary clearing. "Want to tell the rest of the group why you're blaming everything on the guy we thought was a victim?"

"Because he got out of jail free too many times," Saint stated simply.

She didn't have a comeback for that statement. Or maybe she did. This wasn't some boardgame.

"I looked into his life before I came to meet Alice. Not like I was gonna come in blind when it came to the missing. The guy was busted over and over, but he barely stayed in jail even a night. There are two reasons that happens." Saint reached for her hand and twined his fingers with hers. "Either he's bribing the cops and they're giving him free passes, or he's working with them."

Her hand jerked.

"Not like it's the first time Feds have helped an informant vanish. Not even the first time they've faked someone's death."

She shook her head. No, Saint was wrong.

"Could have set the scene so it looked as if he'd had a major fight with someone. He vanishes, the world assumes he's dead, but really Corey gets set up with a new identity." He held up her hand, and his fingers rubbed over her ring finger. "Except there are some things that he just can't let go of. Parts of his old life that he refused to give up. So he kept tabs on what mattered. Hell, maybe he even *paid* someone to watch you and to report back to him. That way, he could stay away, and you'd never know. But then you got close to Shane..."

Alice shook her head. "No."

"And Corey got pissed. So he stepped in. He came out of hiding. You interrupted him when he was stabbing Shane—"

"*No.*" More adamant.

"Uh, excuse me?" Memphis cut in at the same time. "Since *when* did she interrupt a stabbing? Don't you think that's some important information to share with the group?"

The dog whined.

"Easy, Banshee," Tony soothed.

Alice yanked her hand from Saint's. "What are you doing?" She'd *trusted* him.

"Protecting your sweet ass." His jaw hardened even more. He spared a fast glance for the others. "Alice saw the killer. She's not guilty. So I say again, my money is on Corey."

"Well, yes," Tony spoke up. "It has to be if she *saw* Shane getting killed. Fairly safe assumption."

"*Stop it,*" Alice gritted to Saint.

He didn't. "She can't be sure she actually saw Shane die. She got knocked out, so her memories are blurry. But I'm thinking Corey was jealous. He got pissed that he was being replaced so easily, and as a result, he murdered Shane. Everything was fine until I started sniffing around Alice. Things got personal, fast, and he came for me. Only instead of taking me out, he saw Alice save my life, and I think that pushed him over the edge."

"Why would her saving you matter?" Memphis asked.

Saint smiled down at her. All tender-like. That dangerous, disarming smile of his. "It mattered because Corey finally saw something that Alice had said would never happen."

A whisper from her, "Stop."

Saint didn't stop. "He saw Alice in love."

Enough. "You wish I loved you."

"Fucking fondest wish in the world." Flat. "And I've set the stage in motion, don't worry."

That just made her *worry* extra hard. "Saint?"

"Full disclosure, I didn't really come here to look for the bodies. I know Tony needs more to go on."

"Yes, I do," Tony grumbled. "I'm not some psychic who can get visions of the dead. I use science. Clues. Evidence."

His gaze softened as Saint revealed, "I came here so that Tony and Memphis could keep watch on *you* while I went hunting."

Goose bumps rose onto her arms. "Not happening."

"Already in motion," he said. "Why do you think I *carried* you inside while the cameras were rolling? I'm thinking our perp saw the scene. Thinking it made him crazy. So crazy that he will be chomping at the bit to come for me." He shrugged. "I'll just make sure he has the opportunity."

"No."

"I didn't need to see the message inside the ring to know it was him," Saint said. "Just needed the ring itself. He never gave it up because he never gave *you* up. He's been eliminating anyone close. Eliminating threats."

Like Tracy?

"Now he thinks he will eliminate me, but he's wrong. I'll take care of him." He looked over his shoulder at Memphis and Tony. "Do whatever you have to do, but don't let Alice leave this hotel room."

Not happening. She was walking the hell out, right then. She'd like to see them try and stop her.

But Saint wasn't done. "I'm sure he had eyes on us when we left the house. Something tells me he can't take his attention off me." A smirk. "So when I leave alone, he'll be ready to come after me."

"That's *not* happening!" Alice cried. Did the man not hear her speaking?

Saint leaned in close, and his voice turned low and lethal. "Yes, baby, it is. I'm walking out of this hotel room, and you're staying behind. You're staying *safe*."

"While you take the risks?"

"You're worth the risk. You're worth saving. Didn't you tell me that once?"

"I lied. Absolutely lied." This was ridiculous. She spun for the door, grabbed it, yanked it open, only to have Saint immediately slam it closed. His hand slapped against the wood as he leaned in behind her.

"No," he rasped against her ear, "you didn't. You think I'm worth saving, and I'm telling you right now, you are worth *everything* to me."

CHAPTER EIGHTEEN

"Ah, Saint..." Memphis began.

"Stay with her." He had one arm locked around Alice's waist. The other pressed to the door. "Keep her safe. I need you to keep my Alice safe."

His words seemed to vibrate against her because he held her so close.

"I'm not going to kidnap the woman, Saint!" Memphis snapped.

Good. At least someone in the room was being reasonable.

"Look," Memphis continued, voice sounding frayed at the edges, "you are not thinking clearly and—"

"Police, open up!" A thudding at the door.

Saint's arm tightened around her.

Alice had recognized the voice roaring the order. Heidi. "I was trying!" she called back. "They wouldn't let me."

But now there was no choice. Behind her, Saint swore, and she knew he realized they didn't have an option, too. He eased away from her, just a little, and Alice opened the door. It was either open the door or she suspected the cops would have burst in. When the door swung open a moment later, Saint immediately pulled her back against him.

A team of cops swarmed inside. Heidi. Jamal. Uniformed officers that she'd never seen before. Heidi and Jamal swept a fast gaze toward Memphis and Tony—and the still-at-attention dog—before locking their focus on Alice and Saint.

They're here for me. Figured. Raven had tried to give her a warning, but Alice hadn't heeded it. *So this was why the cops were so excited.* "Ah, detectives." She nodded politely toward them. "Let me guess, you're here to take me down to the station because you have reason to believe that I am a killer—"

"Saint Black," Jamal eyed him with grim intent, "you're coming with us."

Um, no. That was the wrong thing to stay. "You mean I'm coming with you," Alice corrected.

Jamal jerked his head in a very distinct *no*.

"But—"

"We found the audio, Saint." Heidi's hands were loose at her sides, and her badge had been clipped to the pocket on her jeans. "Heard the threats you made to Tracy Eldridge. You didn't want her anywhere near Alice, did you? You warned her to stay away, but she just didn't listen, so you took matters into your own hands."

This was not right. "I think you're confused," Alice tried to say, rather helpfully, she thought.

Heidi didn't even seem to have heard Alice's words. "Then you texted Tracy and told her to meet you at Abracadabra." Heidi's lips twisted in disgust. "The woman thought you were going to help her, but you only cared about Alice. You killed for her, didn't you?"

"No, he did *not*," Alice snapped back hotly. "You have this all wrong!"

"He can come with us and tell us how *wrong* we are." Heidi pulled out handcuffs. "The only question is...will you be coming willingly, Saint, or do we need to put on the bracelets for you?"

"Fuck," Saint growled.

Indeed, fuck.

"Memphis, do not let her out of your sight," he ordered.

She spun in his hold. "Saint?" Alice clutched his shoulders.

"Funny, isn't it? When I first met you, never thought I'd be the one to get locked up."

He would *not* be.

Saint's lips brushed over hers. "I'll be out before you can miss me." Then he let her go. *Let her go.* Like it was nothing. Like going to jail wasn't his version of hell.

Saint stepped toward Heidi.

"No!" Alice cried. "This is crazy." She whirled to confront the detectives. "Saint didn't do anything wrong! He didn't hurt Tracy. He couldn't have. I got to Abracadabra before him. I arrived *first*."

"That's what he wanted you to think." Jamal sent her a look of pity. "You can sure pick them, can't you?"

Saint was led from the room. Alice surged after him, only to have Memphis grab her arm. She turned on him with a fury. "*No!*" Alice yelled. "No, you don't hold me here! You get your ass out there with Saint because he's what matters right now. We are not letting him go to jail again! You stay with him, you prove that he didn't do anything wrong. You get them to *listen* to you!" She glared at him. "We don't leave Saint on his own. We don't abandon him, even if he was just being a serious asshole to me." Her breath heaved in and out.

Memphis's eyes widened. "Holy shit. You love him."

"No one else tortures Saint but me, understand? You're his family. You can *make* the cops allow you to stay close." If not with his family connection, then he could pull some bounty hunting camaraderie shit with them that might work. "Go after him. When you arrive at the station, I'll have a lawyer waiting for him."

"My Alice," Memphis murmured.

She stiffened. "Excuse me?"

"Do you know why he says that?"

She had a general idea. "Because he's a possessive bastard."

Memphis shook his head. "No. Saint doesn't cling tightly to anything. The last time he tried that, the last time someone was part of his crew, the guy turned out to be a killer. He left Saint out to dry."

Yes, she knew that unfortunate story. "*We* are not leaving him."

"No, we aren't." A nod. "I'll stay with him." He hurried out the door.

Excellent. One down...Alice looked over at Tony...One to go. "You're not just going to stand there, are you?"

"I'm trying to figure you out."

"Good luck with that." While Tony was occupied with that bit of uselessness, Alice fired off a text to Raven. *They are bringing in my*—She stopped. How to describe Saint? Then she remembered a conversation that she'd had with Saint once. No way could he be described as a *boyfriend.* So she just typed,

They're bringing in my Saint. Trying to connect him to Tracy's murder. He needs a lawyer.

Three dots showed on her screen. And...

Lucky you know a good one. I'm on it.

Her shoulders sagged. Alice lunged toward the open door. "I think Saint didn't want you to leave this hotel room. He was worried about you."

Tony was still in there. Tony and her eerily well-behaved dog. "Well, Saint is being hauled to jail, so I don't see where he gets a whole lot of options regarding what happens to me." Alice had her own plans. First, she had to clear Saint so he didn't get charged with a murder he hadn't committed. Fortunately, Alice had an idea of how to do that rather challenging agenda item.

Because if Saint was right...

She peered at Tony. "He'll be watching."

Tony lifted her eyebrows. "Excuse me?"

"I thought Saint was crazy. No way my ex has been alive all this time, but...no body, am I right?"

"You're saying you believe your ex is watching...?"

"I think he's watching Saint get hauled away right now. I think he could be very, very close, and I think that means you and I need to get our asses downstairs and search for him." Why was Tony hesitating. "You find the dead, right? Let's put that to the test. Let's see if you can find the dead man walking—the bastard I think is hiding close by. Because no way the cops just randomly get evidence— including a perfectly convenient text— showing that Saint is their big, number one murder suspect. He's clearly being set up." And she was *clearly* wasting time.

"Hate to break it to you, but there might not be anything *random* about it. The cops could have gotten the evidence if Saint is guilty. If he *sent* the text."

Alice raked her with a look of disgust. "And I thought you were on our team. Such a disappointment."

"You haven't even *seen* the evidence. Why are you so sure he's innocent? You don't think for even a second that Saint could be guilty?"

"Not even a second."

Tony held her stare.

"If Saint killed someone, he wouldn't leave tacky evidence like this behind. The man is no amateur." The idea was insulting. *Forget this. She won't help me. I should have known better than—*

"Yeah, I don't buy it, either." Tony nodded. "I was testing you."

"Don't ever do that again. I hate tests."

"Good to know you have Saint's back."

She had his back, front, and everything else.

Tony patted her leg. "Come on, Banshee. Let's find the bastard."

Yes, *yes.*

"He probably is watching," Tony continued as her expression turned thoughtful. "If he's some guy with a mad obsession for you and Saint was in the way, he wouldn't be able to resist seeing Saint get hauled off to jail."

That was exactly what Alice thought. "If Saint is right and it's Corey, he won't look the same."

Another nod from Tony. "Changing his appearance would have been step one. He'll most likely be standing back, watching from the outskirts. But if he sees you, he might be pulled forward. We'll go down separately. I'll keep some distance between us and see what happens."

Nothing might happen. Alice knew that. She also knew she wasn't staying in that damn hotel room. Hadn't she told Saint before that she didn't stay behind?

Alice practically ran down the stairs. No way did she stop for the elevator. When she burst outside, she saw Saint being pushed into the back of a patrol car.

Oh, hell, no. Alice bounded forward as anger pulsed inside of her. "This is so—"

"Alice." Tyler McQuinn jumped in front of her. "Alice, will you tell me why your latest boyfriend is being arrested?" He shoved a microphone toward her. "Is it because he killed Tracy Eldridge?"

His cameraman filmed behind Tyler.

"No, he didn't kill anyone," Alice seethed. "Now get out of my way."

"We got a tip that the police were closing in on their suspect, and now Saint Black is being arrested—"

"He's not being arrested, he's being questioned. There's a difference." She shoved past him. "Get the microphone *away* from me." From the corner of her eye, she saw Tony and Banshee exit the hotel and go to the right.

A crowd had gathered in the parking lot. Not just Tyler and his cameraman, but plenty of other reporters and random onlookers, too. Dammit, apparently, Tyler hadn't been the only one to get a tip. Everyone and their mother waited out there.

Deliberate. He wanted a crowd here. So he could hide better.

He...her stalker. The man who'd been making her life a nightmare for too long. The man who'd made her seem like a monster. "Saint!" Alice called out.

His head lifted. Turned toward her.

She held his gaze. "I love you." Deliberate. Loud. For the cameras. For anyone watching. For the sonofabitch who thought he could control *her*.

No one controlled her. No one made her a victim. Not any longer. Never again.

"*Alice*..." Saint mouthed her name. No, no, it hadn't just been her name...

My Alice.

And something clicked for her. It wasn't about possession. She could see that. See it in the way his eyes lit on her and warmed. The way his face changed.

Possession...belonging...

Fitting.

Like to like.

Mine...because I love you.

He might as well have screamed the words back to her. Alice smiled at him. A smile that she couldn't help, and one that she knew would be caught on camera.

Saint disappeared into the back of the patrol car.

Alice whirled to find Tyler and his cameraman. "Who told you?"

Tyler blinked. He tightened his hold on the microphone. "Excuse me?"

"You want an exclusive, Tyler? Want to hear all my dark and dirty secrets?"

"Yes." His eyes doubled in size. "Please." The man practically salivated.

She inched closer to him. "I'll tell you, but you tell *me* who tipped you off. Tell me exactly how you knew to be at this location."

He licked his lips and cast a glance at his cameraman.

"Get lost," Alice told the cameraman flatly. "Now. Wander away and come back in five minutes." That would give her enough time to get everything she needed from Tyler.

The cameraman didn't move.

"You heard the lady," Tyler said as his shoulders straightened.

Cursing, the cameraman stormed off—off to take footage of the patrol car driving away. Most of the reporters and camera crews had turned their focus to the road and the fleeing cop vehicles.

Tyler looked around, nervously. "You're not supposed to give up info like a tipster's name."

"Do I look like I care what you're *supposed* to do?" Alice shot back.

He inclined his head toward the left, away from the crowd. "Come over here."

She stalked to the left. She saw Tony edging a bit more toward the line of trees on the right. It looked as if Banshee was scenting something. The dog's nose was to the ground and—

"Why the hell did you have to love that sonofabitch?" Tyler burst out, voice low and angry, even as she felt something jab into her side. Fast. Hard. Then cold seemed to sweep through her very veins.

"That's enough morphine to knock out a tiger. It sure as shit will take you out."

Ice. That was what it felt like when the drug poured through her. Cold, flooding her whole body. "Help—" Barely a gasp.

"Too much noise. Too many crews." He locked one arm around her and walked Alice forward, *away* from everyone else. Not that anyone seemed to notice them. "This time, you'll be the one to disappear. Abracadabra, bitch."

Oh, wasn't that...

Fucking annoying. Her fingers fumbled and managed to get her skirt up a little, just enough that she could grab the knife strapped to her thigh. Even as her body iced, she closed her chilled fingers around the weapon. She lifted it and drove it into his leg.

"Dammit!" A low growl of pain.

She sliced again, tried to, but...

Her fingers didn't work just right. The weapon slid from her grip.

"My turn is next..." Tyler promised in her ear as everything grew dim around her. "And I'll give you more than a little scratch. How about I send you straight to hell? Got just the perfect nightmare for you."

***

"Don't say a word." The pretty redhead flashed Saint a hard smile. "Hi, I'm your new lawyer, Raven Scott. Alice sent me."

He'd barely even stepped foot in the police station before she'd zeroed in on him. She gripped a briefcase in one hand, and her direct, intelligent gaze oozed confidence.

"You will be in and out, I assure you," Raven continued breezily. "You don't have to talk to the cops at—"

"Talking to them was the plan," he interrupted to say. "Though I certainly appreciate the offer of assistance. And it's good to know that Alice cares."

Raven blinked. Some of her bright confidence dimmed. "Say again?"

He looked to the right. Jamal Preacher was leaning in close to a uniformed cop at the check-in desk. "Really need about five minutes of chat time with him, and then, if you could swing it, I'd love to be transferred to holding."

"Insane," Memphis muttered. Because, yes, his brother had been shadowing him the whole time. At first, Memphis had tried to get in the patrol car. When the cops had blocked him, Memphis had followed in his own ride.

But his brother was wrong about one thing. "Not insane. Just looks that way." He had a plan.

And at that moment, Jamal looked up. He pointed at Saint. "Interrogation."

"About time." Seriously, could they get this show rolling? "Don't worry, I remember the way." He turned to the left.

Raven jumped into his path. "What are you doing?"

"Getting the truth." Though his masterplan had been thrown off when Memphis joined him. His brother *should* have stayed with Alice. Saint had been counting on Memphis protecting her. But at least Alice was still with Tony and Banshee.

And he could get the answers he needed.

Did you watch me get hauled away, you bastard? Saint knew he had the killer's attention.

"Alice is not going to like this," Raven hissed.

"You are one hundred percent right on that." He could imagine her fury. "So let's not tell her just yet, shall we?"

But Raven was already pulling out her phone, so he figured that answer was a no. Fair enough. Saint sauntered into the interrogation room. Memphis filed in, too. As did Raven, even though she was frantically texting at the same time. Jamal was the last to arrive, and his eyes narrowed when he saw the size of the group inside.

"Do you think this is a freaking party?" he demanded.

"I tend to travel with an entourage. It's a new thing," Saint dismissed.

"You sound like Alice." Jamal's jaw tightened. "This isn't a joke. You don't get to play with the police department."

Saint sat in the wobbly chair like a good interrogation suspect. "Who's playing? By the way, your partner Heidi *is* still at the hotel, isn't she? I figured she wanted to ask Alice some questions." Another layer of protection for Alice. The cop would be with her.

"Yes, she's taking care of Alice." A satisfied curl of Jamal's lips. "And I get to have my run at you." He carried a manila file. "I've got the transcripts from your last voicemail to Tracy Eldridge. Do you want to explain how—"

"I was angry with my client." He perfectly remembered the message he'd left for Tracy. "I told her to leave Alice alone."

"Because *Alice* is what matters to you. A woman you just met, and within days, you were turning on your client for her."

"Tracy was wrong about Alice." He kept his voice mild. "She also neglected to mention a few pertinent facts to me."

"Oh?" Jamal sat down, then he shot a glance at Raven. "You're representing him?"

"That was the plan."

Not Saint's plan.

"Huh." Jamal's stare shifted to Memphis. "Are you going to be a problem? Because I can escort you out right now—"

This was a waste of time. "No one in this room is a problem. We're all solutions. *You* are a solution, detective."

Jamal's eyebrows flew up as he turned his head toward Saint. "Excuse me?"

"Let's talk about Corey Abbott."

Jamal laughed. "This is *my* interrogation."

"Memphis said you were a good cop. He dug into your background after he met you at Abracadabra."

Jamal's face tightened. "Excuse the fuck out of me? Want to say that again?"

"I had some connections," Memphis explained as he stood nearby. "I reached out to them. They vouched for you. Said you weren't the kind of guy who'd roll for money."

Fury flashed in the detective's eyes as he glared for a moment at Memphis. Then, "This circus is over. *Out.* I want you *out* of this room. You have no reason to be in—"

"Memphis is here because he wants to watch my back." Something Saint could appreciate. "I'm here because I want your help."

But the detective laughed. The sound held zero humor and a whole lot of mocking anger. "You're here because I brought you in for questioning—"

"No." Saint shook his head. "I brought you in." Just so they were clear.

Silence.

"No wonder Alice likes you," Jamal finally said. "You're as crazy as she is."

They weren't crazy at all. "Corey Abbott." Saint's target. "I want to know why he was able to get out of jail so many times.

Why every single charge against him would vanish as if by magic." *Abracadabra.*

Jamal leaned forward. His hand slapped on top of the manila file. "You think I didn't wonder the same thing?"

Great. Now they were making progress. "Was he working with dirty cops?"

Jamal's mouth tightened.

"Or was he an informant for someone? Maybe for the Feds? Because I figure it has to be option A or option B. I came to you—"

"You didn't come to me. I dragged your ass in for questioning—"

"Because I wanted your take. Which option was it? Why did he keep walking away?"

More silence.

Come on, Jamal. We are wasting time.

"Why did you text Tracy and tell her to meet you at Abracadabra?" Jamal asked in an obvious effort to take charge of the interrogation. "Was it because you'd decided that Alice's life would be a whole lot easier without Tracy in it? Or did Alice ask you to get rid of her?"

Beneath the table, Saint's hands fisted. "I didn't text her. Whatever data you were given, it's wrong. Not like it's difficult for someone in the know to do a little phone hacking." Hell, he'd done it himself when he tracked Tracy to Abracadabra. "Just takes a bit of skill. I'm absolutely certain that a man with Corey's connections would have a few hackers at the ready. Seemed like a ton of people owed him favors. I'm sure he always collected on those favors."

Jamal eased back in his chair. "Are you forgetting that Corey is *dead?*"

"Not so sure about that. So, how about we circle back to my question. Was it option A? The dirty cops? Or option B? Federal help?"

The detective's gaze shot toward the one-way mirror, then back to Saint.

"A," Saint murmured.

No change from the detective.

"B," he said.

Jamal's head tipped toward him.

Saint's hands uncurled, only to clench again. Now they were getting somewhere. "And no one ever considered that maybe the bastard had gotten a little bit of help with his disappearance? Or was everyone so eager to put nails in Alice's coffin that no one ever stopped to consider other possibilities?"

"I did," Jamal admitted quietly. "But nothing came up. And then Shane Madison vanished. All the pressure was on Alice at that point."

Victim number three.

With Alice as the perfect villain. Only, she wasn't. Saint's phone vibrated. He ignored it. This talk with Jamal was important. It was giving him the intel he needed. Because maybe Corey wasn't dead. Maybe the bastard was out there, always watching Alice.

Memphis's phone beeped. "Sorry," he said, not particularly sounding it. "I'll just turn the volume off."

Saint cut a glance his brother's way. He saw Memphis pull out his phone and...

"Fuck." Memphis snapped his head up. "Problem, Saint, *problem.*"

Saint's phone vibrated again.

"Oh, by all means," Jamal said with a wave. "Not like we're in the middle of an interrogation or anything."

But Jamal's phone rang in the next moment.

Frowning, he, too, pulled out his phone.

Saint already had his gripped in his hand. He read the multiple texts that had come through from Tony.

Alice is missing.

Banshee found blood.

I'm so sorry.

He jumped to his feet. "No!"

Jamal was talking into his phone. "What do you mean she's not on scene? I thought Alice was in the hotel?"

"*No!*" Saint thundered. This wasn't happening.

"I..." Raven cleared her throat as she stepped away from the wall. "Is this about Alice? Because...she's not answering any of my texts."

This wasn't part of the plan. Alice couldn't be *gone*. There couldn't be *blood* left behind. Not her blood. Not Alice.

Not my Alice.

Saint rushed for the door.

He could hear Memphis on his phone. No doubt talking to Tony. Asking to know what was happening at the scene. Asking was she *certain* that Alice was gone.

Alice can't be gone.

Then, in the next instant, one thought obliterated everything else.

I will fucking get her back.

Before Saint could yank open the door, Jamal jumped up. Grabbed his shoulder. "Wait, man, *wait!* You're not going after—"

"Put me in fucking lockup," Saint demanded. *"Now."*

Jamal blinked. "What? Are you crazy?"

"Yes. When it comes to Alice, I absolutely am." He whirled on him. *"Put me in lockup."*

***

The cell door clanged shut behind Saint. It was a familiar sound. One that used to send a chill down his spine because it meant he was trapped in hell.

I am in hell.

Alice was missing. Tony had confirmed that she'd seemingly vanished from the parking lot of the hotel. Alice's phone had been found tossed in the grass, not too far from the damn *blood* that Banshee had scented.

Rage burned inside Saint as he stared at his prey.

There was only one other man in that cell, and his head slowly lifted as the guy shot a curious look at...

"Oh, hell," Logan groaned. "What are you doing here?"

Saint smiled at him. "I'm here to kick the ever-loving shit out of you."

"What?" Logan jumped up from the cot. "Hey, guard? *Guard?*" he shouted. "They can't—*who even let you in here?*"

Saint stalked toward him. "I didn't trust you from the beginning. Didn't like the way you hung around Alice so much."

Logan backed up—tried to—but there was nowhere for him to go. "Where is the *guard*?"

"Probably on break." He stopped right in front of Logan. "Alice is missing."

Logan blanched. "Wh-what?"

"He's going to hurt her because he knows that she loves me. He doesn't want her loving anyone else, does he? Possessive bastard. He couldn't even let her go when he was supposed to be dead."

Sweat beaded Logan's brow. "I don't know what you're talking about—"

"I can break every bone in your body long before the guard comes back." Saint smiled at him. "I got good at doing things like that back when I was locked away. You know about that time, don't you? Because you investigated me for Alice."

"Sh-she told you I did that?"

"Alice tells me everything."

"G—"

This time, Logan didn't get to call out for the guard because Saint had wrapped his fingers around the bastard's throat. "Do you know," he said, conversationally, "how very easy it is to kill a person?"

Logan's wild eyes rolled as he sought help.

"You've been selling out Alice. She thought she could trust you, but you were working for someone else."

Logan began to shake.

"You're afraid of him, but that's a mistake." Saint smiled. "You see, you need to be afraid of *me*."

The shaking grew worse. Good.

"I'm going to lift my hand off you, and you're going to tell me what I need to know. Or else I will hurt you, very, very badly. Are we clear?"

Saint heard the scrape of a shoe behind him, but he didn't look back.

Logan also didn't look away from him.

Saint lifted his hand.

"Sh-she thinks you...you're different from them," Logan rasped. "She's wrong."

"Alice knows exactly what I am." He didn't move. "You told him that Tracy was harassing her, didn't you? Said that you were afraid of what she'd do to Alice."

"I-I just wanted Alice safe!"

"He killed Tracy."

Instead of making a denial, Logan's body sagged. "Why do you think I was searching Abracadabra when you and Alice arrived, huh? I was trying to find evidence. I wanted to help!"

Bullshit. Like Saint was gonna buy that story. "He's taken Alice."

A hard shake of Logan's head.

"She's not *safe* with him," Saint added, voice grim. "You know it."

"No, no, no...he *wouldn't* kill Alice. He's not like that! Look, he just—he wanted a story, okay? Just stories and—"

This time, both of Saint's hands closed around Logan's shoulders. "What in the hell are you talking about?"

"The...the reporter." Logan's breathing hitched. "He wanted a big story. That's why I told him about Tracy. And l-look...I had to do it, okay? He was blackmailing me!"

The reporter?

"He knew. He *knew!* I don't know how," Logan burst out. "But he knew I was the one who screwed up the swords so long ago."

"What? Bastard, what are you—"

"When Alice got sliced by the sword during her dad's act! Dammit, he knew it was my fault! I screwed up! I put the wrong swords out. Somehow, he knew, and he said he'd tell her. He'd tell Alice unless I fed him info, and I didn't want to lose Alice. She's my only family. I didn't want to *lose* her!"

This didn't make sense. "I'm talking about Corey Abbott." Saint tightened his grip. "Where is he? Where did he take Alice?"

Logan's mouth opened. Closed. Opened once more. "Corey? But...he's dead."

Saint's heart thudded into his chest. "Which fucking reporter are you talking about?"

"Tyler. Tyler McQuinn."

Saint shoved him against the wall. "Did you leave a broken wand for Alice to find after her dad died?"

"I—what?" He squinted. "Yes, I, uh, left the wand. I loved her dad, okay? He was the closest thing to a father *I* had. It was just—just my way of saying goodbye."

What the fuck? Alice had thought the wand had been a message. It hadn't been. Did that mean the other stuff— "You're telling me that you've been feeding info to *Tyler McQuinn?* Not Corey Abbott?"

"Why would I be telling a dead man anything?"

Saint spun and rushed back to the cell door. "Open it up!"

Memphis appeared. "Getting a little close to the edge, aren't you?"

You have no idea. "I'll do whatever is necessary to get her back." Tyler McQuinn? Saint hurried away even as he heard Logan call out behind him. The reporter hadn't been on his radar. He'd been locked and loaded on Corey.

The revelation about Tyler changed everything. They'd get an APB on him. They'd track his phone, the same way that Saint had tracked Tracy's phone when he'd located her at Abracadabra. She'd disappeared but then she'd shown up there, waiting like a freaking present for Alice, along with that ring.

The ring.

It was in Saint's pocket. He'd shoved it in there earlier, not even thinking, before they left Alice's house. He grabbed it and yanked it out.

Conjure.

"Saint? Saint, what's the plan?" Memphis barked.

He glared at the ring. *I get Alice back. I kill the bastard who took her. End of story.*

CHAPTER NINETEEN

"I have to get back."

The voice drifted to her. Alice's lashes fluttered.

"Told my cameraman I was running down a lead, but I can't be gone forever. Can't let anyone miss me too long."

Who was that? She tried to sit up...

But her head bumped into something. And her body felt funny. Tired. No, heavy. And so cold. Super, super cold. A cold that seemed to come from the inside. Like her veins had frozen.

"The bitch cut me with her knife. Can you believe that? I thought the morphine would take her out. Thought it was supposed to work instantly, but she managed to slice me. That's why I dumped her in the box. Wanted her to wake up to her own hell."

Dumped her in the box. Her breath shuddered out.

"Now I have to change clothes before I go back. Dammit, that is gonna take time I don't have!"

That was Tyler's voice. The little prick. He'd injected her with morphine? No wonder she was still floating and feeling as if a weight dragged her down at the same time.

And he'd put her in a box. That explained the darkness. Her hands reached out. Touched a hard surface in front of her. Behind her.

There was a little light coming in from above her. She'd bumped her head before, but...there were slats in the surface a few inches above her head. She reached up. Touched them. And...

*Oh, no. No, no, no...*She knew this box. *My box.*

"You got her, right? She's not going to be a problem?" Tyler pushed.

She strained to hear. Who was Tyler talking to?

"I did everything you wanted," Tyler continued. He sounded nervous. "Now you have to make sure that this doesn't come back and bite me in the ass. I can't be tied to her, not at all. I'll cover the story. I'll make it look like Alice ran because she didn't want to get arrested, but you have to be thorough, got it?"

"Oh, I've got it," a deep voice replied.

Alice stopped breathing. She *knew* that voice. And even though she freaking *hated* Tyler, she wanted to scream for him to *run*. Except Alice knew it was too late because—

"I absolutely believe in being thorough," the voice added.

There was a quick grunt. A rush of breath. Then...

A thud. As if a body had just fallen.

Alice lifted both hands. They were shaking as she tried to push at the wood above her. No give, though, because it had been locked down. She even knew exactly how it had been secured—with the two locks on the right side of the box.

The box.

Alice knew exactly where she was. Her office, at Abracadabra. She'd been put into the magic box. The big, red box that had slats in the top so that swords could be slid inside of it.

The magician's assistant was supposed to stay in the box and magically avoid the deadly blades.

Alice hadn't performed this trick since she was eighteen years old.

She'd kept the freaking box because it was a piece of her past. Now it might be her grave. *No, no, I will not go out like this.*

There were lots of ways she could play this scene. She could try begging. Pleading. She could make the man outside the box a desperate offer. She could...

Fuck it. Fuck him.

She could go out fighting. "Is Tyler dead?" Alice called out. Her voice was only a little bit husky. Not her fault. She blamed it on the morphine. "Or is he still struggling desperately to live? Not that I care, really, one way or the other. Just vaguely curious as I sit trapped in a freaking box."

Laughter greeted her question. "My God, I have missed you."

I have not missed you.

Hinges squeaked. She tensed because she knew he was unlocking and opening the box.

The lid slowly lifted.

"Hello, beautiful," he said.

***

"All right, people, we got a hit!" Jamal thundered. "Tyler McQuinn's phone is near the news station. Let's go, *now!*" Jamal pointed at Saint. "You keep your ass here. You can stay in my office. The last thing I want is you running to the scene and blowing everything to hell."

He didn't intend to blow anything to hell.

"Watch him," Jamal directed a fresh-faced uniform.

Then the detective left. Didn't even look back once. Obviously, he thought Saint was the type of person to follow orders. Why the hell he would think that, Saint had no clue. The minute the detective and his swarming force left, Saint surged forward.

Memphis swore.

But Saint's phone rang after he'd taken all of three steps. The last time he'd ignored his phone, he'd missed info on Alice. So Saint immediately snatched up the phone, frowning a bit at the unfamiliar number. "Who the hell is—"

"Yeah, uh, it's Marcel. Remember me?"

He did. Like he'd forget the bouncer at Abracadabra. Fun fact, he'd kept some secrets from Alice. He had *told* Marcel to go to Alice and reveal what he'd overheard that night. And Saint had given Marcel his number because he'd told the guy he wanted to be kept updated if anything odd happened at the speakeasy. "Can't talk right now. Alice is—"

"Someone is inside Abracadabra. I just—I was here looking for Alice's cat."

The fucking cat again?

"I know she loves that mangy thing, so I was gonna leave it some milk."

Alice and the cat. "The cat's at her place. But who the hell is inside Abracadabra?"

"Don't know. Just saw a man go in. I could have sworn he was carrying something."

Saint's head turned. He met Memphis's stare. His heart thudded in his chest. Every beat felt almost painful. "I need you to get in that building, Marcel. Alice is missing, and she's in danger."

"You think she's inside?"

He was already striding forward. The uniform saw him coming and jumped up.

"I think I want you inside." *Now. Get to Alice. Don't let anyone hurt her.* "And I'm on the freaking way." He shoved down the phone. Glared at the cop. "You do not want to try stopping me." Assaulting a cop would slow him down. He couldn't afford a slowdown.

"Ahem." Raven hurried forward and tapped the cop on the shoulder. "I'll handle this."

The cop whirled toward her.

"So, this will be a lot of legal lingo. I do hope you're ready for it," she informed the cop. Then she unloaded, "You cannot lawfully keep my client here against his will when he has not been charged with..."

Saint didn't hear the rest. He hauled ass for the door. Memphis ran out with him.

"What is happening?" Memphis fired.

"Tyler isn't at the news station." Maybe his phone was. He *wasn't.* "Alice is at Abracadabra." For the final scene. Because the prick holding her thought he was a damn magician.

Conjure.

No, asshole. I'm about to make you vanish.

***

When the lid of the box lifted, light flooded inside. Alice blinked a few times. She wished that she didn't feel so terribly sluggish. If she hadn't been drifting on morphine, she would have shot out as soon as the lid opened. She would have attacked the man smiling down at her.

As it was, she made a show of slowly stretching. "Just...not as flexible as I once was." A smile curled her lips. "You certainly look good."

Corey Abbott's grin just grew. "So do you, love."

He did look handsome. But, then, Corey had always been attractive. His light hair had been dyed to black, and his eyes were now a green, no doubt due to contacts. In the past, he'd always preferred a close shave, but a beard covered his jaw, making his face shape seem a little different. The beard had also been turned dark to match his new hair.

He'd put on more weight, all of it muscle. His smile was even brighter than before.

Alice shook her head. "I have to say, death has been kind to you."

He laughed. The laughter seemed to boom around her. He offered his hand to her.

She reached for him.

But his laughter stopped. "You didn't think it would be that easy, did you?"

No, alas, she had not.

"You're not wearing my ring, Alice."

How wonderful for him to notice. "You had me put in a box, Corey." She could certainly notice things, too. "And I'm pretty sure there's a dead reporter at your feet."

He looked down. "He's bleeding out. Got a knife shoved in his throat. His voice was annoying the fuck out of me."

Do not flinch. "Me, too." A shrug of one shoulder. "Also was a bit pissed about being drugged."

"Ah..." His smile came again. "That's on me, love. I needed you here. Figured you'd put up a fight. So I gave Tyler something to make the trip easier."

Keep him talking. If he was talking, then he wasn't killing her. "You used to feed Tyler tips when he first started on the crime beat, didn't you?"

"I *made* the man. He owed me. Told him the tips would keep coming provided he did favors for me."

"Favors like drugging and kidnapping women?"

"Not women, plural. You're the first."

Her hand closed around the edge of the box. She wanted to jump up and jump *out* of the box, but Alice wasn't sure her legs would hold her. The longer she stalled, the better chance she had of getting stronger. "I'm special that way."

Corey's gaze drifted over her face. "You are." Sad. "You are very special to me. I always wanted us to go away together."

"Really?" Alice squinted up at him. "Odd. I seem to remember you vanishing and then everyone suspecting me of murdering you. My mistake."

His fingers covered hers as they rested on the side of the box. "The night you left me, I was going to ask you then. I knew if I didn't leave town, the Feds were going to turn on me. They'd found that I wasn't always—well, shall we say *truthful*—in my dealings with them. It was vanish or spend my life in jail, and I'm just not a fan of being locked away."

"Know the feeling." *Said the woman in the freaking box!* Alice pulled in a breath. "Donovan's disappearance made it convenient for you. One lover vanished, so why not another?"

He winked. "Exactly."

You bastard. "And Shane? You came after him, so—what? So that there would be more of a pattern? So more people would believe I was a killer?"

His fingers stroked along her knuckles. "That was one of the reasons, yes." Another tender stroke. "A third victim sealed the deal, so to speak. Made my disappearance seem more tied to you, and, well, if you want the truth..."

Another shrug. "Only if you feel like sharing it."

His hand swallowed hers. Tightened so much it hurt. "You were falling for the bastard. I kept watch on you. I *knew* you were getting too close to him. When you came to his place that night and you called out for him, I could fucking hear it in your voice. You *never* sounded quite that way with me."

She ignored the pain in her hand. "Oh, was that you I hit with the champagne bottle? You should have said something."

"He was dead when you arrived. Always wondered if you saw him. I took the knife he was using to make you dinner, and I carved him open."

Do not show him any emotion. Alice lifted her chin. "And then you cleaned up after yourself. Tell me, where did you take his body?"

"Thought about putting it in your backyard." He let go of her hand. "But that seemed too obvious. Cops would search there eventually, and it wasn't like I wanted you to go to prison."

How considerate. He hadn't wanted her to actually *go* to prison. He'd just wanted the world to think she was a monster.

"I actually always thought you'd come back to me." He exhaled. "I was waiting."

"It's hard to come back to a dead man."

"Um. Not really dead, though, am I?"

You will be soon enough.

"I put him somewhere I thought you'd enjoy. A place you visit nearly every day. Seemed fitting." He leaned over her. "By the way, this is the part, Alice, where you promise that if I let you live, you'll love me forever."

"Oh, is that what this is? Sorry. My first time to be kidnapped. You need to explain the rules to me."

His lips tightened. "You beg me to let you live. You beg me to—"

She winced. "Sorry, I'm not supposed to do that. I think the new way is that people are supposed to beg *me* for things."

Fury flashed on his face. "You damn—" But he broke off. Frowned. He jerked out his phone and swiped his finger over the screen. "Someone is in the building?"

Um, yes, she was looking at someone in her building.

"It's your bouncer. Why is he here?"

Marcel? Alarm—and hope—flared in her. Then... "Excuse me, but have you tapped into my building's security feed? Is that what you're looking at? And if so, when did you get access?"

"Right after you moved in. I've been watching you all the time." His head shot up. "Got cameras even you don't know about." His left hand flew out and fisted in her hair. "Didn't like the scene in here with you and the bounty hunter, Alice. *Didn't like it at all.*"

"Too bad," she whispered as he nearly pulled the hair out of her head. "I rather enjoyed it."

Corey leaned toward her. Nose to nose. "I'm gonna kill him."

"Don't be too sure of that. Saint is more dangerous than you might expect."

"No, love." Laughter. "*I'm* dangerous. I'm the one you should always fear." He shoved her down, a hard push that sent her breath rushing out, and in the next instant, he'd closed the lid of the damn box. She heard the locks sliding into place.

No!

"But first, I'm getting rid of the bouncer. He shouldn't be here. Not like I can leave any witnesses."

Were the cops still outside? They'd been at the building when she and Saint came to search. How could they be missing what was happening? Surely, they'd seen Tyler drag her in?

She slammed her fist on the wood in front of her. "Don't hurt Marcel! He's not involved in this!"

"He's involved now."

"Don't!"

But he didn't respond. Swearing, Alice twisted her body around. This was the same box her father had used so long ago. The box that had once soaked up her blood in a trick gone wrong. Her father had found out about the cut, he'd been horrified when he saw the wound after the show, and he'd vowed that nothing like that would ever happen again.

So her dad had gone to work on the box.

He'd put in an emergency escape mechanism. A way for the assistant to get out in case something went wrong. The assistant could push a small button on the bottom...

Alice's fingers slid over the base of the box until she found the button.

She pushed it.

And the back wall of the giant box popped open.

"Abracadabra." Alice climbed out and promptly fell on her face. But then she dragged her ass up. Her gaze flew around the office. She didn't have her knife. She needed a weapon—any weapon. But preferably something that would hurt like hell when she used it on Corey.

Alice yanked open her desk drawers. Searched quickly and...ah, yes, that would do. She closed her hand around the neck of the wine bottle that had been stashed in her bottom drawer. Then she smashed the bottle on the edge of her desk. It shattered, but the base, ah, that base stayed lovely—so jagged and sharp in so many vicious places.

Yes, you will do just perfectly.

Her steps were a little uncertain, but she made her way out of her office. Down the corridor. She could hear shouting. The thud of fists hitting flesh. The fight was so loud that she didn't think the men had heard the sound of the wine bottle breaking.

"I will fucking shoot you."

She wasn't particularly surprised to hear that Corey had a gun. He'd always carried one with him. When she crept into the bar, she could see him standing a few feet from Marcel. Blood dripped from Marcel's busted lip. Alice was sure Corey would have plenty of his own blood flowing, too. Marcel packed one hell of a punch.

She inched toward Corey. She'd drive the broken bottle into his back. Take him *out*.

But Marcel's head jerked toward her. His eyes widened. "Alice, get out of here! Go!"

No! Marcel—*no!* She knew her time had run out. Alice tried to bound forward and attack, even as she knew—she *knew* Corey wouldn't turn to confront her. Not yet. Not until he eliminated the threat in front of him. "Run!" she screamed.

The gun fired. Marcel jerked back and his body hit the edge of the bar counter. Blood bloomed on him.

Where are the cops? Did they hear the gunfire? Is anyone outside?

She was yelling with fury as she surged to eliminate that final distance between her and Corey. He spun to her at the last moment. She drove the broken bottle toward his heart. But he brought his hand down—the hand holding the gun—and chopped hard across her wrist. Her fingers seemed to go numb, and the broken bottle fell to the floor.

Then he raised his gun, and he pressed it to her chest. "Were you trying to cut out my heart, Alice?"

She stared back at him.

"You already did that." His face twisted in fury. "When you fucking *fell in love with Saint!*"

A dull drumming filled her ears. "I thought something was wrong with me." She moved even closer. Let the gun push even harder into her chest. "When I didn't love you, when I couldn't love you, I thought I was broken inside."

"You *are*."

Maybe. But... "There was nothing in you to love. You were wrong, just like Donovan was. I was never going to love you. I *will* never love you. And, yes, yes, I love *my* Saint." She waited for him to pull the trigger. Alice wasn't scared. She was sad, though.

She and Saint could've had one hell of a wonderful life together.

I still hope he has a wonderful life. I hope it's wild and reckless and passionate and—

"If you love him, it's gonna hurt so much when you see him die."

Wait—what? "No! No, you aren't hurting Saint. *No!*"

He laughed and with the gun still digging into her, he hauled Alice back to her office.

CHAPTER TWENTY

"This is a shit plan," Memphis informed him curtly. "You need backup."

Saint slapped a hand on his shoulder. "You are my backup. Give me three minutes, then you come in with guns blazing because you're going to be the distraction I need."

"I'm talking about cops," Memphis gritted out. "You know them, right? The people with badges?"

"Yeah, I think they're across town right now. Feel free to give them a call." There were no longer any uniforms staking out Abracadabra. "Call them *after* I go inside." He checked the gun he'd taken from Memphis's ride.

Perfect.

He also had a knife strapped to his ankle, another item he'd taken from Memphis. The cops had taken Saint's knife, so he'd borrowed this one from his brother. Now, he was more than ready to cut a fucking bastard open if it meant he could get his Alice back.

"You don't even know that she's inside." Memphis glared at the building. "Marcel didn't call you back."

Marcel wasn't answering his phone, and that sure seemed like a bad sign. *Understatement.*

"I'm coming in *with* you," Memphis decided. "Screw this waiting three minutes crap."

Saint squeezed his shoulder. "You have to be my distraction. I'm going in the back. I'm sneaking in because if he has her, I don't want him panicking and hurting Alice." He couldn't think of Alice hurt. If he imagined her that way, he'd lose all control. "Give me time to get in the back, then you start breaking down the front door, got it?"

Memphis's glare hardened even more. "This plan is shit," he said again.

Maybe...but... "I'm glad you have my back."

"Don't get your ass killed!"

He let go of Memphis. Crept around the side of Abracadabra. Getting killed wasn't on his agenda. But *killing?* Oh, yes, that was.

***

"Sorry about the handcuffs," Corey said, clearly not sorry at all, "but I didn't want you trying to grab another weapon and coming at my throat while I was waiting for you boyfriend."

"He's not a boy." Alice jerked on the cuffs. He'd put her hands behind her, cuffed them, and shoved her into the chair behind her desk. He had the gun aimed at her, but he'd walked a few feet away.

Corey's gaze was on the door to her office. He clearly expected Saint to rush in at any moment.

I do, too. And that was what terrified her. When Saint came barreling in that door, Corey would shoot him instantly.

Tony would have reported that Alice was missing. Saint— and the cops—would be looking for her. Though she suspected Saint would be looking harder.

Her stare dipped to the floor. To the giant pool of blood beneath Tyler. He was dead, and she knew it. The knife still hung from his neck. How convenient. It was within grabbing distance.

"Don't mind a little blood, do you, baby?"

Her gaze lifted. "Not at all, *darling.*"

Laughter.

She hated him. "What's the big plan here? You're going to kill Saint? Make me watch him die and then kill me, too?"

His laughter stopped. "No, I'm not killing you."

You'd better. Because if you so much as bruise Saint, I will cut the skin from your body. "Then what are you going to do?"

"Take you away. You have to vanish after your killing spree. Surely you see that makes sense?"

"I'm not the one on a killing spree. I'm not the serial killer."
Ah, Saint's favorite thing. *Saint.* "That would be you."

"Yes." His gaze remained on the door. "But you will take the
fall for it. Then you'll vanish. With me."

"Uh, huh." She was just going to willingly walk into the
sunset with this bastard? Not happening.

"You'll either come to love me or you'll spend your days
wishing you were dead." He didn't seem too concerned either
way. "We'll work all that out sooner or later."

The hell they would.

*I know my weapon. Now I just need my moment to grab
it.* "He's a better lover than you."

Corey's gaze flew to her. *"What?"*

"Saint. Way better. No comparison, really. As in, it's not
even close."

The gun swung toward her, too.

Good. "The orgasms are insane. They seem to last forever."

"Stop it."

"Oh, sorry, was I supposed to be begging instead? My
mistake." She pressed her lips together. Seemed to think about
it, and... "I knew from the first moment that it was going to be
different with Saint. You're right, you see, I think I was falling
for Shane. And if you hadn't—oh, *murdered* him, then maybe
we would've had more together. But you stopped that."

"Damn fucking right I did."

"With Saint, I felt something from the beginning. I knew he
mattered." She tilted her head. "Do you believe in love at first
sight?"

Rage twisted his face as he lunged for—

The door flew open. "Alice!"

She leapt out of the chair. Hell, yes, her cuffs were unlocked.
One was, anyway. She'd had one wrist free two seconds after he
put the cuffs on her. Corey was trying to swing around and fire
at Saint, but Alice jumped between the two men. She swung out
her still-cuffed wrist, and the dangling handcuff slapped Corey
across the face.

He bellowed and fired, and she could have sworn that she
felt the heat of the bullet rip past her side. She tried to hit him
again, but Corey grabbed her. He lifted her up, and then he just

threw her. Tossed her onto the desk, and the back of her head slammed into the heavy surface. Nausea swelled inside of her, and Alice thought she might vomit right then and there. Her body rolled, and she fell off the desk.

Nearly fell *on* to Tyler. Alice missed him by inches, but she didn't miss his pool of blood. It soaked her arms and legs and clothes. She pushed up, wanting to get away as—

Gunfire. Blasting.

"Saint!" Alice screamed.

She whirled back around. Saint was bleeding. Corey was bleeding. Had they both been shot? She didn't see any sign of their guns now, though, because both men were locked in brutal, physical combat. Slamming blows. Powerful fists. Punches that rattled and broke bones.

"She is *my* Alice," Saint bellowed. "You will never fucking touch her again!"

Corey laughed. "I'll be fucking her while you're rotting in the ground!"

Saint slammed his head into Corey's face. Bones crunched. She knew Corey's nose was broken. Saint shoved Corey against the nearby wall and drove his fists into Corey's stomach and ribs over and over again.

Breaking ribs. Doing internal damage.

Kick his ass, Saint.

She made it to her knees and realized she was pretty much soaked in rapidly cooling blood. Absolutely disgusting.

"Look at...her!" Corey gasped out. "You're...too late. K-killed...Alice!"

Saint's head whipped toward her. Absolute horror flashed on his face and in his eyes. "Sweetheart?" He let go of Corey. Staggered toward her. "Alice?"

She was on her knees. The blood was... "No! Not mine!" Alice cried.

Corey—the bastard was smiling behind Saint. *He wants you focused on me so he can attack!*

Alice's hand flew out and curled around the knife still in Tyler's throat. She yanked it out even as she screamed in rage and fear—

Saint seemed to fall. He dropped straight to his knees.

Corey surged at him, but Saint twisted and came up—*With a knife. With a knife that had been in his boot or strapped on his ankle—*

And Saint drove that knife straight into Corey's heart.

"This time," she heard Saint say, "you will stay dead." Then he jerked his hand to the right. Then the left.

Corey gave a grunting, rasping cry. His gaze flew toward her.

"Goodbye," Alice told him.

CHAPTER TWENTY-ONE

"It's not my blood, Saint!" Alice curled her arm around Saint's neck. Wonderful—now he was smeared with blood, too. "I've told you this!"

He just held her tighter. She craned to see over his shoulder. They'd left a river of blood in her office. Corey was dead. Tyler was dead. And...Her head whipped to the front. Saint was taking her back toward the bar. "Marcel!"

"He's okay. Well, he's got a bullet lodged in his shoulder, but he's alive."

Her breath shuddered out. Good. *Good.* Marcel had survived. Saint had rushed in with an avenging fury, and Corey was exactly where he belonged. Dead, with Saint's knife in his heart.

"Saint!" A bellow. "Saint, where the hell are you?"

Before Saint could reply, Memphis appeared a few feet away. He took one look at them and cursed. "Sonofabitch. Alice, are you—"

"Not my blood," Alice told him. "But your concern is touching. Makes me dislike you a little bit less."

He hurried toward them. "I'm actually glad to hear your sarcasm."

She was actually glad to still be alive, so...win. "I don't...feel so good." A hard confession. "Tyler pumped me with a lot of, ah, morphine I believe it was...so if someone could get me to a hospital...that would be great..." Maybe she and Marcel could share an ambulance.

"Alice." Saint's ragged voice.

Her head turned back toward him.

"I was afraid," he rasped.

Me, too. Because Corey had discovered her absolute worst nightmare.

Watching Saint die.

"Go help Marcel," Saint urged Memphis. "He's near the bar."

Memphis ran away.

Saint kept holding her. "I killed him."

"Yes. *You* killed that ex. Can't go..." Little black dots danced before her vision. "Blaming that one...on me."

"I would kill anyone who hurt you."

She wanted to touch his cheek, but she'd already gotten enough blood on him. "I would do the same for you. Any day." Alice swallowed. "*My* Saint."

His stare was dark and angry and turbulent and so beautiful. "I love you."

***

She'd never been a particularly good patient. She hadn't been a very good anything, so Alice didn't intend to spend extra time in the hospital, despite the doctor's advice. When she stopped feeling as if the world were spinning and as if she might vomit at any moment, she turned to Saint—who had been at her side nearly the entire time—and said, "Take me home."

The love of her life, her hero, her villain, replied, "No."

He'd changed into fresh clothes and washed away the blood. That had been the only time he left her. He'd even watched while she'd gotten cleaned up. That protective, possessive stare of his had followed her every move.

But his refusal had her lips curving down. "I need to take care of my cat."

"Tony and Banshee are at the house."

That news made her tense. If the dog attacked her precious Houdini—

"They said there was a litter box in the mud room and the stray had curled up in the cat bed." He sat in the chair beside her bed, holding her hand and stroking her wrist every few moments. "When did you get all of that?"

"A few days ago."

"So you *did* always plan to bring him home."

She stared straight at him. "I planned to make him mine."

"Just like I planned to make *you* mine."

The cops hadn't come to talk to her. Not yet. She knew they would. The doctors had kept them away, for the moment. But when she escaped the hospital, the detectives would close in like the sharks they were. "Marcel got the bullet removed?"

A nod. "He's recovering."

Excellent. She'd need her new manager in top form. "And Logan?" Because there had to be something about him that she'd missed...He'd been involved. She'd suspected as much ever since they'd found him hiding at Abracadabra.

Saint's features immediately tightened. "He's sitting in a cell. He'd been giving intel to Tyler. Then Tyler had been sending it to Corey. I'm sorry, baby, but Logan sold you out."

That hurt. More than she'd expected. "I knew it was him."

Saint leaned toward her. "You knew he was working with someone?"

"No, I-I knew he was the one who had given the wrong swords to my dad. There was so much guilt on his face. I thought...Back then, I thought...he feels so terrible. He can't be bad." But now... "I don't like to be wrong about people."

"When he found out you had been taken, he spilled everything he had. Said that he'd been blackmailed. That Tyler was going to tell *you* that he'd been the one to cause the accident all those years ago."

Her hand turned in his. "Saint, are you defending him?"

"No. No. Hell, no. I'm just saying..." A rough exhale. "Logan didn't know he was dealing with Corey. He thought he was giving intel to Tyler. He's a dumbass, no doubt, but I think he cares about you."

She would think about Logan—deal with him—later. For this moment, she needed to focus on what mattered most. That would be Saint. "The cops will talk to us. Interview us both separately. Conduct some sort of exhaustive investigation." She could already imagine the headlines. And as a result of those headlines...

Marcel will have quite the crowd at Abracadabra. She'd have to make sure he had plenty of time to recover first. Forget just management, maybe he should be a partner. "Oh, by the way, I know Marcel was working for you." She should have probably said something about that sooner.

Saint blinked. "Excuse me?"

She touched his cheek. The blood wasn't on her fingers any longer. "Really, Saint. I can read him like a book." When she'd seen Marcel fighting with Corey, she'd known that Saint would be arriving soon. Marcel would have tipped him off. After all, wasn't that what Saint had asked the guy to do?

As if I didn't get all that intel...

"And me, baby?" Saint breathed. "Can you read me?"

Alice took her time searching his eyes. "Now I can." *My Alice.* There was no way he could say those words without her hearing the love in his voice.

Funny. She'd always thought love wasn't for her. And she'd figured that if she ever did feel it...well, the way she saw it in movies and TV shows, love was some gentle emotion. It filled you with happiness and euphoria and made you want to look at the world and see rainbows everywhere.

Screw that crap. She didn't feel that kind of love. Her love for Saint was dark and deep, and it grabbed her heart and nearly ripped it from her chest. It made her want to fight, to battle anything and everything to stay with him. It drove her with a fierce passion and a hungry need, and she would *not* let him go.

Because he was hers. She was his.

Like to like.

"What are you thinking?" Saint tilted his head.

"That I don't care if I'm twisted, and I don't care if I don't feel everything like the rest of the world. I wouldn't trade the way I *do* feel about you, not for anything."

He leaned in closer. Just a breath away. "You're not fucking twisted. You're not the villain. Never were."

Some would disagree. *Plenty* would. But she didn't care about them.

"To me, you're perfect." His stare seemed so tender as it swept over her. "You think I didn't see you grab the knife...*from Tyler's neck?* You would have killed to keep me safe."

"Only fair." She swallowed a silly lump in her throat. "You killed for me."

"He was dead the minute he took you." Saint's lips feathered over hers. Tender. Careful. "He didn't know it. He realized it when I cut out his heart."

"You say the sweetest things."

He eased back. Shook his head. "No, I don't." A pause. "Is that a problem?"

"Only if you say the same things to the cops."

His brow furrowed.

"Let's practice a bit, shall we?" Her heart beat a little faster. "Instead of... 'He realized it when I cut out his heart,' let's go with 'When he attacked me, I had no choice but to defend myself and fight back. The knife lodged in his chest, and when I tried to take it out, it slipped and cut even deeper.' Something like that."

"Alice..."

"Because it was clearly self-defense, but I do like to play things safe. At least, I do where you're concerned." It was her turn to brush her lips against his. "No one is putting you in a cell again."

"I killed him, Alice."

"And I killed Donovan. And Corey killed Shane." That last part *hurt*. "But I think I know where Shane's buried. Maybe Tony and Banshee can go out with me to find him?" Corey had given away the location when he told her...*I put him somewhere I thought you'd enjoy. A place you visit nearly every day. Seemed fitting.*

Every day, she ran in Forsyth Park. Forsyth Park—where Saint had almost been shot.

Where Shane had been buried?

Tony and Banshee would help her get to the truth.

"I'm sure they will be happy to help," Saint assured her.

That was good. Another loose end tied up. There was just one more thing to cover. "And Donovan?"

"What about him?"

"You tell me." She didn't hold her breath. Didn't give away her emotions at all. Maybe going to the cops and telling them where he was would be the best thing. Maybe it wouldn't be. She didn't—

"Maybe his body will turn up one day. If it does, I'm sure there will be ample evidence to support the fact that he fell to his death. After all this time, such a tragedy, isn't it? A real shame." His words were flat.

Alice wet her lower lip. "Can you live with that?" With hiding the truth? Burying it?

"I can live with anything, as long as I have you."

"I'm not...I'm not going to ever be some sweet, innocent—"

"Good. I like you fierce, Alice. I like you tough and wild. I like you dragging a knife from a dead man's throat because you want to protect me. Screw sweet. I'll take you just the way you are any day of the week."

Saint. "I like you, Saint. I like you dark. I like you bad. I like when you make me go wild in bed." Wild, with no restraint. With no part of herself held back because she was with a man who understood her. "I like you when you fight for me. When you bust in the door and come rushing in because you want to save me." She hadn't ever wanted a hero. Never wished for one. Instead, she'd wanted a fighter. She'd gotten him. "I love you."

Saint smiled at her.

"Now take me home."

Once more, he pressed a kiss to her lips. "No."

"Saint!"

"Not until you get the all-clear from the doctor."

Alice glared, but then the door to her hospital room opened. Jamal and Heidi stepped inside, and Alice realized the cops weren't going to wait for her doctor to release her before they came for their little chat.

No, they weren't going to wait at all.

Time for the big show.

Alice allowed Saint to keep holding her right hand. Her left pressed to her chest. Fluttered. "It was such a nightmare..." she began.

It had been, actually.

Waking up in that box.

Seeing Marcel get shot.

Fearing that Saint would be killed before she could save him.

Nightmare.

But they'd survived and nothing—no one—would ever tear them apart.

***

Twenty-four hours later...

"Houdini, I don't know why you're meowing at me. Not like I wanted you to have to bunk with the dog, but we both had to deal with unpleasant situations." Alice scratched the cat behind his ears.

The cat arched into her touch.

Saint watched them as he leaned against the doorframe in Alice's kitchen. She'd finally been released from the hospital. She'd definitely been unhappy that Saint had refused to bust her out of the joint, but he hadn't been about to leave. Not until he was sure she was safe.

"So, yeah, you guys all good here?" Memphis asked.

Saint inclined his head toward his brother. "Thanks for the ride."

"Any time." But Memphis didn't move to leave. He lingered. And his stare darted toward Alice.

She kept scratching the cat's ears.

"If you have something to say," Saint invited. "Say it."

Memphis sidled closer. "Do you know what you're doing?"

He kept watching Alice and the black cat. "Absolutely."

"And? Want to tell me the master plan?"

"I'm gonna marry her. See if she wants kids. Give in to her every wicked desire." He hadn't bothered to lower his voice, so he knew Alice heard each word quite clearly. He figured it was better if she knew his intentions.

After one final stroke for the cat, Alice straightened. "You no longer want to take me down?" She took a step toward him.

"No."

"See me locked away?" Two more steps.

Hell, no. "Not on the agenda."

Fucking her all night long? *That* was on his agenda. Making her come over and over again. Giving her more pleasure that she could stand. Making her scream. Oh, yes, there were plenty of things on his to-do list.

Alice paused in front of him. She offered him such a tempting smile. Her eyes lit up with warmth.

"Right." Memphis cleared his throat. "Clearly, you are not as bad as they say."

The warmth dimmed. Her head turned toward Memphis. "I am. Don't forget that. And when it comes to Saint, I am especially bad."

Memphis grinned. "That is good to know. Because he deserves someone to love him like that. Happy to hear that you'll be watching his ass when I'm not around." He dipped his head. "With that, I'll be leaving. Tony said to tell you she'll be by in the morning. She and the cops are going to start the search at Forsyth Park. She said you can ride with her."

The search for Shane Madison's body.

A shadow swept across Alice's face. She watched Memphis leave, and when the door closed behind him...

"I hate it when you're sad," Saint muttered. He didn't like to see her in any kind of pain.

"It's okay. I think Shane deserved a bit of sadness from me." Her hands curled around his shoulders. "Just like I think you deserve some happiness."

He was happy. He had Alice, safe, standing right in front of him. A woman who saw the real man he was. He didn't have to hold back with her. No pretending. No constant control and toeing the line.

She understood him.

Loved him, despite everything.

He thought of their first meeting. Beautiful Alice, standing behind the bar. Making him the best old-fashioned in the world. He'd followed her into the parking lot. Stroked her cheek even as he'd warned her, "I came to take you down." Fuck, but he needed to apologize. He'd been wrong about her back then. The world was wrong. Alice had been painted as the villain for so long.

She was so much more. To him, she was everything. *Everything.* "I'm sorry."

"Why?"

"You've been through hell, baby."

"That just makes me appreciate heaven."

She staggered him. Stunned him. "I will give you paradise every day of my life."

"You'd better," she warned him. But she was teasing. And her face brightened with a soft glow. A warmth. He could *see* her love for him.

"I was mistaken." Gruff. "When I found you that first night, when I said I was going to take you down..."

The memory was in Alice's eyes. "Told you, Saint, you said that wrong."

This time, he nodded. Because she was right. "What I meant was that I came to fall in love with you."

"Damn straight, you did." She rose onto her toes. "Now kiss me."

And he did. As he held Alice close, the last thing Saint felt was cold. He wasn't locked away any longer. Wasn't trapped by control.

Fire burned in him. Need. Lust. Love. All because of...

My Alice.

He pulled her even closer and knew he would face any threat, fight anyone, to always keep her at his side.

THE END

A NOTE FROM THE AUTHOR

Thank you very much for taking the time to read ICE COLD SAINT. I appreciate you taking the journey into the world of the Ice Breakers with me. I've always been a bit of a cold case addict, and these books are giving me a chance to blend romance and sleuthing.

Alice was a very complex character, one with an extremely painful past. While researching her story, I learned that nearly twenty people are abused every minute by their partners. A staggering number that breaks my heart. If you or someone you know is the victim of domestic violence, please call the National Domestic Violence Hotline (800-799-7233).

ABOUT THE AUTHOR

Cynthia Eden is a *New York Times*, *USA Today*, *Digital Book World*, and *IndieReader* best-seller.

Cynthia writes sexy tales of contemporary romance, romantic suspense, and paranormal romance. Since she began writing full-time in 2005, Cynthia has written over one hundred novels and novellas.

Cynthia lives along the Alabama Gulf Coast. She loves romance novels, horror movies, and chocolate.

For More Information

- *cynthiaeden.com*
- *facebook.com/cynthiaedenfanpage*

HER OTHER WORKS

Ice Breaker Cold Case Romance

- Frozen In Ice (Book 1)
- Falling For The Ice Queen (Book 2)

Phoenix Fury

- Hot Enough To Burn (Book 1)
- Slow Burn (Book 2)
- Burn It Down (Book 3)

Trouble For Hire

- No Escape From War (Book 1)
- Don't Play With Odin (Book 2)
- Jinx, You're It (Book 3)
- Remember Ramsey (Book 4)

Death and Moonlight Mystery

- Step Into My Web (Book 1)
- Save Me From The Dark (Book 2)

Wilde Ways

- Protecting Piper (Book 1)
- Guarding Gwen (Book 2)
- Before Ben (Book 3)
- The Heart You Break (Book 4)
- Fighting For Her (Book 5)
- Ghost Of A Chance (Book 6)
- Crossing The Line (Book 7)
- Counting On Cole (Book 8)
- Chase After Me (Book 9)
- Say I Do (Book 10)

- Roman Will Fall (Book 11)
- The One Who Got Away (Book 12)
- Pretend You Want Me (Book 13)
- Cross My Heart (Book 14)
- The Bodyguard Next Door (Book 15)
- Ex Marks The Perfect Spot (Book 16)
- The Thief Who Loved Me (Book 17)

Dark Sins

- Don't Trust A Killer (Book 1)
- Don't Love A Liar (Book 2)

Lazarus Rising

- Never Let Go (Book One)
- Keep Me Close (Book Two)
- Stay With Me (Book Three)
- Run To Me (Book Four)
- Lie Close To Me (Book Five)
- Hold On Tight (Book Six)

Dark Obsession Series

- Watch Me (Book 1)
- Want Me (Book 2)
- Need Me (Book 3)
- Beware Of Me (Book 4)
- Only For Me (Books 1 to 4)

Mine Series

- Mine To Take (Book 1)
- Mine To Keep (Book 2)
- Mine To Hold (Book 3)
- Mine To Crave (Book 4)
- Mine To Have (Book 5)
- Mine To Protect (Book 6)
- Mine Box Set Volume 1 (Books 1-3)
- Mine Box Set Volume 2 (Books 4-6)

Bad Things

- The Devil In Disguise (Book 1)
- On The Prowl (Book 2)

- Undead Or Alive (Book 3)
- Broken Angel (Book 4)
- Heart Of Stone (Book 5)
- Tempted By Fate (Book 6)
- Wicked And Wild (Book 7)
- Saint Or Sinner (Book 8)
- Bad Things Volume One (Books 1 to 3)
- Bad Things Volume Two (Books 4 to 6)
- Bad Things Deluxe Box Set (Books 1 to 6)

Bite Series

- Forbidden Bite (Bite Book 1)
- Mating Bite (Bite Book 2)

Blood and Moonlight Series

- Bite The Dust (Book 1)
- Better Off Undead (Book 2)
- Bitter Blood (Book 3)
- Blood and Moonlight (The Complete Series)

Purgatory Series

- The Wolf Within (Book 1)
- Marked By The Vampire (Book 2)
- Charming The Beast (Book 3)
- Deal with the Devil (Book 4)
- The Beasts Inside (Books 1 to 4)

Bound Series

- Bound By Blood (Book 1)
- Bound In Darkness (Book 2)
- Bound In Sin (Book 3)
- Bound By The Night (Book 4)
- Bound in Death (Book 5)
- Forever Bound (Books 1 to 4)

Stand-Alone Romantic Suspense

- It's A Wonderful Werewolf
- Never Cry Werewolf
- Immortal Danger
- Deck The Halls

- Come Back To Me
- Put A Spell On Me
- Never Gonna Happen
- One Hot Holiday
- Slay All Day
- Midnight Bite
- Secret Admirer
- Christmas With A Spy
- Femme Fatale
- Until Death
- Sinful Secrets
- First Taste of Darkness
- A Vampire's Christmas Carol